D1239358

Good People
A Grace Howard Mystery

By Kelly Adamson

Copyright © 2014 by Kelly Adamson

All rights reserved. No part of this book may be reproduced or transmitted in any form or by any means, electronic of mechanical, including photocopying, recording, or by any information storage and retrieval system, without the written permission of the Publisher except where allowed by law.

This is a work of fiction. Names, characters, businesses, places, events and incidents are either the products of the author's imagination or used in a fictitious manner. Any resemblance to actual persons, living or dead, or actual events is purely coincidental.

Printed in the United States of America

First Printing, 2014

ISBN13: 978-0-615-96425-6

ISBN10: 0-61596-425-7

Acknowledgements

Thanks to my dad for teaching me that life, like poetry, doesn't always rhyme. To my mom, for every wonderful story she has ever told me. And to my husband, for loving me no matter what.

Special thanks to Joan Kennedy, Ken Bishop, and Lucy Merrill. I couldn't have done it without them.

Table of Contents

Chapter 1 – Touchdown

Nothing was going to ruin this trip for Grace. Not the unrelenting rain or being stuck in this stuffy airplane for an hour and a half waiting to be cleared for take-off. Not even the dead man in the airport.

Of course, this last monkey wrench was strictly hearsay, overheard by Grace on her first trip to the miniscule bathroom while the plane was still at the gate. The two flight attendants looked stricken when they saw her there, so close to their little galley. She caught them whispering that the police were holding all flights while they investigated. A man had been found in a stairwell with one bullet in his leg and another in his head, shot through the eye at point blank range. His blood had dripped down the stairs and seeped out under the door, where it was spotted by an employee in the baggage room. The poor employee almost had a "come apart," according to the older of the flight attendants, whose southern accent was even more pronounced than Grace's own.

They could get in big trouble for spreading rumors like this, of course. The official word was that the delay was due to the thunderstorm, a much more plausible explanation. So, Grace just smiled at them and acted as if she hadn't heard a thing.

She did, however, pocket this juicy bit of gossip and make a mental note to add it to her vacation scrapbook when she got home.

After all, she had wanted this trip to be exciting, a break from her too-ordinary routine. And what could be more exciting than a dead body in a stairwell? It definitely trumped a little rain, and would sound even better in the retelling.

A barrage of thunder rattled the plane and an uneasy rumble rose from some of the passengers. Grace couldn't keep from grinning on the way back to her seat. She wondered if she should tell her husband, Nick, about the possibility of a murderer running around the airport with a gun. She decided to save that one for later. Much later.

After all, Nick was a bit of an anxious flyer, though he would never admit it. She knew it stemmed from the fact that he didn't like being a passenger. He wanted to be the driver, or at the very least, be able to look over the shoulder of the driver. Pretty tough to do in a Boeing 757. Grace thought if they had let him sit in the cockpit and pinned a little pair of wings on him, like they used to do with kids back in the 60's, he would have been just fine.

Nick held the *Atlanta Herald* up in front of him, a shield from the other passengers. She could see the top of his head above it, his brown curls in their usual disarray. The headline on the front read, "Queen's Necklace Stolen from Cairo Museum." There was a photo of a domed building the color of red clay. Uniformed men carrying rifles stood in front of yellow caution tape at the entrance. Grace sighed. She'd never really cared for museums. Why did people get so excited over a bunch of broken pottery? What was the point? She wasn't interested in people who died thousands of years ago. Let the dead bury their dead.

Instead, she leaned back in her seat and picked up her copy of *Bright Star* magazine. Glossy photos of Johnny Depp, Killian Ross and Brad Pitt smiled up at her. Headlines on the cover included, "The nose knows: Which leading man has had the most plastic surgery," and "Is it splitsville for good for Trina and Jake?" Now here was news worth reading. Movie stars were more exciting than mummies any day.

Three hours later, safely on the ground in Las Vegas, Nick was back to his usual easy-going self. It didn't even bother him when he found out his suitcase had been placed on the wrong plane and wouldn't be arriving until the next morning. Grace just shook her head. Nothing ever seemed to make him angry, which sometimes made her even angrier. She saw no shame in a little righteous indignation now and then.

They picked up their rental car, a white Subaru with a scuffed bumper, and followed the lights to Las Vegas Boulevard. Less than an hour after first spotting that unmistakable skyline from the airplane window, they got their first glimpse of the famous "Welcome to Las Vegas" sign. Grace snapped a blurry photo as they passed. She had forgotten all about the dead man in the airport.

Their hotel was the newest on the center strip. It wasn't long until the blue and gold lights of the Egyptian-themed Isis came into view. Palm trees lined the circular drive, and a three-story waterfall almost hid the hotel's entrance. It was supposed to give the impression of stumbling on a desert oasis and a hidden pharaoh's tomb.

All of the employees wore brass nametags engraved with the eye of Horus. A tall man with "William" on his tag loaded their lone suitcase and carryon bags onto a bell cart and followed them to the registration desk.

While Nick checked in, Grace inspected the contents of the sparkling cases set into the walls around the lobby. All housed Egyptian artifacts, apparently fragile and priceless, and painstakingly labeled. All useless objects, like little statues of goddesses and cats. She wandered from one case to the other snapping photos and wondered if these were the sorts of things the thieves had taken in Cairo. At least she understood bank robbers — everyone could use money — but stealing knickknacks seemed utterly pointless.

From behind her, William the bellman said, "If you'll step this way, I'll show you to your room."

Grace turned to see Nick's smug smile.

"What?"

"Look what the power of positive thinking has brought me." He motioned with a flourish toward the bell cart and his suitcase, now sitting beside hers. "I told you there was nothing to worry about. They sent it over from the airline. Turns out, it got here even before we did."

Grace rolled her eyes. "You and your positive thinking."

They followed the bellman toward a large opening on the other side of the lobby that was made to look as if blocks had been chipped away, rubble piled strategically against the wall along with archaeological "finds," broken pottery, jewelry and coins. The opening revealed a curving stone passageway that led into the casino and hotel. Statues, at least ten feet tall, stood on either side of the tunnel's entrance.

"Who are they?" Grace asked the bellman as they drew near.

"The man is Osiris, the Egyptian God of the Underworld," William said, "and the woman is his wife, Isis, who lends her name to this resort. The baby she's holding is their son, Horus." He pointed to his nametag. "Like the eye of Horus."

"Huh. You must be a real history buff."

William shrugged. "You have to be to work here. Mr. Clifton — he's the owner — he's one of the richest men in America and he's got one of the biggest private collections of Egyptian artifacts in the world. They say he's even going to be mummified when he dies — old school — canopic jars for his organs and the whole nine yards. Anyway, he's in here all the time, and you never know when he's going to stop some employee and start asking questions. When we're hired, they give us a bunch of facts to memorize. He wants to make sure we can answer the typical questions guests have." He grinned, his face suddenly boyish. "You'd be surprised how many times I've been asked who those statues are."

The walls of the passageway were carved floor to ceiling with hieroglyphs. Nick said, "I could work here then, because I can read all this."

"Oh, really?" William said. "It's from the *Book of the Dead*. What does it say?"

Nick ran his finger along the wall as they walked. "Big bird, little bird, wavy line, snake, feather, eyeball. Let's see, two birds were swimming in a lake and a snake swallowed them and spit out a feather and an eyeball. See? That's pretty easy."

"You'll have to pardon him," Grace said. "He doesn't get out much."

The tunnel opened up, and the threesome stepped into the warm golden glow of ancient Egypt — if ancient Egypt had had slot machines. Grace stopped in mid-stride. "Wow, I feel like Dorothy going from black and white to color."

William draped his lanky frame over his brass-railed cart and gave them a genuine smile. "Welcome to the Isis," he said.

The room was the size of a football stadium. The walkway under their feet was sand-colored stone that rose up gradually into actual sand on either side. It meandered through Sago palms along the edge of the two-foot-wide Nile River, which gurgled along south to north, just like the real one, and separated the hotel from the casino.

"Over there," William pointed to the far quadrant of the room at a massive stone structure surrounded by carved columns bigger than oak trees, "is the Temple of Isis. That's where they play high-stakes poker."

He pushed the cart and Nick and Grace followed mutely.

To their right, on the far bank of the Nile, couples dined under palm trees at linen-covered tables. Oil lanterns hung from ropes that crisscrossed high above their heads, casting a warm glow and glinting off the crystal stemware.

They took a right past the restaurant onto the rustic bridge that joined the casino and the hotel across the river. "See the Sphinx back there," William said. "Behind that is our after-hours nightclub. It's called The Eye. You've probably heard of it. You can see a lot of famous people clubbing there."

Kelly Adamson

Grace's eyes lit up even more. A line of people waited to get in. She strained to see if she recognized any celebrities.

William stopped in front of a set of carved stone columns. He touched a button on the wall and a door opened to reveal an elevator. They filed into the torpedo-shaped elevator car, squeezing to the sides to make room for William and his cart.

The doors slid closed, immediately shutting out the universal clanging, beeping, and jangling that came from a casino floor. Inside the elevator door was a projection that showed a loop of the different restaurants and bars on the property. Nick put his hand on his stomach and groaned. "Oh, look at that prime rib. I almost forgot how hungry I am. Let's put our stuff up and go find that buffet."

"I should have pointed that out," William said. "When you get off the elevator, it will be straight ahead, past the craps tables. It's in the building that looks like the Temple of Philae."

"Can you be a little more specific? I'm a little rusty on my temples," Nick said.

"It's guarded by two stone lions. Take the escalator to get to the buffet line. You can't miss it," he assured them. "But they close at midnight, so don't wait too long."

William held open the door to room 1404 and then followed them in. They'd been saving over a year for this trip, and the hotel room didn't disappoint. It was easily the nicest either of them had ever been in.

Grace sidestepped into the bathroom while William told Nick about the hotel's spa. The walls were mirrored on both sides of the room and Grace could see herself reflected into infinity. She sucked in her stomach and stood up straight, critical as always. Nick came up behind her in the mirrors, his mop of wavy brown hair framing his smiling face. Grace liked the little lines that appeared at the corner of his dark eyes when he smiled. She thought they made him look distinguished.

"You happy?" he asked. "You've been wanting this trip for a long time."

"Absolutely. How about you?"

"If I was any better, I couldn't stand myself."

William stood in the doorway with his now empty cart. If he were much taller, he would have to duck to keep from hitting his head on the door frame. Other than his height, he had a look that would blend in any crowd, late twenties with short, dark hair, dark eyes and an easy smile.

"It's been my pleasure showing you folks around. If you need anything while you are here, just pick up the phone and ask for Guest Services. Feel free to ask for me personally. If I'm on duty, they'll find me." He pocketed the tip Nick handed him, and rolled his cart out to the sand-colored corridor. As the door closed, he called, "Good luck!"

"What's that supposed to mean?" Grace asked. "That's an odd thing to say."

"No, it's not," said Nick. "We're in Vegas, remember? Where people come to gamble?" With that, he fell back on the bed, spread eagle. "Ahhhh!" he groaned. "I don't think I can get up. This is the most comfortable bed in the entire world, hands down. I'm going to spend my whole vacation here."

Grace picked up one of the overstuffed pillows and squeezed it. "Wow. What do you suppose these are made of?"

"Angels and unicorns," Nick replied, his eyes closed, a smile curving his mouth.

Grace rolled her eyes and tossed the pillow at him. She crossed over to the window and pulled back a heavy silk curtain.

"What's our view?" Nick asked.

"Hmmm… I think it's an access road."

He came up behind her and put his arms around her waist. "I guess you have to be a high roller to get a view of the Eiffel Tower. Maybe next time."

He tucked her hair behind her left ear so he could kiss her neck. He kept his mouth there and mumbled, "I'm not used to your hair being this short, or this color. I feel like I'm with another woman." She made an indignant sound and he added quickly, "I like it. Don't get me wrong. I'm just not used to it yet. The color suits you. I could get used to you as a red-head. But you know I thought you looked perfect already."

She wasn't sure she liked it herself, actually. It didn't turn out like she thought it would. She wanted it to look like pop star Leah Love's hair. It was supposed to curl in under her chin but the left side always curled out, giving her the appearance of just having come inside on a breezy day.

"I wanted something different," she said. "I'm tired of being boring and ordinary. Don't you ever get tired of that?"

Nick shrugged and nibbled at her earlobe. "I suppose one man's boring could be another man's perfection."

She pushed him away half-heartedly. "Be serious. I thought you were hungry."

"I am," he said with a wicked grin.

"For *food*."

His stomach growled audibly. He shrugged. "All right. You and my stomach may have won this round, but the night is still young."

Moments later, they were out in the open sunshine and sand of Ancient Egypt again. They wound their way through the palm trees and across the bridge into the casino and stopped, looking for a sign for the buffet.

Casinos are notoriously stingy with signage. It is their fond hope that anyone looking for a bathroom or an exit will be sidetracked instead into playing a few dozen hands of poker.

They found the craps table. They continued on through roulette and blackjack tables. They saw Pai Gow, Baccarat, Keno, and Texas Hold 'Em, but they did not see two stone lions guarding a buffet.

"Okay, he said we couldn't miss it," Nick said.

"I think he overestimated us."

"That's got to be it right there." Nick nodded toward an oddly shaped building across the casino floor. "He said it looked like some temple, right? Well, that looks kind of temple-y."

"I don't see any lions."

"Look, there's an escalator." Nick hurried forward. "He said we took an escalator up to the buffet line."

"I still don't see any lions," Grace said.

The drone of slot machines grew softer as they neared the top of the second bank of escalators. They stepped off into a darkened mezzanine surrounded by tall, black doors that led into meeting rooms that were just a few teamsters and some sliding walls away from becoming a 75,000 square foot ballroom. Above the doors were names like "Giza" and "Thebes."

The open area was filled with tables and chairs. Only hours from now, this space would host a breakfast for the Ping-Pong Table Manufacturer's Association, or the Snow Globe Collectors of America, or some other inane conglomeration of people. They would fill their plates with made-to-order omelets and mingle around the dripping ice sculptures. But for now, it was just naked plywood table rounds and nicked metal folding chairs, waiting for their black linen and silver sashes like the emperor with no clothes.

"You'd think the biggest buffet in town wouldn't be this hard to find."

Grace stepped to the railing and peered down two stories onto the casino floor. It was incredibly quiet up here for being so close to the crowd and the noise below.

"There it is. I see the sign. Temple of Philae Buffet. There's a different set of escalators behind the craps tables." They turned to head back down the way they came, but the escalators were both moving up, getting ready for the onslaught of conventioneers in the morning.

"All right, where are the elevators? I feel like a mouse in a maze trying to find the cheese." Nick groaned. "Mmm, now I want cheese."

They turned just in time to see movement in the darkened corner of the hall. "Did you see that?" asked Nick. "Somebody just went in that room. Come on."

"Are you crazy?" said Grace indignantly. "I'm not going in there. Horror movies start this way. I'm staying right here."

"No way; it's got to be an employee. Who else would be up here?" Nick disappeared into the dark room marked "Cairo." "Hello! Is anybody in here?" Grace could hear his echoing call, but no one answered.

Then, like a cork popping out of a bottle of champagne, the door marked "Aswan" opened and a man almost fell in his rush to get out. Grace gave a startled yelp and the man froze, mid-stumble, eyes wide.

Nick came rushing back out at the sound. "Oh, hey. Do you work here?"

The man hesitated, then shook his head. The three of them just stared at each other. The man looked like he'd been caught stealing, though there could be nothing in any of these vacant rooms of value and his hands were empty. He looked to be in his mid-thirties, with a shaggy beard and shoulder-length, sandy colored hair that was desperately in need of a brush. There was something oddly familiar about him, thought Grace. The fact that he might be homeless flickered briefly in her mind, but his clothes were too nice. His designer tennis shoes alone had probably cost several hundred dollars. He shifted nervously from one foot to another as she looked at his shoes.

"Well, do you at least know how to get to the buffet?" Nick asked, a note of desperation in his voice.

The man shook his head again, still silent.

Nick sighed. "All right. Well, thanks anyway." As they turned to leave, Nick motioned to the man's arm and said, "Hey, your tattoo. Is that Special Forces? Navy Seals? I know I've seen that somewhere before."

Grace looked back at this odd stranger. His short sleeves didn't quite cover an intricate shield on his upper right arm. When he finally spoke, it was just above a whisper. "It's my family crest."

At the sound of his voice, Grace gasped. He turned his green eyes back to her as she said, "Oh, my God! Oh, my God! Oh, my God! It's *you*!"

Chapter 2 – The Host With the Most

Grace had one hand over her mouth and the other hand was pointing. "You're Killian Ross," she said breathlessly, and then to Nick, as if he hadn't heard, "That's Killian Ross."

The man looked like he wanted to melt into the floor. He made frantic shushing gestures with his hands.

Nick looked closer at the bearded stranger, clearly unconvinced. "Can't be," he said.

"Yes, it is," Grace insisted, "The tattoo, the voice…those eyes," she finished with a smile, her own voice trailing off.

The stranger didn't bother to deny it. He just stood looking around as if a silent alarm had been triggered.

"Really?" Nick asked skeptically. "You're Killian Ross, the movie star?"

In answer the man said, "Please don't tell anyone you saw me here," and his Shakespearean actor's voice gave him away.

Grace stood still, one hand over her mouth, staring in happy astonishment. Nick looked around, trying to find whatever it was Killian kept looking for. "What are you doing here? Are you hiding from someone?"

"It's a long story," he whispered.

They heard voices from the escalators. No more than two or three people, but enough to make Killian jump. He motioned for them to follow and bolted down a dimly lit hallway beside the ballroom, silent as a ghost.

Kelly Adamson

Nick grabbed Grace by the sleeve and pulled her after him. They ducked through a wide swinging door at the end of the hallway into the glare of bright fluorescent lights and the scuffed doors of a service elevator.

"Why are we running?" Grace whispered.

Killian shushed them. He pushed the "Up" button for the elevator, then flattened himself against the wall beside the door. He gestured for them to do the same. For a long minute they all stood, backs against the wall, waiting. Nick and Grace exchanged puzzled looks, but neither spoke. When the elevator finally opened, Killian darted inside. They followed. Heavy gray quilts hung inside to protect the walls, and when the doors slid closed, it was like being in a padded cell.

Killian waved his room key in front of a mounted card reader and pressed a button marked "PH." Grace didn't remember seeing that button on the guest elevator when they arrived. The car rose noiselessly.

"Okay, seriously, what's going on?" Nick demanded. "Are we in danger here?"

Killian seemed to relax a bit. "Look, I know this sounds quite mad, but there is a perfectly simple explanation for all this. You see, I don't want anyone to know I'm here, so I'm trying to avoid being seen. If the paparazzi find out I'm here, it will surely get back to…" He faltered. "Well, the only people who know where I am right now are my mum and my manager, and I want to keep it that way."

Of course, Grace and Nick, total strangers to him, now also knew his whereabouts. With that thought in mind, the absurdity of the whole situation hit Grace, and she fought back the urge to laugh.

They'd started out for dinner and now were hiding in a dirty elevator with an Oscar-winning actor.

At that, the elevator doors slid open. No bell of announcement on this floor.

Killian stepped out, but Nick put out his hand to hold the door open. "Look, I don't mean to be rude, and I'm sure this is fascinating and all, but I'm gonna pass out if I don't get something to eat soon. So now that I know we're not all in danger of being killed, we're gonna go."

"No, no, don't go! If food is all you need, I have plenty. Please join me." Killian motioned down the hallway. Nick and Grace hesitated and he added, "I have a fully stocked kitchen, and anyway, I think the buffet is closed now."

Nick glanced at his watch as his stomach growled. He sighed and looked at Grace.

Under normal circumstances, she would have protested. *'No, we couldn't possibly put you out, Strange Man we just met in a dark room who might try to poison us!'* But instead she was wearing a silly smile she couldn't seem to wipe off her face. "If you're sure it's no trouble," she said.

"No. Honestly, I would really love some company." Then Killian smiled his dazzlingly white smile. With a start, Grace realized she had seen that smile many times before, only it was usually six feet long up on the silver screen. And now, here they were, in the actual presence of *the* Killian Ross, the British Bombshell, the hottest actor in Hollywood – or the *world*, for that matter – and they were about to go into his hotel room. The very thought made her a little dizzy. She felt like a schoolgirl. Even the fact that he was probably just being nice to them to convince them to keep his secret didn't bother her.

They made their way down the service hall, Killian leading the way, a new spring in his step now that he had company. They stopped at a plain door marked "P3" and waited while he first entered numbers on a keypad and then swiped his card key in front of another reader.

It was the service entrance into the kitchen of his suite, full of black granite and stainless steel appliances. The island in the center was lit from above by hand-blown globes highlighting a tiered tray of fresh fruit and an assortment of pastries under a glass dome.

Nick's growling stomach would not allow him to stand on formality. He immediately reached for a banana and began peeling it.

Killian's demeanor had changed in an instant from wary to hospitable. "Make yourselves at home, please. I haven't had guests since I've been here." He pulled wine glasses off a rack over the bar, then took two chilled bottles out of the wine cooler and began uncorking them.

"How long have you been here?" Nick mumbled through a mouthful of banana.

Killian looked at his watch. "A little over three weeks now." There was something melancholy in the tone of his voice that seemed surprising to Grace. How could anyone be depressed when they were surrounded by all this?

Killian took plates out of the industrial-sized refrigerator and placed them on the bar. Nick set to removing the plastic wrap, stopping to taste from each plate. There were stuffed mushrooms, huge Gulf shrimp, and a number of things Grace didn't recognize. "Mmm, mmm... What is this?"

"I think that's cherry tomatoes with some sort of crab or lobster stuffing," Killian said.

Grace felt a rush at his short â pronunciation of "tomatoes." She picked up a mushroom and stuffed it in her mouth so he wouldn't see her silly grin. Why couldn't she get her face to cooperate?

While Nick admired the variety of beers in the well-stocked refrigerator, Killian pushed a button on a remote control and the rest of the suite became visible. It looked larger than Grace and Nick's house.

Killian pressed another button and short pale flames rose up from the center of a free-standing fireplace. Another button and heavy silvery silk curtains on the far wall began to part, revealing an unbelievable view of the Strip. Grace laughed out loud; she couldn't help herself. She walked towards the windows in slow motion and touched the glass as if she expected it to be a mirage.

"Wow," Nick said. "Who needs a helicopter tour when you have a view like this. What floor are we on?"

"I think it's technically about the twenty-first," Killian said. "I suppose it really is a splendid view. I guess I just haven't noticed."

Nick settled into a corner of the red leather couch and balanced a plate on his knees. "Okay, so I've just got to ask," he said between bites. "If an internationally recognized movie star is trying to hide from the press, why would he come to a swanky hotel in Las Vegas? I mean, that's not exactly off the radar."

Killian sighed and shrugged his shoulders. "Poor planning," he said, sitting in a white leather armchair facing the couch. He leaned back and crossed his feet at the ankles, all of the tension gone out of him. He looked tired and surprisingly human.

"That's it? Poor planning? That's all you've got?"

Killian shrugged again.

Grace joined Nick on the couch. "Are you filming a movie here?"

"No."

"Well, certainly this isn't some sort of weird, solitary vacation. Because if it is," she added, "you don't really seem to be enjoying yourself."

Killian didn't respond and Nick said, "Grace, maybe it's none of our business. Maybe he doesn't want to talk about it."

Grace doubted the existence of a movie star who didn't want to talk about himself, but she held her tongue.

Killian leaned forward in his chair, rubbing his closed eyes with the heels of his hands, then ran his fingers through his unkempt hair, usually cut short and neat. "Actually, I think I really would like to talk about it. And that's odd, because I haven't wanted to talk at all for over three weeks." He walked to the window, maybe to admire the view he hadn't noticed before. "Ruth, my manager, she's tried to get me to talk, but I just couldn't, especially to her." He turned to face them with a puzzled expression. "And now, here I am with two total strangers — who, for all I know could work for *People* magazine — and for some foolish reason I have this terrible urge to tell you everything. Ah, the irony."

Nick inclined his head toward Grace. "Would she look this star-struck if she worked for *People*?"

She nodded earnestly. "It's true. You're the first star I've ever met. I think I saw our local weatherman in the mall once, but that's about it."

Killian refilled his wine glass for the second time and sat back down in the white chair. "Well, at least I don't see any cameras."

Grace made a funny sound in her throat. She just remembered that her little pink camera was in the pocket of her jeans. The irony, indeed. Here she was, six feet away from Killian Ross and she couldn't even take a picture of him. Maybe she could work up to that. For now, she would encourage him to talk, to confide in them. Maybe later she would broach the subject of a photo.

"Look, we're just average people," she said. "You've been very nice inviting us into your beautiful suite and sharing your food with us." She reached for a piece of cheese on Nick's plate. "And you didn't have to do all that. So, in return, if you want to talk, we promise whatever you tell us will go no further than right here." She held up her right hand like a Boy Scout.

"Unless you are about to confess to a murder or something," Nick added quickly. "I mean, the deal's off then."

"No, no murders," Killian shook his head. "Though I won't say it didn't cross my mind." Grace laughed a little nervously, but no one joined in. She wondered if he meant it.

Kelly Adamson

"All right, it's not as if it will stay a secret forever anyway. Nothing ever does in show business. But, at least tell me something about you first. I don't even know your names."

"Fair enough. I'm Nick Howard and this is my wife, Grace. We're from Alabama and we're here to celebrate our tenth anniversary, which is day after tomorrow."

Grace added, "I'm a secretary and Nick is a carpenter. We live in the suburbs with three dogs. Nick's hobby is target shooting and mine is…" she started to say 'photography,' but thought better of it. Instead she said 'gardening.' Nick looked sideways at her. She knew he was wondering when she'd ever gardened, but he didn't say anything. "That's about it." She shrugged. "We're pretty boring."

"What kind of dogs?" Killian asked, filling up his wine glass yet again.

"Mutts," Nick answered. "One part beagle, one part terrier, and one part long-gone smooth talker."

Killian raised his glass in a toast. "To dogs. Always loyal. They will never lie to you."

"Here, here."

Grace and Nick drank to dogs with Killian. Then, a little tipsy, he began his story.

Chapter 3 – Makar

A few miles away, two men, one tall and thin and one short and fat, picked up their car from the long-term-parking lot at McCarren International Airport. Neither had spoken since they left Atlanta. They truly believed they were justified in their actions, but doubted their boss would see it the same way. All he would see was their failure. The closer they got to Las Vegas, the more uneasy they became.

Makar had been on their side once, an ally. Their boss would be angry they'd killed him, and angrier still that they hadn't disposed of his body properly. He also wouldn't like the fact that they'd left their pistols in a locker in Concourse C. But, most of all, their boss would be angry because they hadn't done the job he'd sent them to do.

They had tried. They'd tailed Makar in a rented sedan for three days and had gotten as far as Georgia. But one of the men was six-foot-eight, and the other, though less than six feet, weighed almost three hundred pounds. Not exactly a duo who could blend into the shadows.

And so it was that Makar spotted them in the Atlanta airport. He became evasive. Casually, at first. They followed him to get ice cream. They followed him to the newsstand. Then they followed him into the vast, open baggage room beneath the terminal. It smelled like diesel fumes and axle grease. The roar of the planes was deafening. They almost lost him among the baggage carts. They finally spotted him hurrying toward a stairwell that would take him back out, and that was where they stopped him.

The stairwell was poorly lit and smelled of insecticide and cigarettes. Makar made it to the first landing before they put a bullet through his calf from behind. He didn't beg for his life and he didn't tell them where the package was, even with a gun pressed in his eye socket. They had to respect him for that.

The package they'd been sent to retrieve wasn't hidden on Makar's body. They'd searched him thoroughly after they killed him. All they found was a receipt for ice cream.

Chapter 4 – A Very Nice Cell

"It all started almost a month ago," Killian said, with just the slightest bit of a slur thanks to the wine. "No, that's not true; I suppose it began three years ago in a little night club in Monaco when I met Astrid LeBeau, the most breathtakingly beautiful woman in the entire world."

The fact that Killian Ross and supermodel Astrid LeBeau were an item was no secret. Grace remembered well the magazine covers that proclaimed them "The World's Most Beautiful Couple." Seeing their perfect, smiling faces made standing in line at the supermarket a little more enjoyable. "Perfect looks, perfect lives, perfect love." This type of headline almost always made her buy the magazine.

"I still remember what she was wearing that night," he said. "Hell, I still remember what she *smelled* like that night. She was a goddess among mere mortals. A dozen preening men swarmed around her, vying for her attention. A bunch of bloody peacocks. She just looked bored with them all. The French are good at that. I caught her eye and winked. Then I turned and went outside. She followed, as I knew she would. We spent the rest of the night on the floor of my hotel room; we never even made it to the bed."

Grace shifted on the red leather couch. This was even better than the tabloids. Had she really just promised she wouldn't tell any of this?

His voice hardened as he continued, "Little did I know she would one day rip my still-beating heart out of my chest and set it ablaze in front of my eyes." He held up his hand, staring at the imaginary remains of his heart like poor Yorick's skull.

Grace and Nick stole a quick glance at each other. This was a little more melodramatic that the unlucky-in-love stories their friends told. She might have laughed if Killian hadn't looked so miserable.

"She moved to London to be close to me, but wouldn't live with me," he said.

Grace nodded. Of course she knew that; she'd seen pictures of both of their houses in *Bright Star* magazine.

"She said she didn't believe in living together before marriage." His lip curled in a sneer and he paused to pour more wine. "So what did I do? I bought her the biggest damned diamond I could find and I got down on one bloody knee and I asked her to marry me."

Grace remembered seeing photos of the engagement ring, too, some emerald cut thing, ludicrously large on Astrid's bony finger.

Killian's face was getting flushed from all the wine. He was staring absently at his glass, swirling the crimson liquid around and around. "Three and a half weeks ago," he continued in an obvious effort at controlled calm, "we finished filming in Vancouver. Astrid never came with me on location. She said she didn't want to *distract* me." He made a noise of disgust at ever believing such a lie. "We finished filming early, which almost never happens, and I took the next flight home. Ruth sent a driver to the airport for me, of course, and I went straight to Astrid's house. I asked the driver to wait, I would come back and get my things in a minute. I wanted to surprise her." He drained his wine glass in one gulp, refilled it and continued. "Well, I surprised her, all right.

"I let myself in the front door. I could hear the sound of the TV coming from her bedroom. Quite a torrid sex scene, from the sound of it – all moans and groans and bedsprings." Killian stared at his wine glass, but Grace knew he was seeing the interior of Astrid's darkened house, seeing his own feet climb the stairs.

"I could see her through the open doorway, though she couldn't see me. I could see her... and the man she was on top of." He squeezed his eyes shut again, like he was trying to squeeze the memory out of his head. "Needless to say, it was not the television I was hearing. It was my beautiful, angelic..." His voice cracked and he stopped.

Grace glanced at Nick. He was frozen to his seat, trying to blend in to the surrounding leather like a chameleon. Why in the hell was Killian telling them this? Was he really this desperate for someone to talk to? Maybe this was one of those hidden camera, practical joke shows where a celebrity tries to make some unsuspecting couple uncomfortable. If so, it was working. Maybe they were filming right now and Astrid was going to jump out in a minute and yell, "Surprise!"

Nope.

Killian sprang out of his chair and began pacing back and forth in front of the long window like a caged lion.

"How...could...she...do...this?" he managed to spit out, though each syllable sounded like it cut him. "I *never* cheated on her, not once in three years! And I had plenty of opportunities." He stopped and turned to them as if waiting for an explanation. "We were about to be married, for Chrissake!"

After a pause, Nick asked, "What did you do then?" Grace gave him a scathing look. He shrugged.

"I…I left. I didn't want her to see me and I didn't want her to talk to me. I didn't want any hollow apologies or crocodile tears. I just wanted to get as far away from her as possible. I came here because I thought it would be the last place she'd look. She loathes Las Vegas. She says it's *fake*. That's rich, coming from her."

"She hasn't tried to contact you?" Grace asked.

"Of course. E-mails, voice mails, text messages; I've deleted them all. I don't care to hear what the bitch has to say."

He was a little calmer now as he reclaimed his seat on the white chair and wiped his wet eyes with the backs of his hands.

"Ruth wants me to come home. I do miss her. And I miss my dog, Zeus. Ruth is taking care of him for me. Funny, he never really liked Astrid. I used to think he was jealous, but it turns out he was just smart." He drained his glass again and refilled it immediately. "Darling Ruth. She's telling everyone I'm on holiday. She said every time she drives by my house, a couple of photographers are hanging around in the street. They know something's going on. They know my schedule better than I do, and they know I am supposed to be there. And they know Astrid's not with me. That's the main reason I've been staying in my room here. If the paparazzi find me, Astrid will soon follow. And I just don't want to see her yet. I know I'll have to face her eventually, but not just yet."

He leaned over and put his head in his hands. "Oh, God," he groaned, "I don't want to talk about her anymore. I mean, I really thought I would burst an hour ago if I didn't get it all out. But now, I just don't have the strength."

Grace cleared her throat and tried to divert the subject away from cheating fiancées. "Um, where were you going tonight when we saw you in the ballroom?"

Killian shrugged. "I don't know, just out of here. I guess I was a little stir-crazy. I mean, it's a beautiful suite, but it's...lonely. His mouth twisted into a wry grin. "Ha! I guess that's why I accosted two innocent people looking for the buffet and bribed them with camembert to listen to my tale of woe. I apologize for that, incidentally." He gestured toward the empty plates that now littered the coffee table. "The least I could have done is order you some fresh food; the chef is really quite good."

"I believe you," Nick said, patting his full stomach.

After a pause, Grace said, "So, you really haven't been out? You've eaten every meal in this room for over three weeks?"

Killian nodded.

"Well, we've got to get you out of here," she said. "You can't stay cooped up in here like a prisoner in a cell." She looked around, "Okay, a *really nice* cell. But, that's beside the point; after almost a month in solitary here, it's still a cell."

Killian looked at her doubtfully, then said, "Be that as it may, I think going out would rather defeat the purpose of remaining hidden. Don't you agree?"

"Look," Grace said, "I've seen every movie you have ever made, even the bad ones" – Killian winced – "and until you spoke downstairs, I didn't recognize you. You're always the dashing, debonair man-about-town, even off camera. I've never seen your hair this long, and I have absolutely never seen you with a beard, and definitely not in blue jeans and tennis shoes, and I don't think anyone else has either. I think if you just don't talk to anyone, you'll be fine. We can at least take a walk outside, get some fresh air and see the sights. Besides, it's late; everyone out on the street now has their beer goggles on anyway. No one will recognize you."

"She has a point," Nick agreed. "I didn't have a clue who you were until you said something."

"Do you really think it could work?" Killian sat up a little straighter, like a prisoner with new hope of parole. "The hair and beard were for the movie I just finished, but no one has seen any stills from it yet. And, I really would love to see the Grand Canyon, but even if we just walk down the sidewalk, well, you know I've never done that here. That's rather exciting."

Nick shook his head. "You've met the Queen, had love scenes with some of the hottest women in the world, and it's common knowledge that you do most of your own stunts, but what you're excited about is the thought of walking down the sidewalk?"

Killian grinned. It was good to see him grin.

"First, you'll need to put on a long sleeve shirt to hide that tattoo. And do you have any sunglasses?" Grace asked.

"Only dark ones. I couldn't see a thing if I wore them outside now. You'd have to lead me around like I was blind." He looked thoughtful for a moment. "You know, I've never played a blind person before."

"Well, there's no need to start now," Grace said. "There has to be a shop around here somewhere that's open all night."

"Oh, yes," Killian nodded, "there's a twenty-four-hour chemist at the mouth of the Bazaar that has everything."

"I thought you hadn't been out," Nick said.

Killian pointed at the television. "Channel fifty-six is all about The Isis. I know more about this place than the concierge."

"So you were just lying to us when you said you didn't know where the buffet was earlier?" Nick shook his head in mock disgust. "Unbelievable."

Killian made a face, looking apologetic. "Sorry, mate."

The Delta Shop was indeed open twenty-four hours. Nick loitered with Killian just outside the front door while Grace bought a cheap pair of amber-tinted aviator glasses and a red baseball cap. Killian stood with his hands in his pockets and his eyes on the ground, trying to avoid meeting anyone's gaze. It didn't take long and they were on their way.

"Here. Put these on."

Killian slipped the glasses on and blinked, looking around, nodding.

Grace handed him the cap. He turned it over in his hands to look at the front. The word 'Lucky' was embroidered in big block letters on the front over a pair of red dice. "You must be joking," he said. "I'm not wearing this."

"Would you rather have 'Bikini Inspector'? Or perhaps 'I Heart Las Vegas' in rhinestones?" Grace drew a heart in the air with her two index fingers. "Those were the choices."

"Well, I can't be seen in this," Killian said indignantly. "I'll look like a… what do you call them? A redneck. Why don't you just black out a few of my teeth as well?"

"Oh, really? I thought you were trying *not* to look British," Grace snapped.

Killian raised his eyebrows in surprise. For a moment, Grace thought she'd gone too far. Then he turned to Nick and said, "Get this one, will you? She thinks she's Ricky Gervais." Then his face lit up and he clapped Nick on the shoulder. "You two are all right, you know."

"Don't worry," Nick said. "No one's going to know it's you under there."

Killian blew out a deep breath. Reluctantly, he put the cap on and turned to the nearest store window to check his reflection. He ran one hand over his shaggy beard and adjusted his new glasses. Then he turned back around with a grin. "Let's go."

As they stepped out into the dry night air, Killian inhaled deeply, as if he were walking through a field of fragrant wildflowers. Grace watched him out of the corner of her eye. The smell of car exhaust and diesel fumes were the easiest aromas to pick out – and probably the least offensive – but to each his own. His smile never faded as they jostled their way down the crowded sidewalk. It had to be two a.m., but the night owls rule Las Vegas. Up ahead a woman wore fairy wings and a tiara. A young Elvis in a gold lamé jacket was crossing the street in front of the Bellagio. Here and there, the ground was littered with colorful business cards, each with X-rated photographs of call-girls for hire. Killian scooped one off of a low wall as they passed. "I think I know her!" he quipped to Nick.

"Shhhhh…" Grace warned.

He looked contrite and slipped the card in his pocket. "Souvenir," he mouthed.

A construction site stood to their left and across the street, right next to the CityCenter, filling a whole huge Las Vegas block. Another themed mega-resort going up where a landmark had been. They could see the strings of bare light bulbs twinkling high up in the steel skeletons of the buildings. The massive cranes sat motionless, like dinosaurs in a museum. They stood poised to resume their work in just a few hours, hauling I-beams and vats of concrete. For now, it was the only spot in four miles that was quiet.

The Eiffel Tower at the Paris hotel stood ahead of them. Killian pointed like a tour guide. "Not as large as the real one, but much cleaner, eh?"

The fifteen-foot-tall replica of the Fontaine de les Mers stood in front of the hotel and the water seemed to glow with a blue light as it cascaded over the sides. Grace pulled her camera out for the first time since meeting Killian. "Hey, Nick," she called, "Let me get your picture in front of the fountain."

She wasn't expecting Killian's reaction. He held out his hand and closed the distance between them with two strides. "Here, let me take a photo of you together," he said.

He held the little pink camera in front of him and backed up a few paces, checking to make sure everything was in frame. Grace joined her husband and leaned against the fountain. A concrete fish spitting water was visible over their shoulders. "Okay," Killian said, "put your arm around her."

Click.

"Good. Now look at each other, not at me."

Click.

"One more," he said, squatting down like an umpire to look up at them, undoubtedly getting as much of the tower in the frame as possible. "Big smile."

Click.

"Hold it right there." He stood and joined them at the fountain, standing next to Grace and putting his arm around her shoulder. He turned the little camera around and held it at arm's length. He leaned in to join them in the frame and said, "Say camembert!" The little flash popped brightly at such close range, leaving stars in their eyes. But, Grace already had stars in her eyes. She got a photo of Killian without even having to ask, and with his arm around her, no less. Of course, it was unlikely anyone would believe her, considering how he looked at the moment. They would think a street person had wandered into the photo.

"Can we go up in the tower?" Killian asked.

"It's probably not operating at this time of night," Nick answered. "Maybe we can come back tomorrow."

Killian flinched and looked around nervously. "Come back in the daylight?"

"What? It's not like you're a vampire," Grace said. I know you played one in *Poseyhurst Manor*, but even *he* could go out in the daylight."

Killian relaxed and smiled graciously, instantly back in movie star mode.

"Actually," Nick said, "we planned to check out Red Rock tomorrow. If you want to go with us, it would be great. The weather is supposed to be perfect, and you probably won't run into a lot of people there."

"Really?" Killian asked. "You'd let me join you? I wouldn't be imposing?"

From the expectant look in his eyes, Grace wondered who could ever say no to him. "The more, the merrier," she answered brightly. It was a date. She, her husband and *the* Killian Ross were going to hike around Red Rock. Life was good.

From Paris, they made their way across the street toward Caesar's Palace. Killian was drawn like a magnet to the eight-acre lake that housed the dancing waters fountain at the front of the Bellagio. "I can see this from my window, you know, but of course I can't hear the music." He hurried onto one of the round balconies overlooking the huge expanse and leaned on the railing. "I hope they play *Viva Las Vegas* next; I like that one." He looked at his watch. "When is it set to go off again?"

"Um, three p.m., I think," Grace said.

"Three p.m.?" He turned exasperatedly to Grace. "You mean we're too late for this, too? I thought this was the city that never sleeps."

"That's New York." Grace pulled a folded piece of notebook paper out of her back pocket, where she'd made her cheat sheet for the trip. "It says here it plays every fifteen minutes from three p.m.

to midnight." She looked back up at Killian, but he was looking past her, and it looked like he was seeing a ghost.

Nick said, "What are you looking at?" then a dull, "Oh," as he turned to follow Killian's gaze.

The Number 333 city bus to Henderson idled noisily at the traffic light. Only in Las Vegas, thought Grace, would a bus run this late. Then she saw her: six feet tall and eighteen feet long, stretched out in a pink and white baby doll negligee on the side of the 333 to Henderson. Astrid LeBeau's flawless face smiled demurely back at them. "Twilight Lingerie. Why wait until dark?" read the advertisement.

The light turned green and the bus rumbled up the street. Killian stood looking at the spot where it had been like the image was burned into his eyes.

"Are you all right, man?" Nick asked.

As if on cue, Killian's cell phone rang. Whitney Houston's "I Will Always Love You." Not the first surprise of the evening. Without looking, he pulled the phone out of his pocket and pressed a button to disconnect the call. It must have been Astrid's song. He turned around slowly to stare at the still expanse of black water. He stood so quietly, so perfectly still, that he could have been one of the stone statues that dotted the landscape at the Bellagio.

Then he pulled back his arm like a major league pitcher and lobbed the cell phone out into the fountain like a grenade. It arced high, fifty feet in the air, and came down with a graceful "plunk" among the air cannons.

"That *bitch*!" He choked out between clenched teeth. "That lying whore! She never loved me. She just wanted to be seen on my arm. She wouldn't go on location with me, but you can bet she never missed an opportunity to walk the red carpet."

Then he ripped off his wristwatch and held it up in front of Nick and Grace. "*She* gave me this," he said spitefully.

"That's nice. Is that a Rolex?" Grace asked, trying hard to sound calm.

"Do you see what's engraved on the back?" Of course they couldn't. He was shaking it around too much. "It says *Until the End of Time*." His voice was full of venom. "Have you ever heard a bigger lie in your entire life? And I fell for it. What a bloody fool." Before they could stop him, he launched the watch with a vengeance into the same watery grave as the cell phone.

"Hey, buddy, if you're trying to be incognito, this is not the way to do it," Nick said softly, edging toward Killian. "I know it sucks. She screwed you over and she's a bitch and all that. We get it. But people are beginning to stare."

Sure enough, several people had stopped what they were doing to watch the crazy man throw his possessions into the fountain.

"Not to mention the fact that security is probably on their way out right now. So, maybe we should get out of here," Nick added.

Grace nodded, looking around for guards. "Nick's right. Let's go get the car and drive somewhere that's less obvious, somewhere off the Strip. Somewhere you won't find any photographers." She held her hand out to Killian. "Trust me."

Chapter 5 – Reprieve

Pavel Alkaev's normally tan face was a dangerous shade of crimson as he confronted his subordinates. His eyes flashed menacingly from one to the other of the two men, who seemed unable to meet his gaze, but chose instead to focus on the matted orange carpeting at their feet. He was furious at their ineptitude and wanted them to feel his wrath.

"If I didn't have to clean up the mess, I would kill you both right now," he hissed.

Then, inspired, he pulled a pistol from beneath his Armani jacket and leveled it at the shorter man's chest. "On second thought, I could just kill one of you and let the other one clean it up. Hmm?"

The two men struggled to stand as still as possible, although the shorter one's hands began to shake and beads of perspiration formed on his round face.

Alkaev looked at him in disgust and lowered his gun. "You are the only man I know who is so fat you even sweat in the desert."

He paced back and forth in front of them, swinging his gun as he walked. He loved the feel of it, the reassuring weight of it in his hand. He'd carried a Berretta M9 since moving to the states, not the antiquated Cold War Tokarevs of the two incompetents who now stood before him. They didn't even *try* to blend in, he thought. And now they had left two of their guns in a locker in the Atlanta airport. Imbeciles.

He turned to face them, making sure there was less than a foot between them, uncomfortably close. "What were your orders?"

No answer.

Alkaev let out an exaggerated sigh and then slapped the shorter man hard across his fat face with his empty hand.

The man spluttered, "You told us to bring you the traitor."

"And what did you do instead?"

The two men shifted uneasily, but remained silent. Alkaev had to reach up to the taller man, the sound of his open-handed slap echoing in the motel room.

"I'll tell you what you did. You dumped a dead body in an airport stairwell. A dead body with ties to our operation."

"But, he was a traitor…" the shorter man began weakly.

"Yes, and he would have been dealt with, by me. Did it ever occur to you idiots that I might want to question the man? Did it enter your empty heads that he might have information that would be useful to us? Now we may never know who his intended buyer was. And you bring me *nothing*."

He resumed pacing, hands behind his back, talking to himself, but purposely loud enough for them to hear. "And now I have to decide what to do with the pair of you. You are useless and incompetent, but I can't let you go; you know too much. But, how would I dispose of your bodies? I could take you out in the desert and make you dig your own graves." He hesitated, really giving it some thought. "No, that would take too long. I don't have all night."

He glanced sideways at them. Sweat dripped off the fat one's nose. The tall one had his head bowed, his hands stuffed in his pants pockets like a guilty child. Then he brightened a little as he pulled out a scrap of paper.

"Um…Boss. It might not mean anything, but he had this in his pocket."

Alkaev reached out and snatched the paper. It was a receipt for ice cream. He clenched his teeth and was about to slap the big idiot again when he saw handwriting on the back of the paper. In small, cramped letters, it read: "Nick Howard, LAS 238."

"Where did you say you followed him?" Alkaev asked.

"To the big room with all the luggage," the tall man said tentatively. "Where they take the luggage to the planes."

Slowly, very slowly, a smile softened Alkaev's face. "Of course," he said, as if the information he sought had been obvious all along. "How kind of Makar to do half the work for us and even leave a note. The greedy bastard was nothing if not resourceful." He wouldn't admit it to these two, but he was glad they'd killed him, just not happy they'd left him in the Atlanta airport.

Chapter 6 – The Barrelhouse

The three of them walked back to The Isis, Killian simmering in silence. He kept his eyes on the ground, letting Grace lead him. She marched straight through to the bell desk and asked for William.

The unlikely trio was loitering by a brightly lit museum case that held items for sale in the Isis Boutique when William arrived. "That's a real beauty, isn't it?" he asked over Grace's shoulder. She was looking at a gold necklace in the shape of a hawk, with its wings almost touching as they fanned out in a circle above its head. And it really was a beauty. Each feather was a different piece of inlaid stone, orange, white, blue and green. "That's a replica of the Amulet of Kavayet, belonging to King Tut's mother. They found her tomb under 120 feet of sand, in what you might call a pauper's grave. That necklace was the only thing in the whole tomb worth a dime and it's worth…well, it's priceless. It proved she was Tut's mother. You can't put a price on that." He grinned and handed her a flyer he took from a Lucite holder next to the display. "Here, this will tell you all about it."

"Thanks for the history lesson," Grace said, "but your mummy-loving boss isn't here right now, and what I need is some non-Egyptian information."

"Fire away," William said.

"I need to know somewhere fun we can go this time of night that's decidedly un-touristy. We want to know somewhere the pretty

Kelly Adamson

people don't go, somewhere the pretty people wouldn't be caught dead."

"You're asking me where the ugly people go?" William asked.

"I guess I'm asking you where the locals go, the working men, the salt-of-the-earth types."

"I get it," William said, nodding. "You're looking for the Barrelhouse."

"I am?"

"Sure, it happens sometimes. People come out here and they want to see the gritty underbelly of the beast instead of all the velvet rope clubs. I totally get that. I can't stand all the strobe lights and overpriced drinks in those 'ultra lounges.' But, you didn't hear that from me."

"So, what's this Barrelhouse like?" Nick asked.

"It's a dive, a real hole-in-the-wall, but if you like good blues music, it's the best place in three states. And, I guarantee you won't see any pretty people."

"How do we get there?"

William drew a map on the back of the gift shop flyer. It would lead them straight to the corner of Dartmouth Avenue and Warrior Road. With a wink, he said to tell the bartender, a woman named Skye, that "Black Mountain Willie" sent them. He said she would take care of them.

Once in the car, Killian finally broke his silence. "I would like to apologize for my disgraceful outburst earlier. That was totally unforgiveable. And I want to thank you for ushering me away before the police arrived." They rode on for a minute in silence before he added, "That was silly of me, absolutely ridiculous. I'm obviously going to see photos of her, after all. They're everywhere. I'll just have to get used to it. I'm sure I'll even see the 'Killian and Astrid Split' headlines before long, and I'll just have to ignore them. I'm a grown man, for God's sake. It's not as if I've never been dumped before." He paused. "Well, okay, perhaps not in this magnitude, but, well, I have been. And you know if I let her get to me like that, well, it's hurting no one but me, is it? And I'll be honest with you; I'm tired of being the loser in this equation."

He continued this soliloquy for several miles, not really needing or asking for their input. Each time Grace thought he was through, he would start up again. By the time they turned onto Warrior Road, he seemed in considerably better spirits. Grace finally said, "I hate to interrupt, but listening to you talk just now made me realize something. It seems to me that the two things that give you away are your eyes – they're just so...*green,*" she felt her face flush, but continued, "and your voice – everybody knows that voice.

"We've addressed the eyes; they look sort of brown with those glasses on. Now we need to address the voice. I was trying to think of a movie where you had an American accent, but I can't remember a single one. Haven't you ever played an American?"

"Well, of course, I have. I did six months on Broadway as a yank. How's this?" He cleared his throat. "Jimmy, why don't you and Big Sal take Pauley for a ride and show him how we do things around heah?"

"Hmmm.... Do you have anything that doesn't sound like the Godfather?"

Killian looked sincerely offended. "I'll have you know I spent a lot of time and effort learning to sound like that. Are you telling me that no one in America talks that way?"

"Not since they repealed prohibition," Nick said. "Try to sound more like us."

"No offense, mate, but you two sound like the cast of *Gone With the Bloody Wind.*"

"You *say* 'no offense,' but I really think you intend offense," Grace said.

Killian folded his arms across his chest and looked out the window, pretending to ignore her.

"Children, children," drawled Nick. "Let's focus here. We obviously can't call you Killian in public. We've got to call you something else. How about Bobby? That's nice and common."

"Bobby?" Killian said. "Bobby, Bobby, Bobby." He said the word like he was trying it on, like he was tasting it. "Hmmm… That's a policeman, you know. How about Bubba? I always wanted to play a Bubba. Then I can say things like *howdy* and y*'all*."

Grace shook her head. "Nobody says *howdy*. And there's no way you're getting away with y*'all*."

Killian sighed and leaned back in his seat, as far as anyone could lean in the back of the little Subaru. "Fine. I won't say *howdy*, as long I can be Bubba."

It wasn't far past Freemont Street that the people and the lights began to thin out. Many of the buildings looked abandoned. This was definitely not touristy.

William had assured them they couldn't miss the Barrelhouse, but then he'd also assured them they couldn't miss the Temple Buffet either. Consequently, they circled the corner of Warrior and Dartmouth several times before Nick finally spotted faded gray letters stenciled on a single metal door that read: "The Barrelhouse, est. 1965." There was no parking lot to speak of, but a number of well-worn cars lined the street, and the chrome of several nicer motorcycles gleamed in the light of street lamps.

Lowell's Plumbing Supply Shop across the street was closed, of course, at two-thirty a.m., but a bright security light lit up the small parking lot. Nick pulled in beside a faded red pickup truck with a primered driver's door and no tailgate.

Just as Grace was about to say this might not have been such a good idea, Killian hopped out of the backseat rubbing his hands together. "This place is *brilliant!*" he said, "and not a camera in sight. Howdy, y'all!"

"Okay, hold it right there," Nick said. "If you're not gonna take this seriously, we might as well go back to the hotel."

Killian stopped. He grinned and shrugged at Nick.

"And you can wipe that smile off your face, too," Nick said. "It doesn't work on me. And it's not gonna work in there with a bunch of bikers either, that's for sure." He pointed at Killian. "Nothing is *brilliant* around here. I assure you, the people in this place do not use that word. Where's your Bronx accent? Get into character or get back in the car."

"Sorry," Killian said. "You know, you might make a good director." He hung his head, took a deep breath, let it out slowly. Grace and Nick watched as he shook out his arms and legs like an

Olympic swimmer getting ready for a relay. When he looked up again, his face was different. His grin was slick, his eyes were narrowed, and his movements were smooth and deliberate. He hunched forward, looking like a coiled spring or a rattlesnake waiting to strike. He reached up to rub his bearded cheek, and when he said, "Let's do this thing," it was pure Jersey Shore.

They followed him as he swaggered across the road, amazed at his transformation.

The place seemed so deserted that, as Killian reached for the metal door, Grace half expected it to be locked, or at least for the hinges to creak. Instead, they were greeted with an onslaught of noise that almost rivaled the casino floor. Loud masculine voices and ribald laughter surrounded the "clunk" of billiard balls into corner pockets. A lone figure with a guitar played Robert Johnson's delta blues at the far end of the room. There was no stage, just a space with a microphone, a stool and a couple of spotlights. The dark space in front of him was littered with small round tables and mismatched chairs full of patrons paying rapt attention to this middle-aged man whose fingers flew across the strings like he could do this in his sleep.

A tall, thin man with a long, thin beard suddenly blocked their view. "Ten dollar cover charge."

Killian, in character, waved away Nick's hand. "I got this," he said in his hard gangster accent. "Your money's no good here." He handed some bills to the doorman and they nodded at each other as if sharing some dark secret.

The smell of cigarette smoke and beer encircled them before they even stepped inside. Grace was glad she was still in the jeans and tee shirt she'd worn on the plane. She would certainly have been out of place if she'd been dressed for a night out at The Eye.

Killian seemed oddly in his element as he sauntered over to the end of the bar to place his drink order. A beautiful Native American woman, her long hair worn loose, was making change at the register. When her big doe eyes caught site of Killian — six feet of blonde self-assurance, handsome even in a six dollar baseball cap and five dollar sunglasses — she leaned toward him like a moth to a flame. The brown suede vest she wore as a shirt fell forward as she leaned, offering an up-close and personal view of cleavage as well as a couple of otherwise-hidden tattoos. "What can I do you for?" she asked in a husky purr.

Ah, this must be Skye, Grace thought. She looked like she could take good care of whatever she chose.

Apparently this dawned on Killian too, because he said "Black Mountain Willie sent us."

Her smooth dark face broke into a smile, a much different look than she was wearing before. It was a sweet, genuine smile that made her look like a teenager. "Oh, Big Willie. How is my favorite harp player?"

"Just fine," Killian said smoothly, although Grace could tell he was probably picturing angels, or maybe even Harpo Marx.

Skye turned to get their drinks and Grace leaned in and whispered, "She means he plays the harmonica. A harp is a harmonica."

"Well, why didn't she say that?"

Skye passed them three draft beers in plastic cups. No glass bottles were allowed in the Barrelhouse, and no choice of brands,

Kelly Adamson

either. It was just 'beer,' whatever they happened to get from their distributor that week, but Skye poured it with very little head, and it was good and cold. Grace couldn't remember the last time a beer had tasted this good. She usually preferred a glass of wine, the sweeter the better.

They walked around to the other side of the pool tables to get a better look at the guitarist, a wiry, white man in his fifties, wearing a sleeveless tee-shirt and baggy jeans. His guitar looked older than he did, and was patched in places with silver duct tape. It sounded different than any guitar Grace had ever heard. The notes were sharp, crystal clear and resounding, even when playing Muddy Waters. This guy was good, way too good for a dive like this, but as she looked closer at his smiling face, she could see there was no place he would rather be.

"Hey, Lucky," came a booming voice from behind them. They turned to see every single person around the pool tables with their eyes fixed squarely on the three newcomers. So much for blending in. The speaker's arms were folded across the broad expanse of his chest. A huge moustache hung down on either side of his mouth, making him look a little like a walrus. He wore a faded, gray flannel shirt with the arms torn off at the shoulders, probably, noted Grace, because the sleeves would not have gone around his massive biceps. The man inclined his head toward the pool table and said, "You want in?" It didn't seem as much an invitation as a challenge, but Killian seemed oblivious to that. He actually looked pleased at this new turn of events.

The cues hung on a rack behind Nick and Grace. Killian picked one out and said confidently to them, "I was a billiard player in *One Dark Night*," as if that solved everything. He turned the cue horizontally in front of him, eyeing it for straightness. Nick whispered to Grace, "He played one in a movie?" She nodded. "Did he at least play a good one?" She didn't answer because the walrus was talking again.

"Eight ball. Five bucks a point." He pushed the rack of balls out onto the felt and said, "Lucky breaks."

Killian rolled the white cue ball around with the end of his stick. It was a lazy motion, as if he had all the time in the world. Maybe he was good. On the other hand, thought Grace with a sinking feeling, maybe he was stalling. Maybe he didn't know the first thing about pool.

He leaned over the stick, took aim once, twice, then *crack*, the sound of the cue ball smacking the yellow one ball was like a firecracker. If everyone in the area wasn't already watching, they were after that. Three balls went in three pockets, the four, the five and the seven.

A murmur went around the table. Killian never looked up. He only had eyes for the game. He stalked around to the right side and pointed at the far corner pocket with the cue stick. He didn't look up to see if his gesture was acknowledged. He just slammed in the one ball. The cue rolled slowly back down to his end of the table, and he only had to adjust a few inches to the right to make the next shot. He pointed with the stick to the side pocket across the table and then, *crack*, in went the two.

Nick hung his head and whispered, "Oh, shit."

Grace closed her eyes. She could see tomorrow's headlines in her mind, and they weren't good. Maybe paparazzi didn't frequent this neighborhood, but she bet police photographers did. She wondered if they really made those chalk outlines or if that was just for the movies. She was afraid they might have a chance to find out.

Killian moved clockwise, chalking his cue, never taking his eyes off the table. A petite woman with peroxide-blonde hair, a tight Harley-Davidson halter top and a pair of cut-off blue jeans sat on a bar stool beside the nearest support post. When Killian leaned over the table for his next shot, she was right behind him. She didn't hesitate, just reached out and slapped him hard across the butt. It made a nice loud sound, and the crowd roared in approval. To his credit, Killian didn't even flinch. He simply took the shot – which he made – then turned slowly to smile at the woman. He wagged his finger back and forth playfully and said, "Now, wouldn't you have felt just awful if I missed that shot?"

The woman was inspecting her hand, with its long nails painted fire-engine red. She looked up with a gleam in her eye and said, "I think you hurt my hand." She stuck out her bottom lip in a mischievous pout and extended her hand to Killian. "You should kiss it and make it better."

"Oh, shit," Nick whispered again.

Still smiling, Killian cut his eyes left and right, waiting for a reaction from someone, anyone. He had about five seconds to figure out what was expected of him here. Would it be worse to look like he was making a pass at someone's girl, or would it be worse to look like he was disrespecting her? No one moved. Several other women flanked his accuser, all grinning widely now, waiting for his next move. Not one man took even a single step toward her. That was a good sign.

He bowed at the waist and took her outstretched hand. "Please accept my apologies," he said, like a true gentleman mobster. He touched his lips to her hand and she giggled like a schoolgirl. Her friends giggled too.

Movement shimmered around the group like a wave. Perhaps a faux pas had been averted.

Grace knew they weren't out of the woods, though, and as Killian lined up for his next shot, she leaned in to Nick and whispered, "Do you notice the one thing all the men here have in common, besides the tattoos and black leather? They're all *bald*. And I don't mean *chemo patient bald* and I don't mean *receding hairline bald*, I mean *I got tired of people grabbing my hair in knife fights so I shaved it all off with a straight razor bald!*"

Play resumed and Grace watched the women, all five of them, all sitting together, ignoring – and being ignored by – all the men in the bar except one. They had adoring eyes for no one but Killian, watching as he sank first the six and then the eight with little fanfare and absolutely no effort.

Meanwhile, Nick counted the steps to the nearest exit. These guys really didn't look like the skinheads he'd seen and, after all, they were listening to the blues. Ah, the irony that would be. But they were certainly some sort of gang, and there were probably a dozen of them all wearing the same emblem, "Vegas Vipers," on the backs of their jackets.

Grace held her breath as Killian offered his hand to the walrus. Everyone was watching, and the big man knew it. He hesitated, but Killian's hand never wavered. "The name's Bubba," he said. "And I believe it's your break."

Finally, after what seemed like an hour but couldn't have been more than ten seconds, the biker grabbed Killian's hand, shook it once. Everyone breathed a sigh of relief.

The man counted out the money he owed Killian and said, "I'm Sunshine." He nodded toward the men nearest him and said, "This is Shady and that's Little Frank."

If this was Little Frank, Grace didn't want to meet Big Frank.

"Why do they call you Sunshine?" Killian asked as he racked the balls for the next game.

"I'm named for my personality," grumbled Sunshine. "It's my sunny disposition." Little Frank chuckled at this.

Grace and Nick were dumbstruck. What just happened here? It sounded like a bad joke: Three idiots walk into a bar. The king of the idiots runs the table against a big scary biker and then the biker shakes his hand and suddenly everything is okay?

Play began again and was a little more evenly matched this time. Killian took some good-natured ribbing from Sunshine as play switched back and forth, the two men basically taking turns running the table, though Killian was definitely the better player. Skye poured them some more ice-cold beer in plastic cups, and everyone seemed to relax a little. Music floated over from the other end of the room. *"I got me a good woman, she love me like no one else. I got me a good woman, she love me like no one else. But these evil-hearted women, they want to keep me for themselves."*

Nick kept his arm draped casually around Grace's shoulders. Marking his territory, she knew. Any other time, it would have annoyed her. But tonight, she just leaned in closer.

As Killian waited his turn, the red-nailed woman in the Harley halter addressed him again. "My name's Di, like Princess Di." She batted her eyes at him. Her fake lashes looked more like spiders than eyelashes.

"Yes, *just* like Princess Di," Killian murmured, smiling broadly.

"And these are my friends, Fay, Brandy and Terri Lynn."

"Ladies." They all grinned and smoothed their hair as he nodded to them.

"So, what's your story, Blondie?" Di asked, putting her hand on his arm.

"My story?"

"Yeah, me and the girls here think you look awful familiar."

"Aw, shucks, ma'am, I get that all the time," Killian said with an ingratiating shrug. "I guess I've just got one of those faces."

"It sure is a nice face," Fay said. She reached up and stroked his bearded cheek with her tanned fingers. Killian took her hand and brought it up to his lips, much the same as he had Di's.

The next moment, he was on his knees on the concrete. Nick caught him by the back of the shirt before he hit the ground, and he wavered to remain upright. Half a broken pool cue clattered across the floor and his red baseball cap stared up at him from three feet away.

Grace stifled a gasp. She rushed over and knelt in front of him. His green eyes were unfocused. She slapped his cheek lightly. He looked around slowly, trying to find her. "Ten more minutes, Ma," he mumbled. Grace pulled her hand back and smacked him across the face. His head twisted and she felt guilty immediately.

Kelly Adamson

"Bubba!" she called right in his ear. He groaned in protest. She put a hand up to touch the back of his head. No blood. That was good. He squeezed his eyes shut and Grace helped him to his feet.

Nick stood between him and the crowd of angry men. "My friend didn't mean any harm," he said. "We didn't come here looking for trouble."

Killian stood beside him, trying to focus on the scene. "What the hell just happened here?" he demanded dazedly, thankfully remembering to use the accent.

"I don't know. You tell me," growled Sunshine, still wielding the rest of the broken cue stick. "I turn my back for one minute and you're hitting on my woman."

"Your woman?" Realization was slowly dawning on Killian. "No, no, no, no," he said calmly. "To begin with, I assure you I was not hitting on anyone.

"And secondly," he searched his foggy brain for a secondly, still trying to clear the stars out of his head. "Wait, no one seemed to mind when I kissed Di's hand. What's the difference?"

"Di is a free agent. She doesn't belong to any of us. She can do whatever she wants to whoever she wants."

Grace's mouth fell open. What century was this, anyway? Maybe they were farther removed from civilization than she thought.

"Belong?" Killian squeezed his eyes shut. Grace couldn't tell if it was from the wine and the beer or the blow to the head, but he was definitely looking a little green. He inhaled slowly and said, "In my defense, how in the world would anyone possibly guess that Fay was your...woman? I mean, you haven't spoken to her since we've been here."

"Yeah, well I've had my eye on her, and all she's been looking at is you, like a hungry wolf looking at a jackrabbit. And...I...don't...like...it." Sunshine slapped the remainder of the broken cue into the palm of his left hand as he spoke.

Killian took a step back. "I can't help it if someone looks at me. I have no control over that."

"Like hell you don't," snarled Shady, standing shoulder to shoulder with his comrade. "Darlene is *my* woman and she's been eyeballin' you ever since you walked in the door! You and your tight shirt and your white teeth," he scoffed. "Teeth like that ain't natural."

There was a general rumble of agreement from the other bikers. Someone in the crowd said, "I think he needs to be taught a lesson."

Another rumble of assent circled through the crowd.

"Gentlemen, I *beseech* you to see reason," Killian urged.

At that, Sunshine and Shady exchanged a puzzled look. Apparently, "brilliant" was not the only word they never used around here.

Nick whispered in Grace's ear, "As soon as someone makes a move, you head for the door as fast as you can." He slipped the car keys into her hand. "Get out of here and call the police." Grace's heart was racing, but her feet were frozen to the spot. She wondered with a jolt if her legs would be able to move when the time came.

A melodic voice rose above the looming fray. "If I've told you boys once, I've told you a hundred times, I don't allow fighting in here." The group turned as one to see diminutive Skye pointing a shotgun across the bar at the troublemakers. It looked like it weighed as much as she did, but she brandished it like a pro. "Now, Sunshine, you put down that stick. I think this fellow has a very good point after all. You boys never pay the slightest bit of attention to these ladies. I've always wondered why they put up with you."

Sunshine's mouth fell open in disbelief. "Don't tell me you're taking his side, Skye."

"He's telling the truth. I always take the side of the truth," Skye said. "Not to mention that, in this instance, I'm backing up my girls."

This seemed to empower the women, who were now on their feet, most of them with their hands on their hips. "You know, she's right," Darlene said. "Why do we put up with you?"

"Yeah," Fay added, "and we are *not* your property! We have feelings, you know."

"We get all dressed up to try and impress you and you don't even look at us all night!" added Darlene, her arms folded in front of her, pushing up her already ample cleavage. "You don't know how lucky you are to have us." She turned around to the other women and said, "Come on, ladies, let's go somewhere we can be appreciated."

As every woman in the place, except Grace and Skye, moved in the direction of the door, Shady lurched toward Darlene. "I'll show you about appreciating," he snarled.

"One of these barrels has birdshot, and one of them has buckshot. Which one do you want me to use?" called Skye sweetly.

Shady stopped cold. Apparently, nobody doubted Skye's intentions.

Grace sidestepped behind one of the support columns, trying to put something between herself and the shotgun.

"All right, all right! Hold your horses now," Shady said, his hands in the air in surrender. "No need to get your panties in a wad."

"Don't you worry about my panties, Shady Eustes," Skye said. "Now, if you boys can't behave, you're gonna have to leave. You know the rules."

"Aw, we're just having a little fun," said Sunshine. "Just a little of that male bonding you always hear about. Right, Bubba?"

Killian smiled, relief evident on his face. "Sure, sure," he said. "All in good fun."

Skye was still pointing the shotgun at Shady. "All right, then let me see you boys shake hands."

Shady pulled himself up to his full height, a good four inches shorter than Killian, and with as much dignity as he could muster, stuck out his beefy hand. Killian shook it, still grinning.

"That's better. Now we can all play nice," Skye said, though she didn't lower her weapon. "You know, I think I see the light at the end of this tunnel. You," she nodded toward Killian, "you obviously have a way with the ladies." The bikers groused but she continued over them. "And I'm not stupid enough to think it's by accident." She looked him up and down with a thoughtful expression on her pretty face. "Well, not *entirely* by accident, anyway. I mean, the good Lord gave you some of that, but if you don't know how to treat a woman, it doesn't matter what you look like. So, here's what's gonna happen. I've watched these big lugs act like cavemen for about as long as I care to. So, we're gonna have ourselves a little schoolin'." She looked pointedly at Shady and Sunshine. "A little *charm* schoolin'."

They stared back at her blankly.

Kelly Adamson

"You all walk around beating your chest like a bunch of gorillas and just expect these girls to follow you. If you think that impresses a woman, then you are sadly mistaken. And if you're acting like that to impress other men, well, that's another set of problems altogether. And this ain't that kind of bar."

The men all huffed indignantly. "Now, see here, Skye. Everything was going fine until this fellow showed up. We never had any problems with our women before," Shady said.

"Oh, really? Well, let me just ask you one question. And you answer me truthfully. Do you or do you not want your women to look at you the way they look at him?"

There was a pause, during which all eyes were on Killian. This was what it all boiled down to, of course.

Sunshine was studying him like he was a Harley with a Japanese carburetor. "How *do* you do it?"

Killian opened his mouth to reply, but wasn't sure what the question was. The back of his head throbbed, his mouth was dry, and he'd almost lost his beer buzz.

Sunshine elaborated. "Look, you were okay to start with. You came in here looking like a fish out of water, all duded up like a Christmas tree, but you didn't try to shark me, which you damn sure could have. You didn't look like you knew which end of the stick to use. You could have played me for a fool, but you didn't. So, I'll make you a deal. You tell us how you do it, what your secret is with the women, and we'll let you go."

Killian looked helplessly at Nick and Grace. Grace gave him what she hoped was an encouraging smile, but it looked more like she had a toothache. She was impressed by Skye's command of the room, but wondered how long she'd be able to keep order if Killian couldn't come up with something to "teach" them about women.

"My secret?" Killian looked queasy, but appeared to be giving the question some serious thought. He had to say something, and it had better be good. He slid onto one of the rickety bar stools, took a deep breath and began slowly.

"Well, my pa died in prison when I was just a baby. I never knew him. Broke my ma's heart. She never remarried. It was just me, my ma, and my three older sisters from then on. My Grandma May came to live with us when I was eight. Wonderful woman, a true matriarch. But, it wasn't an easy life, I can tell you. There was never enough money to pay the bills and we moved around a lot, usually to escape a horny landlord who wanted an alternate payment from my mom or my sisters. By the time I was thirteen, two of my sisters were strippers and I heard the way they talked about the guys who came in the club. I knew the contempt they felt for those men. So, yes, I was raised by women and maybe I do have an insight into them that some men don't." He glanced at Skye. She looked up at him like she wanted to hug him. He cleared his throat and continued.

"For instance, I know that the one thing a woman wants more than anything else in the world is for her man to listen to her."

Skye nodded like she was listening to the preacher in church.

"Now, you may think that you listen, but you've got to remember, it's not what's actually happening that counts; it's what they think is happening. Perception is reality. You've got to make sure they *know* you're listening, and that you value what they're saying. Look into their eyes when they're talking. Pay attention. Make comments on what they're saying." Then he added hastily,

Kelly Adamson

"nice comments. Say things like *'that's a good point'* or *'tell me more.'* And for God's sake, don't bring a woman to a bar and ignore her all night. Catch her eye across the room and wink at her." He demonstrated on Skye and she blushed vividly. "When you walk by her, touch her hair, give her a little kiss. Maybe tell her she looks nice. Compliment her clothes or," he had a fire-engine red flashback, "or her fingernails. Because, believe me, gentlemen, if you don't, eventually someone else will." His audience had fallen silent, all of them looking as thoughtful as was possible.

"You may not believe me, but it really is that simple," Killian finished. "That's my secret."

Grace took a shaky breath and got ready to run.

Then Killian's face clouded over as he added, "And I should know. Because it just happened to me."

Sunshine shifted his bulk from one foot to the other and asked, "What did?"

"I walked in on my…woman, the woman I loved more than life itself, the woman I was planning to marry, in bed with another man. And all because I didn't pay her enough attention."

Murmurs of discontented brotherhood rumbled from the audience, along with much muttered cursing. They may have been ready to kill him only moments before, but now he was a kindred spirit.

"What did you do?" Little Frank asked.

Killian shook his head and looked away. "I don't want to talk about it."

In biker lingo, that was as good as saying he'd killed the man. Sunshine and Shady nodded in sage understanding.

Grace stole a quick glance at Skye. She'd finally laid the shotgun on the bar and was now propping her elbows on it, staring at Killian in precisely the same manner that had started all this fuss. "He's right, you know," Skye said to Sunshine and Shady and anyone else who was listening. "And if you big galoots were paying attention, you might have learned a thing or two."

Next to Sunshine sat a large gray barrel filled with discarded plastic cups and paper napkins. All eyes on him now, Sunshine added his broken cue to the trash. Then he began, slowly, to cover the dozen or so steps toward Killian. The two men stared at each other for a long moment, two men with much more in common than either would have suspected half an hour before. Killian stood tall, determined to appear undaunted. Finally, Sunshine's face broke into a jagged grin beneath his moustache and he growled, "Beat it, kid. Get the hell outta here before I change my mind."

Chapter 7 – Alive

Grace had been two steps from the door of the Barrelhouse as Sunshine finished speaking. She, Nick and Killian fought to play it cool until they were out of earshot of the Vipers, but once the little Subaru was back out on the road, all pretense was gone. Killian leaned out the rear window, the warm wind whipping his hair wildly around his face. He punched the night air overhead like a boxer. Then, drunk on the feeling of deliverance, he yelled up at the stars, a crazy, ecstatic war cry.

Grace began to laugh. She felt lightheaded. She held her hands in front of her, palms down. They were shaking violently. She clamped her teeth together to keep them from chattering. Still, she couldn't control her laughter. Nick gripped the steering wheel at ten and two, his knuckles white. He stared ahead, unmoving, but his face was covered with a huge grin.

In the back seat, Killian bounced up and down like a kid. "That was bloody brilliant! Did you see those blokes? They could have killed us and left our bodies out in the desert for the coyotes and scorpions. I can't believe that just happened. I feel so… alive!"

"So, near death experiences are your thing, eh?" Nick said. "I never would have pegged you for one of those."

"No, no. It's not that. It's just…" Suddenly, Killian seemed at a loss for words. He ran his hands through his hair and shoved the lucky cap back on his head, wincing as it touched the spot where the cue had hit him. "I don't know. It's just…you know, so much of my life has been this elaborate façade, with me always pretending to be something I'm not. I've done it as long as I can remember. Maybe on screen I was slaying dragons or jumping out of burning helicopters, but in reality, it was all very controlled – all harnesses and airbags, no real danger, you know." He stared out the window at nothing as he spoke, maybe seeing the green screen in his mind. "But, this…this is *real*. Life is supposed to be real."

"Yep, that was real, all right," Nick muttered.

"You know, in acting school, they tell you to draw on your own experiences to recreate the emotions you're attempting to portray. I never told anyone this before, but I always thought that was a load of rubbish. Mainly, because I was never able to do it," Killian admitted with a shrug. "Mine has always been a complete masquerade. I suppose I'm more comfortable acting my emotions than I am feeling them. Besides, most people tend to like me better when I'm someone else. But maybe that happens to all actors eventually."

No one had anything to say to that. The wind whistling through the back window was the only sound for several minutes.

"Was that stuff you said back there true – about your childhood, I mean?" Grace asked. As soon as she said it, she wished she could take it back. Nick made a noise, somewhere between a sigh and a cough. She'd heard that noise before. Maybe it was true that she should think about things a little more before she said them. But surely this wasn't prying; after all, this relative stranger had already told them some of his most intimate secrets of his own free will.

She turned in the seat to look back at Killian, to apologize for her boldness, and she could see that he was grinning again.

"My dad is a retired naval officer and my mum taught primary school for years. I had a wonderful childhood. But I knew the bikers didn't want to hear that. That would have been curtains for me – for all of us."

"It was all a lie?" Grace said.

"Well, I did have a Grandma May. Truly wonderful woman. A saint. She made the most magnificent pumpkin tarts."

He clapped Nick on the shoulder over the back of the driver's seat. His hands were still clamped on the steering wheel. "Loosen up, mate. This is living!"

Grace turned back around in the seat. Her hands were still shaking a little. "I don't know, Killian. Nick and I are just normal, everyday people. I don't know if we can handle this kind of living."

Killian chuckled. "Oh, I'm not about to try and beat a train or play Russian roulette. I just feel as if I've woken up from a long sleep, that's all. At any rate, I think this calls for a celebration. What do you say? Let's celebrate being young and alive and in Las Vegas."

In minutes, the brightly colored neon was whizzing by again on either side of them. The familiar camels of the Sahara, the pink and orange of the Flamingo.

Their spirits were soaring, and Killian's suggestion of a celebration seemed incredibly rational and well-deserved. All fear of being recognized had been swept into some unused corner of his subconscious. Nick whipped the little car in to the valet at Caesar's Palace at Killian's urging. It was after three in the morning, and there were still a respectable number of night owls at the slots and die hard gamblers at the tables. Killian strode purposefully through the casino, under the marble archways and past the Roman statues, as if he knew exactly where he was going. Nick and Grace followed him hand in hand, hers having finally stopped shaking. She scanned the faces as they passed. Funny how so many people would forego sleep to lose their last dime. Luckily, no one took a second glance at them. No one seemed to notice the international superstar in cheap sunglasses. Almost no one.

Chapter 8 – The Spider's Web

If the Russian had believed in such things, he would have thought it was divine providence that caused the Howards and their shaggy friend to head to Caesar's Palace that morning.

He had followed them since they left The Isis on their way to the bar in the slums. When they circled the block twice in that near-deserted part of town, he was certain they had seen him. But he parked in front of a body shop two blocks away and the three idiots had never even looked in his direction as they crossed the street.

He searched their car while he waited and found nothing. He hated waiting, and by the time they came back out, he had almost talked himself into following them back up to their room, hotel security be damned.

But instead, divine providence – or luck, or kismet, or fate or whatever other bullshit lesser minds tended to believe in – steered the rental car right into the parking structure at Caesar's, where he knew for a fact that his boss was playing cards.

He smiled and reached for his phone. His boss answered on the second ring.

"The flies are walking right into the spider's web," he said. "You should be able to see them momentarily. Both men are about six feet tall. One is thin, with dark curly hair. The other is blonde, more muscular, with hair like a broom and a beard like a derelict. The woman is a red-head. She's wearing ill-fitting jeans and no make-up. She looks like she doesn't own a hairbrush."

His voice dripped with contempt and on the other end of the line, his boss laughed. The Russian smiled. It was good to hear that laugh. When the boss was happy, everyone was happy.

Chapter 9 – Eleven Black

When Nick headed for the cashier's cage inside Caesar's, Killian stopped him. "No. I insist. I'm your bankroll tonight – both of you."

Nick shook his head and kept walking. "No way, man. We didn't bring you with us to pay for everything."

Killian stepped in front of him and said in an undertone, "Do you have any idea how much money they pay me to pretend to be someone I'm not? I assure you it is an obscene amount. So, please, I don't want to hear another word about it."

"I'm a terrible gambler," Grace said. "I would just lose all your money."

"I don't care about that," Killian said. "I would never gamble with money I couldn't afford to lose. No one should. Besides, unless you can count cards – which I'm sure would get us thrown out on our arses – gambling is just luck anyway." He didn't wait for any more objections, but headed for the blackjack tables.

It was easy to find an empty table at this time of morning. The dealer, a plump, middle-aged woman with steel gray hair, stood up straighter as they approached. She smoothed a wine colored velvet vest over her black silk shirt, the same uniform all the other blackjack dealers wore. Killian smoothly slipped back into his gangster-esque accent. "*Buon giorno, bella*," he crooned.

"Good morning, sir," she answered, color rising to her cheeks.

Out of the corner of her eye, Grace saw Nick shake his head, clearly as amazed as she was by the response women had towards Killian. If they'd recognized him, it might be different, she thought. It was understandable they'd be excited about meeting such a big star, but these women didn't know him from Adam. And here he was, still wearing his silly hat with the dice on the front, Mr. Nobody from Nowhere, as far as any of them knew. Yet, he still had the power to make them swoon with his slightest smile.

Grace felt something brush her hip, someone too close. She looked around, expecting to see a drunk trying to cop a feel, but instead saw a stunning, leggy blonde. She wore a skin-tight gold lamé dress that only partially covered her enormous, perfectly round implants. "Ooh, sorry, Hon!" she said in a sweet, girlish voice Grace was sure she had practiced for years. "I get one or two drinks in me and I just get so clumsy."

Directly across the pit from them another blackjack table mirrored their own. The blonde walked over and sat down with the man who was playing there. She kissed him on the cheek and smiled happily at him. He was much shorter than her and when he turned, his eyes were almost level with her cleavage.

"Wow, she's really proud of those, isn't she?" Grace snickered. She turned to Nick to find him staring intently at the woman's ample assets. She waved a hand in front of his face.

"What?" he asked, not changing focus.

Grace rolled her eyes. "You know you'll go blind if you stare at those too long. It's like the sun."

"So those would be the last things I would ever see? Hmmm..." He chuckled at her disapproving scowl. "Well, she obviously paid a lot of money for those. I just want her to know they're appreciated. I want her to know her doctor does good work." He raised his hands to the woman and mimed applause.

Grace inclined her head toward the man sitting next to the blonde. "No, I think Grandpa paid a lot of money for them. Maybe you should applaud him."

"Ha! Yeah, I think I *should* applaud him. Way to go, Grandpa."

The man was at least seventy. His thinning hair was black but the thick tufts spilling over the top button of his Hawaiian shirt were snow white. He wore a thick gold chain around his neck and a pinky ring with a light blue stone the size of an English pea. It flashed in the light when he moved his hand. It looked vaguely familiar somehow. His skin was leathery from years of relaxing by pools. His whole bearing was that of a man who had not wanted for anything in a very long time.

As they watched, the blonde looked up and caught them staring. She winked at Nick and blew him a kiss. Grace made a show of being indignant. "Who does she think she is?"

Then the dealer said something and the blonde squealed with delight and hopped up and down in her seat.

Grace rolled her eyes again. "Great. All that and luck, too. Maybe she can buy some nicer perfume. Did you smell that? It was like someone dropped a bunch of lilies in a bottle of gin. Besides, I think she tried to pick my pocket just now."

Nick shook his head. "Jealously doesn't become you."

"Jealous? What's she got that I haven't got? Don't answer that."

They joined Killian at the blackjack table. He sat in the center chair and pushed two stacks of black chips down towards them. Grace started to object again, but he raised his voice to speak over her to the dealer. "My friends will be playing as well. Norma Jean, is it?" He peered at her nametag. She nodded. "Lovely name. That was Marilyn Monroe's real name, you know?" She grinned and nodded again.

It took a few seconds for her to realize she was supposed to be dealing cards. With a start, Norma Jean set to work, two cards up for each of them, with one up and one down for herself. The one that was visible was an eight of hearts. She looked at Killian, awaiting his next move. Grace did the same. She had never played blackjack before in her life and the only thing she knew was that the object was to get twenty-one.

They played eight hands in rapid succession, Killian winning seven, Nick and Grace both winning three. Each time, Killian left his winnings to increase his bet until finally the dealer told him that, regrettably, he had reached the table limit.

"Color me up, would you, doll?" he said to Norma Jean, pushing all but a few of his black chips toward her.

"Certainly, sir." In return for his mountain of black chips, he received three short stacks of orange chips. Grace thought it didn't look nearly as impressive that way.

"Let's find something else, shall we?" Killian said, pushing back his chair and getting to his feet. "I like to spread the love around." He left three black chips on the felt and said "For you, Bella."

Grace picked up her chips and Nick his, and they followed the man with the silly red cap through the casino. The big-bosomed blonde watched them go.

Killian finally stopped at a roulette table where three Asian men stood chain smoking and adding more chips on top of the bets they had just made. They never stopped until the dealer waved them off each time the ball started to slow on the wheel.

The dealer changed out some of Killian's orange chips for stacks of green table chips and slid them across the felt to him.

"Fourteen black," the dealer called.

The players grumbled. It seemed that their well-thought-out plan of putting as many bets on the table as humanly possible had somehow allowed all three of them to miss fourteen black. The dealer swept all of their bets toward him, where they fell through a saucer-sized hole on the table's surface. Grace followed the chips, sidestepping around so she had a better view of the machine that separated them by color and stacked them all up again in neat columns. Ingenious.

The wheel never stopped spinning, the same steady, hypnotic speed, as the bets were placed all over again. This time, Killian added his to the pattern, three red, twenty-four black, and eleven black.

The dealer released the ball and Killian sat back. The ball fell, click, click, click, bouncing from one number to the other before landing on thirty-five black. No winner again.

Killian leaned over the table again. Three red, twenty-four black, and eleven black, just like before.

"You play those numbers every time?" Nick asked.

Killian nodded. "I always win within three or four spins."

"Why is that?" Grace wasn't sure she could understand some complex mathematical system, but felt compelled to ask.

Killian grinned and pointed at his hat. "I'm lucky, remember?"

It occurred to Grace that she had no idea how much these table chips were worth or even the ones in her pocket, for that matter. She pulled out one of her black chips and held it up where she could read it. It had the Caesar's Palace logo on it and — she gave a little gasp at the sight of it — $100 stamped in the middle. She tugged at Nick's sleeve and held the chip in front of him. "Did you know these were hundred dollar chips?" she whispered.

He nodded.

"Well, if these are a hundred, what are those orange ones?"

"A thousand." He grinned at her wide-eyed reaction. "Hey, it's his money. He can do whatever he wants with it."

The ball fell and while Grace was still marveling over the chip, Killian grabbed her in a bear hug, twirled her around, and slapped hands with Nick again. When she regained her balance, she turned to look at the wheel still revolving at the same hypnotic speed. Sure enough, the little white ball was sitting right in the lap of eleven black.

"Thirty-five to one, with three chips on there," muttered Nick, shaking his head in disbelief. "That's over a hundred thousand. Damn. Does this guy ever lose?"

The Asian men nodded and smiled, congratulating him on his win. Killian was being gracious, bowing and saying, "Arigato gozaimasu," in return.

Out of the corner of her eye, Grace saw the pit boss approaching. Evidently, winning more than one hundred thousand dollars after only losing ten thousand made you a sudden person of interest. She slid quickly between Killian and the man with the clipboard and said "Reign it in, Bubba. You don't want to be the center of attention, remember?" She glanced back over her shoulder and saw the pit boss had been stopped by one of the other dealers to handle an altercation at another table. Thank Heaven for small favors.

Killian cashed in his table chips and they were on the move again as quickly and inconspicuously as possible, making their way back outside into the night air and neon. Killian had left one orange chip for the dealer, leaving Grace open-mouthed. He ended up with five mustard yellow twenty thousand dollar chips and the rest in orange and black. They easily fit into his pockets. Grace finally convinced him they had pressed their luck enough in Caesar's, and coupled with the fact that it was four-thirty in the morning, she also convinced him to call it a night.

Chapter 10 – Room Service

Bam, bam, bam, bam. An indistinct male voice sounded outside their door.

Nick groaned.

It was the middle of the night. No, it couldn't be. They didn't get back to the room until almost dawn. But whatever time it was, it was way too early for anyone to be knocking on their door.

"Did you order room service?" Grace mumbled.

"No, I did *not*," he said irritably, getting to his feet. As he groped around for a pair of shorts, the knock cut into the quiet and darkness again.

Bam, bam, bam!

"Coming!" Nick growled.

He stomped to the door and Grace saw the crack of light grow larger as he opened it wide and then heard a familiar voice, "Good morning, campers!"

A familiar voice? A familiar *British* voice?

She bolted upright in bed, holding the sheet up tight in front of her. She was still groggy with sleep. This must be a dream.

The entrance light came on and in rolled a room service cart heavily laden with covered dishes. The cart was being pushed by a slight man in a tall chef's toque and white jacket who respectfully turned his back on the bed as he entered. Close at his heels, bright eyed and buoyant, was Killian Ross.

"Anyone hungry?" Killian asked. "I had Thomas here whip up some of his best dishes for us."

No one spoke, but Killian didn't seem to notice. He stood there at the end of the bed, in an oversized blue and white striped golf shirt untucked over long, khaki hiking shorts. Brown leather boots, a camouflage boonie hat and a pair of dark sunglasses hanging around his neck made him look every inch the tourist. He tugged at his shirt. "What do you think? I sent out for the gear about an hour ago. Will I blend in?"

No one answered, and Killian looked around, finally noticing that Grace was still in the bed and that the lights had been off. "Oh…," he faltered, "I hope I wasn't interrupting anything."

Grace glanced sideways at the clock. The red glowing numbers said it was nine-thirty-four a.m. The blackout curtains had provided the darkness. She groaned and slumped back down on the fat pillows. They had gotten in around five a.m. and her exhaustion wrapped around her once again like a heavy blanket, the momentary burst of adrenalin at seeing Killian long gone.

"We're still going to Red Rock today, aren't we?" Killian asked.

Grace felt a weight at the foot of the bed and heard the metallic clang of one of the silver domes being lifted off of a plate.

"Of course we are," Nick said, the sight and smell of the food soothing any animosity he may have felt. "As soon as we finish eating."

Grace made a grunt of protest and he patted her foot through the covers. "We can sleep when we're dead," he told her bracingly. "But, right now, let's eat."

Thomas closed the door behind him when he left and it put the room back in near darkness. Killian switched on the nearest lamp and began pouring a cup of coffee, making himself at home.

"This is great," Nick said with a mouthful of bacon. "Extra crispy, just like I like it."

Grace rolled over to face the wall, determined to ignore them both. But soon, the smell of fresh coffee became overwhelming. She breathed in deeply and opened one eye to see a steaming cup just inches from her nose. Killian was holding it steady, grinning, and gently waving the aroma towards her.

"Rise and shine. If a hot Colombian can't get you up, then nothing will," he teased.

She sat up slowly, resigning herself to four-and-a-half hours of sleep, and grudgingly took the offered cup. She slumped forward and began sipping.

By the time the white porcelain cup was almost empty, the caffeine was working its magic and the fog was beginning to lift a little from her head. Her stomach did a little flip when it finally registered that Killian Ross was sitting at the foot of her bed, eating Eggs Florentine and discussing cars with her husband.

Yesterday had not been a dream.

"The Maserati I drove in *No Secrets* was the fastest by far," he was saying. "It handled like a brick, but man, could it fly!"

Grace closed her eyes tight, then opened them again. He was still there. The events of the previous day were a blur, something that happened in someone else's life. Bits and pieces began tumbling through her head, the Eye of Horus, the sound of a blues guitar, a walrus holding a broken pool cue, a red ball cap with dice on it, and casino chips, lots of casino chips.

"Did they really let you drive an M1A1 Abrams in *Ground Assault?*"

"Yes, a bit, just to get the feel for it. But you know that's seriously complicated machinery…"

Gradually, she felt a grin spread across her face. She scrambled out of bed, grabbed whatever clothes were topmost in her suitcase, and dashed to the bathroom to change. Baggy olive green denim shorts and a coral and olive zip-up jersey top. Her tennis shoes still lay on the floor where she'd kicked them off only hours before.

She scurried around as though Nick and Killian were about to leave her, but they were still enmeshed in their talk of torque and horsepower.

Her eyes darted around for the hairbrush. Oh, right. Nick had thrown it in his case as they were leaving the house yesterday. She ducked back around to where his suitcase stood, undisturbed since they brought it up from the bell desk. She threw it open, plunged her hand down in the side of the case and felt around for bristles. Her fingers brushed across them and she tugged, but the handle was caught on something. She pulled harder, impatient, and heard the faint sound of paper tearing. She stopped. She had packed this suitcase. There was nothing paper inside. She shoved her other hand in and pulled out a small package, long and thin, wrapped in layers of tissue paper with foreign writing on the outside. She could feel something hard and flat inside the paper.

With her second pleasant surprise of the morning, she realized what it was, what it must be. Tomorrow was their tenth anniversary and undoubtedly Nick had hidden her present in his suitcase. She grinned and stuffed it back down under his socks and shirts.

But, as she stood in front of the bathroom mirror brushing her hair, she knew there was no way her curiosity would let her just leave it there. She hesitated, trying to talk herself out of it, but not for long. She slipped back around the corner and, with a covert glance at her husband, quickly fished the package out and dashed back around the corner with it, closing the door softly behind her.

The little bundle was bound with packing tape. Her fingers fumbled, trying to find a weak spot in the tissue paper. She finally managed to rip one end. She tipped the bundle, hoping the contents would fall out into her open palm, but it was wrapped too tightly. A glimpse of gold caught her eye. She hesitated. If she pulled too hard, she might break it. She couldn't wait to see what it was. Nick's gifts were usually painfully practical. For her birthday last year, he had given her a toaster oven. She'd dropped a lot of hints for jewelry this year. It looked like he had finally paid attention.

As the paper fell away, she had to suppress a delighted squeal. It was one of the Kavayet necklaces from the shop downstairs, the one on the flyer where William had drawn the map. It was beautiful. This one looked even better here in her hand than the one in the glass case. Must be those harsh lights downstairs. Or perhaps this one just looked better because it belonged to her.

It fit in the palm of her hand, but just barely. It was a hawk with wings outstretched, the tips almost touching over its head. In the center of its chest was an ankh. The whole thing was a colorful mosaic of stones set in gold and the chain appeared to be interlocking gold loops. The hawk held an orange-red ball in each claw.

Her clothes from yesterday were in a heap on the marble floor in front of her. She pulled the map out of her jeans pocket. There it was, the whole story. The flyer said the necklace had been given to King Tut's mother, Kavayet, by his father, Akhenaten, to commemorate his son's birth. Kavayet, a maid in Akhenaten's household, died, or was murdered, three days later. The necklace was the only thing in the tomb that connected her with Tut, but it was enough. This had all been a mystery until last summer when workers in el Amarna unearthed her tomb. No one had ever been able to say with certainty who Tut's mother was. Some scholars had maintained it was Queen Nefertiti. But the inscription on the back of the necklace was proof even they could not deny.

The flyer said the stones were carnelian, turquoise and lapis lazuli. Well, the ones in the original anyway. These were man-made turquoise and quartz, but Grace couldn't tell the difference. It listed the price as $138. Nick shouldn't have spent so much. This anniversary trip was costing a bundle already. For a second, she almost felt a twinge of guilt for opening it. After all, their anniversary wasn't until tomorrow and he'd taken great pains to hide it, tucked away in the bottom of his suitcase. Still, she had to admit that he obviously hadn't bought it until yesterday. Nothing like waiting until the last minute. But, his taste was improving. This was much better than a toaster oven.

She began to maneuver it back into the tissue paper, but stopped. She had a mischievous thought. What would he do if she just put it on? How long would it take him to notice? How long would it take him to say something? She held it up in front of her, admiring the effect in the mirror.

A knock on the door made her jump. "Can I come in? I've got to brush my teeth," Nick called.

"Yeah, yeah, just a second!" She fumbled clumsily with the clasp. She'd never seen one like this before. They were really overdoing it on the authenticity. She gave it one last admiring look in the glass and then zipped the front of her shirt so only the head of the hawk showed from underneath.

"All yours." She breezed past Nick in the doorway, not wanting him to see just yet and spoil the surprise. This was going to be fun.

They had to retrieve their rental car from the valet at Caesar's Palace, having left on foot and in rather a hurry early that morning. Killian kept his boonie hat pulled low while they waited, carefully avoiding attention from the Caesar's patrons checking in and out. Two young couples waited alongside them for their car, and he kept his back turned to them as they discussed movies, specifically their favorite love scenes of all times.

"Ooh, I love the one in *Diamond Dust* with Killian Ross and Jennifer Hart where he climbs up to her balcony in the middle of the night!" said one of the women.

"Oh, yes," agreed the other. "He looked so hot in that one."

"He could climb on my balcony any time," said the first.

"Hey, we're standing right here," huffed one of the men. "You could at least wait until we're out of earshot to drool over beefcake."

"Besides, he's obviously gay," said the other man. "You can tell by the way he walks."

The girls giggled and nudged each other. "You're just saying that because you're jealous. Besides, what are *you* doing studying his walk? You like what you see?"

Grace glanced sideways at Killian. She couldn't see his face, just the hat, dark glasses and beard. He stood very still. The couples continued to argue about his sexual orientation. Grace wondered how it would feel to be talked about like that, to have people who didn't even know you, idolize or revile you as a matter of everyday conversation. She wondered what the two girls would do if they knew who was standing only six feet away. Living in a fishbowl was something she'd never given much thought to before, but she suddenly felt a little sorry for Killian Ross.

Chapter 11 – Red Rock

They were already lost, following what Nick referred to as a cartoon map from one of Grace's travel guides. Killian sat in the back seat, gazing out at the passing scenery and sipping the coffee he'd convinced them to stop for at Starbucks.

"It looks like we were supposed to take 95 to Charleston Boulevard and that just curves around and…it looks like we can't miss it," Grace said.

"Funny how everything in this town is so easy to find until we start looking for it," Nick said.

Grace started to make a snide remark about Nick's ability to miss things that were right under his nose, but refrained. She was a little miffed that he hadn't even looked at the necklace she was wearing, her anniversary present, much less commented on it.

"All right, the next exit is Powerline Road. Is that on the map?" he asked.

Grace scanned it, but had to admit it left a lot to be desired. "It's not on here." She sighed dramatically. "You were right and I was wrong. Is that what you wanted to hear? I guess we really do need a roadmap. And now I don't even see anywhere to buy one."

As far as the eye could see in any direction, was nothing but sand and sagebrush and cactus. They'd passed the suburbs with their slate-roofed stucco houses and boutique shopping centers, and now the only thing that appeared in front of them was an endless strip of highway.

Grace looked back at Killian. He hadn't said a word since Starbucks, probably the longest he'd been quiet since she met him. "You all right back there?" She hoped he wasn't thinking about his ex again. She really didn't want any more drama today. To her relief, he turned from the window with a smile. "Brilliant," he said. "Just thinking about how no one on God's green earth is expecting a damned thing from me today. I'm just going to go and have fun and forget about the rest of the world."

The view from the Powerline Road exit was unobstructed all the way to the surrounding mountain range. There was a grand total of one building at this exit. The road continued past it, disappearing into the hills.

A metal road sign proclaimed they were now on the Paiute Indian Reservation. Killian perked up at once. "Are we going to see some real Native Americans? This is fantastic!" He leaned closer to the car window, as if expecting to see a line of warriors on horseback on the top of the ridge.

"Skye is a Native American," Grace said.

"She is? She wasn't dressed like one."

Grace chuckled. "Did you expect her to have a feather in her hair?"

"Well, all I know is I definitely hope we see more like her. So, let's keep following this road to the reservation."

They pulled into the freshly paved lot of the Great Eagle Smoke Shop. It was a large, relatively new building with gas pumps out front under a massive metal canopy.

Killian said, "Look, those people are following the road. There must be something down there." A black Chevy Tahoe with dark tinted windows rolled past the Smoke Shop in the direction of the hills.

"I'll bet that's their chief," Nick said. "He had to drive the medicine man into town to get some aspirin."

A flicker of excitement crossed Killian's face before it turned to embarrassment. "Oh, you're pulling my leg. I had this vision of them in their war paint going in to the chemist."

"You watch too many movies, man."

Grace opened the door of the shop, and the warm, rich smell of tobacco engulfed her. It was so much more inviting than the spent, stale cigarette smoke of the Barrelhouse. She closed her eyes and inhaled the aroma of cherries, pineapple, and fresh cut lumber. It reminded her of her favorite uncle's house when she was a child.

A walk-in humidor covered the back wall of the store. The left side of the building was a souvenir shop, selling dream catchers, tee-shirts, hand woven blankets and rugs. The right side was your standard convenience store, stocked with sodas, candy bars and pre-made sandwiches.

While Nick and Killian looked for a map – Grace knew it would really be Nick looking for a map and Killian looking for Native American women – she headed for the souvenirs. Her niece was dog-sitting for them, and she wanted to find something different than what was offered in the casino shops. She didn't want to have to resort to a baseball cap that said "lucky" on the front.

She chose a book of Native American stories and a wood carving of a wolf howling at the moon. A pair of turquoise earrings would be perfect for her sister, like the suede moccasins for her parents. She headed to the front, her arms full, and bumped into the woman who'd been standing right behind her.

Grace gasped. "I'm so sorry. I didn't see you there." The woman stood very still, staring intently at Grace. She was tiny, less than five feet tall, weighed maybe eighty-five pounds, and wore a long, straight, faded blue dress with brown and white stitching around the neck and the hem. Worn, buckskin moccasins covered her feet and a small suede pouch on a black leather cord hung around her thin neck. She wore her steel gray hair in a single braid, and her face was wrinkled and weathered from countless years in the Nevada sun. The woman made no effort to move. Grace had to squeeze by, balancing the armload of souvenirs. She looked down at her own shuffling feet.

"Excuse me," she muttered. For some reason, this tiny woman was a bit intimidating, with inky black eyes that followed Grace as she passed. They seemed to burn into her back as she headed toward the front of the store. She couldn't resist a peek back at the woman when she reached the cashier. She was gone. Grace looked around the store, standing up on tiptoes to get a better view. But the old woman was nowhere to be found. She must have gone in the back room, Grace thought. She must work here. That was it.

Nick had already paid for a roadmap and was studying it by the front window of the store. Killian, two plastic bags full of purchases at his feet, held up a tee-shirt with a drawing of a beautiful young Native American woman on the front.

According to the new map, they had completely missed an exit and driven at least ten miles out of their way.

Grace happily relinquished her duties as navigator and opened the book she'd bought. It was called *How Hawk Formed the Mountains* and it was full of myths and folklore from different tribes. Most were accompanied by illustrations.

"Regale us with a tale, oh, noble bard," Killian said, leaning between the seats.

She let the book fall open to the middle. "How about this one? It's called 'The Bird Woman Who Sees.'" She settled back and began to read aloud.

There once was a woman who had magic, but she kept it all for herself. She could fly in the body of an eagle, far above the desert and the canyons. In the air, her eagle's eyes could see for miles and miles and she could find where fresh berries were growing, or see where the fish were swimming, and then she would come back to her body as a woman and go and get the food for herself. She kept the magic as a secret, even from her own family. She did not want to share with anyone.

One day, while flying in the eagle's body, she saw a great fire spreading across the plains. It was a wall of flames taller than two men, and it burned everything in its path. The flames were moving quickly toward her village and the bird woman turned in the air to fly back and warn her people. 'No,' she thought. 'If I warn my people, they will know I can fly. They will want to steal my magic.' So, the bird woman flew off in another direction, away from the flames and away from her people.

The next day, the woman went back to where her village had been. The flames had been too fast. Her people could not escape. Everyone had been killed in the wall of fire. She stood in the ashes and knew the terrible thing she had done. She could have warned them. She could have helped her people escape, but she did not. The bird woman began to wail and weep. Her tears fell in the ashes around her feet, and she knew she would give up her magic if only she could have her people back. But it was too late.

From then on, the woman could never take the form of an eagle again. And she could not see berries or fish anymore, only trouble on the horizon. She would spend the rest of her days walking the desert trying to warn others, trying to keep them from danger. But she would never fly again.

The white sun was high when they pulled into the Red Rock Welcome Center lot. The trio cast no shadows as they unfolded out of the car. Grace had spent the last few minutes reapplying her 70 SPF sunscreen. The heat was nothing new to her, having grown up in the Deep South, but the sun seemed somehow closer here, as if she were under the broiler in an enormous oven. She tucked her hair behind her ears – it was too short for a ponytail now – and put on her University of Alabama baseball cap.

Ahead of them, a group of teenagers was unloading off of a tour bus and filing raucously into the welcome center. Killian quickly opted to stay outside while Nick went in for a park map. Grace stayed with Killian, who stood so that he was mostly hidden from view by a vending machine. He shifted around nervously, keeping an eye on the tour bus and its passengers. Eighteen-year-olds were definitely a big demographic for him. And forty of them at once were a mob.

Thankfully, Nick emerged from the throng quickly, clutching a handful of colorful maps and photos of flora and fauna. "Look. They have burros here," he said, his excitement only partially exaggerated. "They're just roaming around. We have to look for them." Both he and Killian wasted no time jumping back into the car. "Come on!" he called to Grace through the open door. "The burros might get away."

Grace was already snapping pictures, albeit at a distance, of the Calico Hills. They wound around, well in advance of the tour bus, and had the road to themselves. They skipped the first scenic point so it would take the bus longer to catch up to them, and headed for the foothills in front of the Calico Tanks. The alternating layers of red and white limestone rose up out of the ground to amazing heights. The soft stone was smooth from thousands of years of wind and rain. The mountains looked like sleeping giants covered in striped blankets. Nick slowed the car to a crawl so Grace could take pictures from the car window.

They pulled off the road at the sandstone quarry. Only three other cars had parked in the small lot, so they decided to explore. Each time they passed other tourists on foot, Killian carefully examined a distant outcrop of rock or a low-growing cactus.

Inside the quarry itself, forty-five-degree angles were cut into the earth where giant white blocks of stone had been removed. A few still stood here and there, stacked together like something from the set of *The Flintstones*. Prehistoric cartoon ice cubes or big, blunt dinosaur teeth.

"Oh, Grace," Killian called. "Won't you please take a photo of that elephant for me? I had a camera on my mobile, but..." He made a motion like a quarterback throwing a Hail Mary pass, as if they needed reminding that he had thrown his cell phone into Bellagio's fountain. She raised her eyebrows. He looked sheepish, pointing over her shoulder. "Ruth would love that. She collects elephants – not real ones, of course," he added, as if that were an option. "She told me about a documentary she saw once where two elephants that had been raised together were separated for over twenty years and, by sheer coincidence, they ended up at the same wildlife sanctuary. The keepers said the two elephants knew each other at once. Ruth said it was fate that brought them back together."

Grace turned to see an enormous stone elephant. It sat atop one of the closer hills, one hundred feet above them, resting in profile. The resemblance to an elephant was completely accidental, made by eons of rain and wind chipping away at the softer deposits. Still, it was unmistakable.

"Sounds like you and Ruth get along really well," Nick said. "You hear stories about how awful managers can be. Sounds like you lucked out."

"She's more than just a manager," Killian said with a wave of his hand. "She's also my friend and she's brilliant. *And*, I trust her, which is an amazing thing in this business, let me tell you. The manager I had before Ruth robbed me blind. When Ruth took me on, I was actually in debt. I don't know what I would do without her."

Grace pictured Ruth as a stern, gray-haired woman in a tailored suit, like James Bond's boss, M. Someone everyone said "Yes, ma'am" and "No, ma'am" to.

Back in the car, they put more distance between themselves and the bus. Nick pulled the car onto the shoulder of the road and they hopped out, set their sights on Lost Creek Peak and struck out across the rocky path. This side of the canyon was lush and green compared to the barren rock of the Calico Hills. The trail was steep and curvy in some places, and the brush became thicker as they walked. Gnarled roots of a pine tree crossed the path and were so large that the trio had to climb over them. Grace took pictures of everything, with Nick and Killian frequently posing for her. Killian looked ecstatic. She watched him climbing all over boulders like a big kid and wondered how long it had been since he'd been allowed to be himself.

Nick had been looking for burros since they arrived, but to no avail. He finally gave up and started looking for lizards instead. He was having better luck with them, though he hadn't managed to actually capture one. "You can only catch them before they warm up in the morning," he told Killian, who seemed fascinated with the creatures, too. "Grace won't let me have one as a pet," he said, sounding very much like a ten-year-old who'd been denied a puppy.

Grace rolled her eyes. "You do not need a lizard," She turned to the pair, shaking her head, then gasped. "Look out! Look out behind you!"

They turned to see the waist-high rock behind them was covered in tarantulas, at least a dozen of them, each as big as a man's fist.

Killian sounded like he was choking. He looked like he would have run if his legs would have moved. His voice was hushed as he said, "I must admit I don't really care for spiders."

A woman's voice came from behind them, farther up the trail. Just a few words in a language Grace had never heard before and the spiders all scurried away. She and Nick whirled around to see who was speaking. Killian was slower to respond, his eyes still on the spot where the spiders had been. The tiny, Native American woman in the long faded blue dress and buckskin moccasins stepped out from behind the desert brush. Her dark eyes sparkled and flashed.

Grace's pulse quickened. It was the woman from the Smoke Shop, the woman who'd watched her walk away, then vanished.

"They won't hurt you." Her voice came out strong and level. "You are too big to eat, and spiders are not wasteful like humans."

Questions flooded Grace's mind, but she found herself unable to speak at all. She just stood there, listening to her own rapid heartbeat.

It was Nick who finally spoke. "Well," he said slowly, "thank you for that. I don't think I've ever seen anyone talk to spiders before. That was…um…impressive. But I think we had better be on our way now." He moved backwards along the rocky trail toward the road.

"You are in danger," the woman said calmly. "You are being followed. These are lawless men. Soulless men. They will not stop until they get what they want. Today there is one, but as the sun sets, there will be more."

Grace stole a quick glance at her companions. Nick had stopped, speechless, and Killian's eyes focused on the ground, no doubt looking for spiders. His face was hidden, but Grace knew the old woman wouldn't know who he was. "Why are you telling us this?" she asked.

"Because I must," the old woman said. "You would be wise to leave this place now." She raised a bony hand and pointed behind them towards the road. "They are near."

That was enough to make them all spin around, expecting to see God-knows-what approaching from the distant roadway. The little white Subaru was parked about 150 yards away, and they could just make out the tour bus heading for the parking area behind them. Nothing suspicious. Surely these giggling teenagers weren't the lawless men she spoke of.

"I don't see anything unusual," Grace said. "What are we supposed to be looking for exactly?" She looked over her shoulder at the old woman. It shouldn't have surprised her, but the woman was gone. Without so much as a crunch of gravel or a rustle of a leaf, she'd disappeared.

Chapter 12 – Paper Trail

He knew it was cowardly, but when Pavel Alkaev broke the news to his boss that he did not yet have possession of the merchandise, he was extremely glad it was over the phone. The ten-minute tirade that ensued would surely have ended in a few broken ribs on his part had the information been relayed in person.

And although he secretly believed he deserved some punishment for letting the boss down, he wasn't going to volunteer for it. Instead, he vowed it would not happen again. The next time he would not get off so easy.

It was humiliating enough to have to admit that his once-trusted associate, Makar, had betrayed him, but to know that the rat had outwitted him even in death was outrageous. Stashing the package in some rube's suitcase was quick thinking. Of course, Makar assumed he would live to retrieve it. He still couldn't believe his old comrade was foolish enough to leave a paper trail, and not even in code. How many times had he told them all not to write anything down? An elementary mistake for Makar, but a boon for Alkaev.

There had been a disconcerting moment earlier when he thought the Howards' bearded, shaggy companion spotted him. He'd seen him peeking out from behind a soda machine at the Red Rock Welcome Center, then ducking back in the shadows again. But of course that was ridiculous. He was probably just avoiding this cursed Nevada sun like any sane person. Alkaev couldn't understand why anyone had bothered settling this wretched stretch of desert in the first place, much less why so many people flocked here year after year like pilgrims. You could gamble and get a prostitute in much more pleasant settings than this. There was nothing here but rocks and sand, and in a thousand years it would still be just rocks and sand.

Personally, he preferred New York, where the people on the street didn't dress like Elvis, or even make unnecessary eye contact. But most of all he liked the winters in New York, where the snow reminded him of home, reminded him of how winter should be. Plus, those heavy winter coats made it so much easier to conceal a weapon.

Still, he knew the boss liked it here in this vile sandbox, and that was really all that mattered. So he wisely kept his opinions to himself.

And now, as he headed the big Chevy back downtown from Red Rock, he was confident his problem would be solved before the afternoon was over. It hadn't taken long to find this Nick Howard. Hotels wouldn't give out someone's room number, but they would be more than happy to connect your call, which confirmed that you had the correct hotel. To find the room then was a simple matter of planting a tracking device. If your tracking device was hidden in a bouquet of flowers, for example, you could get the hotel staff to do it for you. Simple. And now that he felt certain Mr. Howard and his two companions would be sight-seeing for hours, Alkaev had plenty of time to find what he was looking for.

Chapter 13 – Vicious

The little restaurant looked like something out of one of John Wayne's dreams. A long, low, single story building, it had dark wood paneling, light fixtures made from antlers, and tables built from solid wood planks, most with the bark still on the edges. Behind a long bar at the back of the room, a smoky mirror hung on the wall, half obscured by dusty liquor bottles. Country music twanged softly from an old jukebox. They were just a few miles from Red Rock but it seemed like it was in the middle of nowhere. It was well off the main road and fairly deserted since it was off-season and the little "Wild-West Town" next door was currently closed. A middle-aged couple wearing cowboy hats were the only other patrons, and they didn't pay any attention to the newcomers.

Grace, Nick and Killian made small talk about the food, the décor and even that kiss-of-conversation-death, the weather, as they ate their burgers and fries. They talked about everything except the old woman and her warning until, finally, Grace could stand it no longer. "That same Indian woman was in the gift shop, you know, where we stopped for a map. She just stared at me. Then she was gone, just like that." She tried to snap her fingers, but the french-fry grease kept them from making any sound. "It really gave me the creeps, and I didn't know why at the time."

"Aw, she probably does that to everybody," Nick said with a shake of his head. "She's probably somewhere right now laughing her ass off about how scared we all looked." He tried to imitate the old woman's voice, "You should have seen them, Little Feather, those tourists, they ran off like they had seen a ghost!"

Killian looked at him thoughtfully for a moment. "Was that supposed to be a Native American accent? I can't believe you had the nerve to ridicule my American accent when that's the best you can do."

Grace laughed, and Nick made a face at her.

"All right, seriously," Killian said, "are you telling me you don't think there was any credence to her warning?"

"Oh, don't tell me you bought that mumbo-jumbo." Nick sounded more amused than amazed.

"Absolutely! Lock, stock and barrel, I bought it," Killian said. "She was talking about the paparazzi. Okay, it might be a little bit of a stretch to call them 'soulless' – well, some of them, anyway – but most of them have a total disregard for the law. They'll stoop to any level to get what they want. The rags pay top dollar for celebrity photos, especially those in compromising positions. And the first one to break the 'Astrid and Killian Split' story with a photo of me disguised as a vagabond and hiding in Las Vegas can take the rest of the year off."

Somehow, this made Grace feel a little less uneasy. She'd been picturing sinister villains, so men with cameras just didn't seem all that bad. "Even if they took a picture of you today, they couldn't prove it's you. With the hat, glasses and beard, there's not enough of you showing to identify."

"Honestly," he sighed, sounding a little surprised at what he was about to say, "I don't think I care if they see me now. It was

Astrid I was really hiding from after all, and I think I'm ready to face her."

Grace folded her arms and tilted her head to one side. "Oh, really?"

"Yes, I am. She should be the one in hiding, not me. I'm innocent." He hesitated, like he was unsure if he wanted to tell them yet another dark secret. "Do you want to know what I really did when I found her in bed with…whoever that was? I ran back down the stairs and out the front door, then I threw up on her rose bushes. Pathetic. But then I saw the garden hose, curled up by the roses like a snake. I closed the nozzle, turned the valve as far as it would go and pulled the hose back up the stairs. They didn't hear me; they were still going at it, making too much noise of their own." He stopped for a minute, his eyes on the floor, and Grace thought he looked like he might throw up again. "When I got to her doorway, I opened the nozzle. The blast was like a fire hose. I sprayed the hell out of them both with that cold water. They were screaming and flailing about. I left the hose spinning around the room like a Catherine Wheel and bolted down the stairs. On my way out the front door, I hit the panic button on the alarm panel." This part of the memory brought a bitter smile to his lips. "I ran to the car. What a good man that driver was. I was soaking wet and running from a house where the alarm was going off. But he never said a word; he just drove."

After a pause, Nick spoke again. "The hose was a nice touch, man. Definitely the highlight of the story."

Grace scowled at him, and he whispered to her, "The guy's a performer. What can I say?"

"You're right, Nick," Killian said. "It was a nice touch. I'm quite proud of it, looking back. And tomorrow night I shall publicly celebrate my independence regained. I'm ready. But, tonight I want to live it up with you lot in relative anonymity. I'd forgotten how much fun that could be. We're going to have a ball, paint the town red, as if I were merely rich and not also famous."

Grace was sure he didn't mean that to be as obnoxious as it sounded.

"And I want tomorrow night to be on *my* terms. I don't want anyone to find me all lurking and depressed. Tomorrow evening, I'll get a shave and a haircut, put on some more stylish clothes," he looked down at the big polo shirt in distaste, "and make a grand entrance at The Eye. I'm going to chat up every woman there, buy drinks all around, and give everyone something to Tweet about." He reached up and scratched his thick beard with both hands. "Besides, this thing is beginning to feel like a bear skin rug.

"I'll have Ruth hire a bodyguard to accompany us. She'll be pleased with that. It's been driving her mad that I've refused one these last few weeks. But, it's not as if I needed one, eh. I hope that won't make you uncomfortable." His smile faltered a little. "Look, I would be honored if you two would accompany me tomorrow night, but I'll understand if you say no. I realize most sane people wouldn't want to be part of that kind of circus."

Grace had been dreaming of just such a circus since she bought her first *Tiger Beat* magazine at the age of eleven. "Are you kidding me? We wouldn't miss it for the world."

The rest of the afternoon was spent doing some of the things they were too late to do the night before, typical sight-seeing like normal people. Now, as the sun set, they leaned against the big white railing that bordered the Bellagio Fountain. The next show wouldn't start for another ten minutes. Nick and Killian were discussing Russia's involvement in World War II, Killian careful to use his American accent. It was hard to believe it was less than twenty-four hours since they stood on this very spot and watched Killian have a meltdown. It seemed like ages ago. She looked up at the passing traffic, hoping fervently that the bus with Astrid's photo on the side had engine trouble today, or a flat tire, or had fallen off into the Grand Canyon – anything to keep it from driving by again.

Then, as she'd done a dozen times in the past few hours, she began scanning the crowd for anyone who might qualify as paparazzi. She didn't know exactly what they looked like, but anyone with an expensive looking camera pointed their way was under immediate suspicion. Earlier, while watching the leopards at the Secret Garden, she'd spotted a man standing alone taking pictures. She casually stepped between him and Killian, blocking his line of sight, before she realized he was actually trying to get a shot of a smiling woman and two kids who were posing in front of the tiger cubs' enclosure. Killian just happened to be standing near them. Oh, well, better safe than sorry.

She caught Nick scanning the crowd a couple of times as well. It was nice to know she wasn't the only paranoid person here, though she was sure he would never admit it. Killian, on the other hand, didn't seem to be paying the slightest bit of attention. Either he was well practiced at pretending not to look, or he really wasn't looking. Grace couldn't tell which.

Behind her, the big air compressors began to hum and the first notes of Sinatra's "Luck Be a Lady" came booming out over the speakers. Nick stuck out his hand to pull her to her feet.

YouTube just didn't do this justice, she thought as she looked up at the huge choreographed show. The water shot over 200 feet in the air at times, momentarily obscuring the façade of the Bellagio. Nick was behind her, looking over her shoulder, his arms around her waist. It reminded her of their first New Year's Eve together all those years ago, watching the fireworks from a friend's apartment balcony. It was the first time he told her he loved her, there with the fireworks booming overhead in the chilly night air. She smiled at the thought of it. He hadn't changed a bit since then. He even looked the same. Nick "Steady-as-a-Rock" Howard. Easy-going and predictable. Grace had to remind herself on occasion that it wasn't such a bad thing to be predictable. He was a planner and she was a doer. His motto was "Measure twice and cut once." Her motto was, "It's easier to get forgiveness than it is to get permission." Still, he knew how to make her laugh, and he knew when not to try. She leaned up and kissed him on the cheek. He smiled at her and wrapped his arms a little tighter.

Ruth had arranged for the three of them to eat dinner in a private dining room at *Boeuf*, a restaurant so exclusive, you had to know it was there in order to know it was there. It occupied the twelfth floor of the Eiffel Tower, just above the public restaurant, and the view was second only to the food.

"You know, Ruth has really got the hookup, hasn't she?" Nick said when his steak arrived tender as a marshmallow.

"That reminds me," Killian said, "Ruth got us on the list for die Nacht tonight. It's a very exclusive club and we can't go looking like this. We'll have to get new clothes."

"I don't know," said Nick. "I don't have to wear a suit, do I?"

"Ooh, I've read about that place," said Grace. "It's like Goth and punk and glam and heavy metal all got together and opened a bar. It sounds great."

Nick made a pained face.

"Oh, come on, be a sport," she said with a pleading look. "It'll be fun. It'll be like Halloween." To Killian, she said, "Nick's not one for playing dress-up. He likes his jeans and tee-shirts."

"Well, jeans and tee-shirts are perfectly fine, just with a few minor modifications. Ruth says there's a store near the club where we can get everything we need. The store's called Vicious, and all we have to do is mention her name and everything is taken care of. We are to ask for a girl named Misty."

They agreed to reconvene at ten p.m. That would give them enough time to shower off a day's worth of desert grime. It was five minutes till ten when Killian knocked on the door of their room.

Grace was glad she didn't have to dry her new hairstyle, just brush it down and under and it would dry all by itself. She was reaching for her rarely used makeup bag when Killian spotted her. "No, no, they'll take care of that at Vicious," he assured her.

Nick said, "I'm not wearing any makeup. I draw the line there."

"To each his own," Killian said.

No one thought twice about the fresh flowers on the table near the window.

The shop was just two blocks away and in the same hotel as the club they were going to, so they decided to walk. The air outside was considerably cooler than it had been the night before, and it was a pleasant stroll. The construction workers on the high rise across the street were getting off for the night. Grace could see them coming down in their cage-like elevators, loaded in like sardines with hard hats. They'd left all of the work lights on in the building and there was something strangely beautiful about the twinkling, now deserted skeleton poised against the black Nevada sky.

Killian wore his "lucky" ball cap and the amber glasses. He still had the beard, but didn't seem to be avoiding anybody's gaze. On the contrary, he was smiling and whistling — Grace thought it sounded oddly like "Sweet Georgia Brown" — and had a bounce in his step.

It didn't take long to find what they were looking for. When Grace saw the storefront, a huge silver glittering skull with an open mouth for the door, she ran inside, leaving Nick and Killian in her wake.

The interior of the store looked like a cave. Embedded in the high, rock-like walls were dozens of television sets all tuned to different channels and set at awkward angles. The TVs were surrounded by everything from galvanized garbage can lids to pieces of broken furniture, old vinyl LP's and even a battered canoe.

"Looks like a high-priced trash heap," Grace exclaimed.

The music was blaring, classic punk — angry, fast and hard to understand. A slender girl in an ultra-short, plaid Catholic-school-girl skirt and what remained of a torn tee-shirt bearing the anarchy symbol asked if she could help them find anything. She wore black patent leather combat boots and her white blonde hair was cut short and spiky. Her left arm was covered in a sleeve of tattoos, and a neon green nametag read Misty. Grace couldn't help noticing how good she smelled, like fresh pears, an odd contrast to the punks she had known in her college days. She knew Nick couldn't help but notice the skirt. She cut her eyes at him, but he was tactfully looking at the assortment of crazy objects hanging from the ceiling, including a turntable, a blow-up doll, a wooden school desk and a chain saw.

"Ruth Averhart sent us," Killian said in his best gangster. "She said you would take care of us."

"Oh, yeah, we've been expecting you. Miss Averhart said to make sure you got everything you need."

Grace could see Misty surveying Killian, looking him over from head to toe like a hungry lioness looks at a wounded gazelle. In a wink, she was next to him, touching his arm. "Don't I know you?" she purred. "I get the feeling we've met before."

Killian grinned wickedly. "Oh, no, my dear. I am sure I would remember you."

Misty smiled and leaned toward him until her mouth was just inches from his neck. Grace hoped she wasn't one of those Goth girls who fancied herself a vampire.

"I can't place your cologne," she said. "What is it?"

"I'm not wearing any," Killian replied, sounding as if he were talking about his pants.

"Mmm…" the girl nodded in appreciation and took another whiff for good measure.

Finally, it was Killian who stepped back, putting a few inches between them on the pretense of looking at a rack of feather boas.

Grace was already sorting through skirts, totally immersed in the shopping experience. Nick, however, stood rooted to the spot, arms folded, looking simultaneously bored and uncomfortable.

Another salesgirl glided up from behind him and looped her arm in his. "Come on handsome. I've got just the thing for you."

The innuendo in her voice made Grace pop her head up from the rack of skirts. The girl, whose bright orange nametag read "Rachel," was a living, breathing tribute to Betty Page, complete with ridiculously high heeled shoes, fishnet hose, a black teddy and an angelic face. As she guided Nick toward the back of the store, Grace found herself following.

In her haste, Grace's arm bumped a rack of hats, sending a few toppling. A pale, thin boy in leather pants and a chainmail shirt caught the rack before it hit the ground. His long, black hair hung halfway down his back in tight, springy curls. Long lashes fringed big, brown eyes, and Grace caught herself staring into them a little longer than she should have. He was beautiful, and he couldn't have been a day over twenty.

The neon blue nametag he wore on a lanyard read Bret and clinked softly against the chainmail as he walked. His voice was surprisingly deep when he asked if he could show her anything.

"Well, to be honest," she said, "I've always loved glam."

Bret raised an eyebrow and nodded. At present, Grace looked anything but glam. As if by way of a sign, the first few notes of a David Bowie song began playing overhead. Bret smiled. "We can do that," he said. "Come with me."

Evidently, Bret had sized her up the moment he saw her, because he was pulling things off shelves right and left and soon had an armload. In the same amount of time, Grace had picked out only one thing, a fitted black tee-shirt that read "Concealed Carry" across the chest in Swarovski crystals. There was so much to look at, so much to choose from, that it was a little overwhelming. After all, Grace usually bought her clothes at Sears. Sears did not sell leather teddies.

As they approached the unisex dressing area, Killian threw aside the silk curtain he had been changing behind. He wore pink and black zebra striped Lycra pants and a black tank top made from some shimmery, see-through material. The pants left very little to the imagination, and Grace turned her head away so quickly she almost hurt her neck. Killian laughed at her response. "I take it that's a no?" he said, turning in front of the full-length mirrors, arms outstretched.

"It's a free country. You can wear whatever you want." She tried to sound nonchalant, but it was too late for that. Her cheeks were already red. Misty, on the other hand, seemed much more appreciative of the ensemble.

Bret ushered Grace into one of the larger dressing rooms and hung her clothes on the outstretched arm of a skeleton. "I'll be right outside if you need anything," he said and pulled the curtain closed behind him, leaving Grace staring at the conglomeration of leather, vinyl, fishnet, feathers and rhinestones that hung before her. She picked up a gold lamé mini skirt and a thin, white tunic with a centaur carrying a bow and arrow on the front.

"How did you know I'm a Sagittarius?" she called to Bret through the curtain.

She heard him chuckle. "Well, Sagittarians are known for being creative, outspoken, and not always looking before they leap. You chose glam, you called the store a high-priced trash heap, and you knocked over that rack of hats."

"Is that all?"

"Are you a Sagittarius?"

"Yes."

"Then it's enough."

Three outfits later, she found one she thought she could live with, at least for one night. Bret had insisted she model each one, which resulted in much head shaking and eye rolling from Nick and a fair amount of clapping and whistling from Killian. They were all either too tight, too sheer or too revealing for Grace's taste. She scrutinized the current outfit in the mirror. The black "Concealed Carry" shirt was tight and low-cut, but it was stretchy and comfortable, something lacking in everything else she'd tried on. She wore a pair of black tights under a "skirt" that consisted of a good number of two-inch wide vinyl strips that hung to mid-thigh. Silver glitter was embedded in the vinyl and they made an interesting slapping sound when she spun around.

By far her favorite part of the costume was the black, patent leather combat boots, just like Misty's. She'd been afraid Bret would try to talk her into some spiky pumps, but he seemed to know instinctively that, even with this crazy getup, Grace was a sensible shoes kind of girl. She would break her leg trying to walk in those torture devices Rachel was wearing.

When she opened the curtain this time, Bret stood with an assortment of necklaces draped from his fingers. When he saw her, he smiled. "That's the one," he said. She grinned in spite of herself, then did a pirouette to make the skirt smack into itself.

"Hey, I just realized you're wearing the necklace they've been showing all afternoon on TV," Bret said.

Grace put a hand to her neck automatically, touching her anniversary present. "Oh, really? What have they been saying?"

"I don't know. We never have the sound up. I just keep seeing the picture and then they show a mummy. I must have seen it a dozen times."

Grace told him about the real necklace having belonged to King Tut's mother and how they sold the replicas at The Isis. "Must be a marketing campaign."

"Well, it's beautiful," he said, "but I don't think it goes with what you're wearing tonight. Try this." He held up a short silver chain with a flat, pearly white skull the size of a golf ball dangling from it. The eyes were iridescent.

As she reached up to unclasp her own necklace, a thought hit her. "What in the world are we going to do with our regular clothes? We didn't even think of that. Now we're going to have to carry them all back to the hotel dressed like this."

"Oh, no," said Bret. "This happens all the time. We'll send your things back to your hotel for you in a 'plain brown wrapper.' We have a lot of powerful people who come in here – congressmen, judges – they don't necessarily want everyone to know they buy chainmail thongs."

Grace's eyes widened in surprise at the idea of chainmail thongs, but Bret just laughed in response.

By the time Bret was through with her hair and makeup, the boys had finished dressing and had come around to find her. Nick started laughing the moment he saw her. "Seriously?" he asked.

She twirled around in the middle of the floor. "Isn't it great? I just love it. I think I'll start dressing this way all the time."

Bret had spiked her hair so it stood straight up on top, with a dusting of silver sparkle. He'd done her eyelids in shiny peacock blue, running it out to a point at her hairline on either side. Her fake eyelashes were an inch long, and her lips were blood red. A finish of pale powder gave her face a shimmering glow.

"I love it!" Killian said. "It's brilliant and mad and crazy and beautiful, just like you."

"Thanks, but how about you? Not too shabby, yourself."

Killian took a dramatic bow. He was wearing a dark blue velvet tailcoat over a shiny white tuxedo shirt, unbuttoned, of course. His pants and pointed toed boots were some sort of leather, a dark indigo, almost black. Misty saw Grace's curious look and said like a true salesperson, "Man-made to look and feel like alligator. Lighter, more breathable, and they're even washable."

Nick, just as Grace expected, hadn't gone too far out of his comfort zone. His arms folded over a vintage WASP tee-shirt that looked like it was two sizes too small, accompanied by a pair of blue jeans with rows of frayed razor cuts all the way from the front pockets to the hem. His shoes were his own, worn Converse high-tops. His one concession to fashion was a bracelet on each wrist, a two-inch wide strip of leather with menacing looking spikes all around. Grace was sure only someone who looked like Rachel could have talked him into that.

While Bret had been doing Grace's hair and make-up, Rachel had been quietly closing up shop. The front gates were locked and the register was counted down. The dressing rooms were cleared and everything hung back in its proper place. She was very efficient for someone in five-inch stiletto heels.

Misty had gathered up all their street clothes and wrapped them in plain, brown cardboard boxes for discreet front desk delivery.

"Well, you know Miss Averhart has taken care of payment, so there's really nothing left to do but go and enjoy ourselves," Bret said.

Misty slung a purse over her shoulder, a cheerful looking quilted bag with a Yorkie puppy embroidered on the front. Obviously not purchased at Vicious. She and Rachel headed for the back of the store. Bret gestured after them with a sweeping bow and a poor imitation of a British accent, "After you, madam."

Nick pointed behind them. "I thought we came in that way."

Rachel laughed, a girlish laugh at odds with her shoes, and took Nick's arm again. "We have our own way of getting into die Nacht."

Misty waited at the rear of the stockroom next to a scarred, industrial looking door. She turned off the flashing televisions and the thumping wall of heavy metal music that had been crashing in over the speakers. The sudden quiet was jarring. "The same person who owns die Nacht owns Vicious. And he requested that we bring you in through his private entrance."

She opened the door to reveal a poorly lit cinderblock passageway running left and right. They all filed in before Misty set the store's alarm and locked the door behind them.

Bret led the way through the empty passageway. Grace soon picked up the vibrations of another thumping bass line and felt a little thrill of excitement.

They stopped in front of a door identical to the one they'd just left. Misty entered a number on a keypad above the lock. Seconds later, a small red light came on over the door and Bret, Misty and Rachel all looked up at the security camera and waved. Someone on the other side pulled the door open and Grace followed the crew inside.

What she saw was not what she'd expected at all. Wherever they were being led, it certainly was not into a nightclub.

Chapter 14 – She is Beautiful

Gravel crunched under the tires of the big SUV as Pavel Alkaev turned into the nearly-deserted parking lot of the motel where his men kept rooms. Night was beginning to fall, and he had his temper back in check again. Now he was glad he had not killed the two idiots this morning. It looked like he would need their help after all. And he didn't want anyone else involved in this. The fewer people who knew that Makar had made a fool of him, the better.

Alkaev thought this afternoon was going to be a breeze and, at first, it was. He'd gone to The Isis alone, wearing a blonde wig and dark glasses, careful to keep his head down and away from security cameras.

A little misdirection employed on one of the maids and, *voila*, he had a master key. He hadn't picked a pocket in fifteen years, but apparently it was like riding a bicycle. He felt like a petty criminal again, stealing from tourists around St. Basil's cathedral, and that made him smile.

One pleasant change since those early days was technology. The little GPS tracker he'd concealed in the flowers was inexpensive and surprisingly accurate. The blip on his iPhone led him to a choice of two rooms. The door to 1404 was the first one he tried, and when it opened, he could see the bouquet sitting on the table across the room.

He hung the "Do not disturb" sign on the door and moved quickly, careful to leave everything just as he'd found it. The suitcases lay open on stands and one, the woman's, was already in disarray. Her dirty clothes were scattered on the floor. What a slob. His search through her case revealed nothing but some garish costume jewelry in a shiny zippered bag. He opened it, then closed it again with a snarl. He knew Americans lacked taste, but this was ridiculous. Even cubic zirconia would be a step up for this woman.

Next, he turned his attention to the man's suitcase. After carefully going through it twice with no luck, he realized that his heart was beating a little faster than normal and he had a tight feeling in his stomach. Was this fear? The very thought made the symptoms worse. Pavel Alkaev did not succumb to fear. That was for the weak-minded.

He began to search in earnest, under the unmade bed, behind the furniture, in the cornice of the drapes, his gloved fingers missing nothing. The little safe in the closet was standing open. It was obvious these people had nothing of their own worth locking in a safe.

Nonetheless, he had to admit after almost forty-five minutes of searching that the necklace was simply not there. A chill went through him when he realized that Makar's note may have been a red herring. Perhaps he knew he was being followed and scribbled Nick Howard's name and flight just to throw Alkaev off the trail. That thought enraged him. He imagined finding what was left of Makar's body and cutting out his old friend's tongue. The image calmed him somewhat.

He made one last pass through the room to make sure everything was as he found it. He was reaching for the light switch in the bathroom when he saw it. Lying behind the small waste basket, almost hidden from view, was an empty tissue paper package wrapped in clear tape. A hole had been torn at one end of the package. Alkaev picked it up and smiled. Written in Russian on one side of it in Makar's cramped handwriting were the words *Ona krasiva*, "She is beautiful."

Chapter 15 – die Nacht

The room on the other side of the metal door smelled of wood and leather and was lined with bookcases and sturdy, comfortable furniture. The massive mahogany desk looked like it belonged in the Oval Office, and there was even a fire blazing in an oversized fireplace. Had it not been for the faint bass line reverberating through the walls, they might have easily been in the study of some wealthy European landowner. In truth, they were standing in the office of the owner of — among other things — die Nacht and Vicious.

The man who rose from behind the mahogany desk appeared to be in his mid-sixties, tall and thin, with a head full of closely cropped white hair and a neatly trimmed moustache. He was wearing an honest-to-goodness smoking jacket with a satin lapel, and Grace had to suppress a giggle at the sight of it. All in all, she thought he looked like something out of a black and white movie, maybe a taller, less macabre version of Vincent Price.

"Herr Koenig, these are the charges you asked us to oversee," Misty said.

He gave her a little nod of approval and a smile.

She seemed pleased with that and turned to the trio. "We'll see you inside," she said with a little wink at Killian. It was obvious they were to stay here, at least for the moment.

Misty joined Bret and Rachel, who were standing in front of the fireplace. The long hearth seemed to dwarf the rest of the room.

Bret flipped a light switch, one of a long row of identical switches. Almost immediately, the fire was extinguished. Gas flames had been shooting up from the rock floor, and with no logs to smolder, it was as if the fire had never existed. The three of them stepped up into the fireplace itself and the whole center began to turn inside the wall. It rotated 180 degrees and stopped. The other side of the wall was obviously a fireplace too, because less than a minute later, the fire was roaring again, just as it had been when they arrived.

Mr. Koenig didn't look at the fire. He had eyes only for his guests. "Please, make yourselves comfortable." He motioned towards two overstuffed leather sofas as he stepped over to a small, but well-stocked bar recessed into one wall. "May I offer you a drink?"

Grace was anxious to get into the nightclub, but like any self-respecting girl raised in the south, she knew it would be rude to refuse the owner's hospitality. She settled lightly on the edge of the sofa and took the offered brandy snifter. She definitely felt like she was in a black and white movie now. All that was missing was the cigarette in a long holder.

Their host smiled broadly at them and raised his glass in a toast, "Prost!"

"Prost," they all echoed.

The crystal clinked noisily and they all drank.

"My name is Wilhelm Koenig and I want you to make yourselves at home here." His accent wasn't heavy, but it was unmistakable. He studied them all intently. His eyes lit up when he got to Killian. "Any friend of Ruth Averhart's is a friend of mine," he said. "You know, she didn't tell me who I would be entertaining tonight, only that you were very special to her. I must admit, from the way she spoke of you, I assumed it was her lover, but now that I see who you are…well…"

"You recognize him?" Grace asked.

"Of course," said Wilhelm with a little bow. "I am honored to have you and your friends in my humble establishment."

Killian nodded, but didn't speak. He looked a little taken aback. A few hours earlier, he was ready to come out of hiding, but now it looked like he was having second thoughts.

"Believe me," Wilhelm assured them, "I understand your desire for privacy, and we at die Nacht are masters of discretion. Your secret is safe with us." He made a motion of locking his lips with an imaginary key, a motion that would have looked silly when performed by most grown men, but he seemed quite sincere.

"Of course, your tab is being picked up by Miss Averhart and she instructed me to tell you not to worry about a thing. Rest assured, if there is something you want – anything – all you have to do is ask. If we don't have it, we will obtain it."

Grace wondered what they would do if she ordered a football helmet full of cottage cheese. She gulped down the rest of her brandy to stifle a grin.

"The VIP section is the balcony level," Wilhelm was saying. "It is private and you will have your own wait staff, but you are by no means confined to that level. Our dance floor is on the main level, and you may wish to join in. There are stairs and an elevator on the south end, near the waterfall. Sentinels are posted at each of these entrances. They will know to let you back up."

"When you are ready to leave, any of our staff members can assist you in getting back to my office through the fire. Any questions?"

"Yes," Killian said. "How do you know Ruth?"

Koenig waved his hand dismissively. "Ah, everyone in show business knows Ruth Averhart. Wouldn't you agree?"

"I wouldn't have thought owning casinos was considered show business," Grace said.

"Owning casinos is not all that I do, my friends. I made most of my money here, yes, but some of it I invest. I like to invest in movies." He looked at Killian as he spoke. "I like action, adventure, danger, a movie with a strong leading man. Those do very well at the box office."

Killian said nothing.

Wilhelm smiled and reached for the switch that would temporarily stop the flames in the big fireplace. "It is my sincere pleasure to meet you all," said Wilhelm warmly. "Now, if you will follow me."

They climbed up onto the hearth and squeezed together – it was a little snug with all four of them – but the platform rotated with no trouble at all. The music grew louder as they turned and Grace smiled as she recognized The Clash. The platform came to a stop and they all stepped off. Wilhelm pressed some unseen button that brought the flames to life again. On this side of the wall, it was not a grand fireplace, but a rocky alcove they stepped out of. Similar pits were dotted around the huge room. Everywhere else was blackness, broken only by intermittent bursts of light. Slowly, Grace's eyes began to adjust. They were on a large, C-shaped balcony, and the flashing lights were coming from the dance floor below.

"I want to know how all these fireplaces are vented," Nick said, peering intently at the one they just exited. "Ventless flames are blue, and these are definitely bright orange. And there's not a lot of heat coming in either. All of this has to go somewhere." He was talking to Killian, as if he thought by sharing a Y chromosome, Killian also shared some knowledge of plumbing. Killian nodded in a brooding, manly way, trying to look as if he had some idea what Nick was talking about.

Then he caught Grace's eye over Nick's shoulder and shrugged. She giggled. The brandy had made her feel warm and happy.

Wilhelm showed them to what he called their own private grotto on the balcony. It was surrounded by artificial boulders on three sides. Nick tapped one with his knuckles as they passed. As they stepped inside, the volume of the music went down a little, making it possible to carry on a conversation without shouting. The interior housed a long, narrow table with velvet chairs on each side.

"Zoe will be your server tonight." The trio turned to see their host now flanked by a tall girl with long red hair. She was so pale, she seemed to glow in the dim light. "I will leave you in her very capable hands."

He disappeared into the half-light of the club. A minute later, they saw one of the fires on the far wall extinguish briefly. Their host had gone back to his office.

Zoe beamed at them, giving every indication she was truly happy to be working as a cocktail waitress in a silver lamé halter top and black satin hot pants.

"What can I get you folks tonight?" Her accent was southern. Shreveport, she said, when Grace asked. She was happy to hear another southern accent, and they talked for a minute about how different the pace was here than back home, and then, just as sweet as you please, she said, "Would you like a fourth for the evening?"

Grace paused a moment and said, "Is that bigger than a fifth? I've never heard of that."

"I'll bet it's more expensive than a fifth, whatever it is," said Nick.

Zoe's pretty face frowned, puzzled by their confusion.

Killian caught on quickly, although his words came out slowly. "You're not talking about a drink, are you?"

Zoe shook her head, all smiles again.

"What kind of fourth are you talking about, exactly, sweetheart?" The gangster accent somehow lent itself to 'sweetheart.'

"Um…a fourth *person*," she said, as if no one had ever misunderstood this question before.

Killian laughed, a low, rumbling sound. "You mean, you're offering us a woman?"

"Oh, no, sir," she replied hastily. "If you prefer a man…"

Now all three were laughing, and Zoe's pale cheeks flushed crimson.

"Can we see a menu of these people?" Nick asked. "I like to see who I'm getting before I order. You can never be too careful."

"That's true," Killian said. "And one bad blonde can spoil the whole bunch."

"Try saying that three times, fast," Nick added.

"Oh, stop!" Grace laughed so hard she was almost in tears.

"All right, seriously, we seem to be embarrassing our lovely waitress." Killian said, making a huge effort to keep a straight face. He inclined his head to Zoe. "My dear, we're fine with just the three of us, but thanks all the same."

A girl with spiky blonde hair ambled up beside Zoe. "I've got this, sweetie. Why don't you go on break?" It was Misty, now dressed in the silver halter and black hot pants of the wait staff. Zoe looked at Misty in surprise, but didn't move. "Shoo!" Zoe turned on her heel and hurried away, long red hair swinging behind her as she went.

Misty carried a serving tray with a silver rail around the edge. She twirled it around and set it on the table in front of them. It contained twelve shot glasses divided into three neat rows of four. "It's called the Monster Mash," she said with a mischievous grin. "If you do it right, I promise you'll be down on the dance floor doing the Monster Mash."

Grace laughed. "Impossible. I don't even know what that dance looks like."

Nick shook his head and chuckled. "Sorry, I don't see that happening."

Misty's smile widened. "I personally guarantee it."

"Oh, yeah? And what if it doesn't work?" Killian asked. "What's in it for us?"

Misty contemplated that for a moment, then said, "Well, I suppose it's only fair that I do the Monster Mash if you don't."

Killian shook his head. "Not good enough. We've already admitted we don't know what that looks like. You could do anything, and we wouldn't know the difference."

"How about the moonwalk?" she said.

"Nope."

"The Cabbage Patch?"

"Uh-uh."

"Do you know the Superbowl Shuffle?" Nick asked.

Misty put her hands on her hips. "I'm afraid not."

"That reminds me of a joke," Nick said. "A string walks into a bar. The bartender says, 'Hey, we don't serve strings in here.' So the string leaves. He goes outside, ties himself in a knot, and ruffles up his ends. He goes back into the bar. The bartender sees him and says, 'Hey, I thought I told you we don't serve strings here!' And the string says, 'You're mistaken, sir. I am no string; I'm a frayed knot."

They were all hooting with laughter, with Nick as the straight man, when Killian managed to pull himself together enough to say, "All right, we're losing sight of the real issue here, which is – what kind of dance are you going to do for us when you lose?" He leaned back regally in a velvet chair as he addressed Misty.

"*When* I lose?" she replied. "You're very sure of yourself, aren't you?"

"Always."

"All right," she said, "I'll bite. How about if you three don't dance after these four shots, I'll do the entire routine from the 'Thriller' video."

"Well, that I'd like to see," said Grace, "but can you do it to this music?" She pointed at the ceiling, indicating the macabre Goth song that was undulating through the speakers.

"I'll take care of that," Misty replied with a wave.

"You're very sure of yourself, aren't you?" Killian tossed her words back.

Misty inclined her head. "Always." Her smug smile was endearing.

Killian looked from Nick to Grace. "Do we have a deal?" They nodded. He turned back to Misty and said, "You're on."

"All right, the rules are simple: First, you have to do the shots in order. Second, after each shot, everyone answers a question. Each of you gets to make up one, and of course you have to answer it as well. We're not trying to force anyone to do any deep thinking, just stay semi-coherent. For instance, you might ask 'Ginger or MaryAnn.'"

"MaryAnn, definitely," Nick volunteered.

Killian shook his head. "No way. Got to go with Ginger."

"Rule number three," Misty continued, "No throwing up. If you do, you're disqualified. Rule number four — and this one is important — you have to keep your clothes on. There are decency laws, you know, even in Sin City."

The first row of shot glasses were filled with a dark purple liquid. Misty said it was a Blackberry Bomber.

They all raised their glasses. "One…two…three," Misty counted and they gulped down the purple liquid and clunked the glasses back on the table.

"Okay, who wants to ask the first question?" Misty looked at Grace and said, "Ladies first."

Grace shivered. She could feel the warm brandy in her stomach and still taste the sweet blackberry flavor. "What's the name of the first person you ever kissed? Mine was Alan." She looked at Nick, waiting for his answer.

He looked wistful. "Ah, her name was Debbie Williams. We met at the pool. Everybody called her Little Debbie, like the snack cakes. She had braces and freckles on her nose and she wore strawberry lip gloss…"

"I just asked for her name, not her life story," Grace said with a wave of her hand. "What about you, K… Bubba."

"Di, just like the princess." He gave Grace a quick wink and she rolled her eyes.

"How about you," Grace asked Misty. "Who was your first kiss?"

"Katy," she replied. Grace, Nick and even Killian looked at her with raised eyebrows. "What?" she said with a shrug. "I went to an all-girls school. You've got to play the hand you're dealt."

She set out the second round. "This one is called a Red-Headed Slut. Hmmm…sort of like Katy," she mused. "You eat the cherry first, then you do the shot."

They all popped the cherries into their mouths. When Killian pulled his stem out, he'd tied it in a knot. He tossed it on the table in front of Misty. Rising to the challenge, she picked it up and put it in her own mouth. A few seconds later, she pulled it out and tossed it down in front of Killian. She had tied two more knots in the same stem. He grinned.

The shot tasted like peaches and licorice. Grace wasn't the only one shuddering this time. She was beginning to get that melty feeling, when all is right with the world and everything is funny, right before you start telling everyone how much you love them.

"I think I like red-headed sluts, too," Killian said.

"Here, here!" Nick said, raising his empty glass in a toast.

"Bubba, why don't you ask the next question?" Misty said.

Killian froze, his eyes fixed on something over Misty's shoulder. Grace, in her warm, red-headed-slut haze, half expected to see the cross-town bus with Astrid's lingerie poster on the side. What she saw instead was much worse. It was Astrid herself. She was just as beautiful as her photos, long blonde hair hanging loosely over her bare shoulders. She wore the same silver halter and hot pants as Misty and Zoe and she carried an empty tray at her side. Grace's first instinct was to hide. She wanted to leap across the table and pull Killian under it with her. But, it was too late. Astrid had seen them. She smiled and headed straight for them.

She stopped beside Misty, giving her a playful nudge. But something was wrong with this picture. Slowly, Grace remembered Astrid was almost six feet tall. This girl was shorter than Misty, and Misty was shorter than Grace.

"Hi, there," she said. "Mr. Koenig asked me to drop by your table. He said I might give your guests a laugh." She looked up at Killian's startled face and her eyes grew wider.

Misty said, "I think you're giving one of them a heart attack. Bubba, are you okay?"

He didn't speak, but did manage a slight nod.

The girl's accent was straight off a Wisconsin dairy farm. This was not Astrid, thank God, but was a very convincing Astrid lookalike. For a second, Grace was furious. Why in the hell had Koenig thought this was a good idea? What was he playing at?

Then it struck her. Of course he thought this girl would be a laugh. He had every reason to believe the real Astrid was still happily engaged to Killian. Ruth wasn't going to tell him any different. Koenig had sent the girl as a lark.

"Wow. You're very convincing," Grace said. She sounded breathless when she spoke, even to her own ears.

"Thank you," she said sweetly. "You know, when I first started working here, I'd never even heard of Astrid LeBeau. Now I feel like I oughta send her a thank-you note on account of all the tips I get for looking like her."

Nick made a noise that was supposed to be "Uh-huh," but sounded more like a grunt. Grace looked askance at him, sitting there with a silly grin on his face, staring at the lookalike. Pathetic.

"Well, I'd better get back downstairs," the girl said. I've got this tall blonde and her sugar daddy in my section, and they are driving me nuts. She must be a real star-gazer because she keeps asking questions about who's up here in VIP. I guess I should keep an eye on her, make sure she doesn't try to sneak up. Of course, the old dude did buy a five-hundred-dollar bottle of Russian vodka, so I guess I shouldn't complain. Anyway, I just wanted to come say hi, so...Hi!" She waved and sashayed back downstairs.

"Sweet girl, that Amber," Misty said, "but dumb as a box of rocks." She sighed. "All right, where were we? Oh, yes, I believe it was Bubba's turn to ask a question." She looked brightly at Killian, waiting for a response.

He took a deep breath. "Here's a question for you," he said. "Have you ever walked in on your fiancée screwing someone else in your bed?"

"Okay, okay," Grace said. "We were doing so well here. Let's try and get back to our happy place."

Misty's smile faltered, but she kept her composure. She looked at Nick. "Why don't you ask the question this round?"

"Um…okay. Let's see," he said, trying to think fast. "If you were stranded on a tropical island and you could only take one thing with you, what would it be? For me, it would be my toolbox. Then maybe I could build a raft."

Grace, who was patting Killian on the arm, said, "That's easy. I would take rum. There are always coconuts on tropical islands and how could I make Piña Coladas without rum?"

"What about you, Bubba?" Nick asked, trying to draw him back in. "What would you take?"

"Ruth," he answered, dropping all pretenses at an American accent. "Because she could get me *off* the bloody island."

He laughed at himself, a harsh laugh, and said, "I'm ready to dance. When do we get to the dancing?" He picked up the third shot and said, "What's this called? I hope it's not a blonde slut, because I've already had one of those, and they leave a bad taste in your mouth."

"That's called the Devil's Kiss," Misty said, "and it's supposed to be flaming." She pulled a wand lighter from the waistband of her shorts and lit the drinks. The little flames danced as she counted. "One...two...three."

They drained the glasses. Killian slammed his glass down on the table, a little too hard. The shot tasted like cinnamon.

"It's my turn to ask a question," he said. Grace opened her mouth to object and he said, "I'll be nice." She wasn't so sure, but she didn't try to stop him. When his eyes met hers, they were full of pain. It made her catch her breath. When he was screaming and yelling the night before, that had been pain too, but a different kind. That was anger and disappointment and hurt feelings, but this... this was the anguish of knowing it was over and there was nothing he could do about it.

Finally, he spoke. "How do you know when someone really loves you?" Grace wanted to look away, but he was staring at her so desperately, she couldn't. "Of course they all say it, but how do you know when it's real?" He was waiting for an answer. She didn't know if she had one.

She finally managed to blink, and glanced at Nick. He looked like he was doing complicated math in his head. She turned to Misty and was surprised to see that she, too, looked deep in thought.

Grace reached across the table and put her hands on top of Killian's. They felt soft compared to Nick's. The life of a movie star versus the life of a carpenter. But a broken heart is a broken heart, no matter who it belongs to.

"I don't think anyone says it if they don't mean it, or at least they think they mean it at the time. It's just that...well, people change, I guess. Circumstances change." Grace looked around for some input, but Nick and Misty just looked relieved that she was taking the reins. "I guess the only way to know if someone really loves you is if they've seen you at your worst, and still want to be with you. Not just in the good times." She could see Misty nodding. "You know, you always hear people say love is forever. But that's a lie. There's no magic spell. The truth is, love is ongoing. It's a work in progress, and both people have to keep nurturing it, to keep it alive. And if one of the people decides they don't want it anymore, there's nothing you can do to stop them." That was as philosophical as she could get after a brandy and three shots.

Killian squeezed her fingers. She knew he was storing his pain away for a later date. It wasn't gone. It would be back, but for now he was in control. Each time it would be a little easier.

He managed a faint smile for Grace and then turned to Misty. "Hurry up, won't you; I can't wait all night to see 'Thriller.'"

She passed the fourth and final shots around the table. "This," she said with a flourish, "is the pièce de résistance. This is the Doc Brown. If this had been the first shot, you wouldn't have needed the other three. But, where's the fun in that? Besides, you have to earn the Doc Brown."

Grace sniffed the concoction and coughed. "What's in this? It smells like paint thinner and feet."

"I know that smell," Nick said. "That's moonshine."

Half an hour before, none of them would have touched the Doc Brown, but now they all toasted and readied for the count without hesitation.

"One…two…three," Misty called.

Grace remembered thinking that gasoline must taste like this.

The next thing she knew, she was doing the Monster Mash.

Chapter 16 – Rooster

It probably wasn't the real Monster Mash, since Grace didn't know what that looked like, but she was giving it her best effort. And she wasn't the only one. Spandex- and leather-clad bodies danced all around her, and Nick was right in front of her, only inches away, doing something that looked like the Twist. She'd known Nick for thirteen years and had never before seen him dance. His eyes were closed and he looked like he was really concentrating on those gyrations.

Fog encircled their feet. Grace realized they must have made it down to the ground floor of the club. She looked around for Killian, but the people were packed in so tightly it was hard to tell who was who.

She heard Nick say something, but couldn't make it out over the music. This floor was much louder than the VIP section. She shrugged to show him she couldn't hear. He grabbed her arms and put his mouth to her ear. "The fog smells like bubble gum!" he yelled with a laugh. At least it didn't smell like the Doc Brown. She wondered if Nick realized he was dancing. Then he grabbed her shoulders and yelled in her ear again, this time even louder. "Hey, look behind you. It's the woman with the bodacious ta-ta's from the casino!" She turned, her hand covering her now ringing ear.

The blonde who'd been wearing the skimpy gold dress at the blackjack tables was now wearing even less. This dress was red and looked like it was made from wide pieces of strategically placed ribbon. Not a whole lot left to the imagination there. Grace caught a glimpse of blue velvet and realized the girl was dancing with Killian. Her hands were all over him, disappearing under his jacket. She had no shame at all.

Misty came twirling out of the foggy throng, smiling and dancing. She leaned toward Grace and yelled, "Is that the Monster Mash?"

Grace nodded, then shook her head. She didn't seem to have enough breath to answer. Maybe the bubble gum scented fog was making it hard to breathe, or maybe too many people were sucking up all the oxygen, or maybe she'd simply been dancing far longer than she realized.

"I have a surprise for you upstairs," Misty called. She waved for Grace to follow and danced her way gracefully through the crowd.

Grace grabbed Nick's hand and pulled him through the bodies. Misty was extracting Killian from the leggy blonde as they passed. The blonde had an exaggerated frown, pouty bottom lip and all. Apparently, she hadn't been invited to see the surprise. Something about that sight made Grace very happy.

They followed Misty's spiky white-blonde hair past the guards and up the stairs to the second floor.

"What's the surprise?" Grace asked when they stepped onto the big balcony.

Misty skipped along in front of them, looking positively ecstatic. "None other than Rooster Hathcock!" she trilled. Who would have guessed Misty was into Southern Fried Rock?

The bubble gum smell of the fog was gone, but it was slowly being replaced by another, very distinctive aroma, something herbal.

Misty stopped at the first grotto. "Knock, knock!" she called out, flashing her best girlish smile for Rooster.

The effort was not lost on him. He straightened right up, spellbound. "Well, well, well, boys. I think it must be my birthday."

Rooster Hathcock was a good ole boy from the bottom of his scuffed cowboy boots right up to the top of his John Deere baseball cap. And he was a very hot commodity. He sang the national anthem in Game One of the World Series and performed at half-time at the Super Bowl in the same year. He'd been touted as the biggest thing to come out of Mississippi since Elvis. It was a known fact that he loved to party, he loved his dogs, and he loved to wave the flag. In Grace's opinion, you could find plenty worse things to love.

Misty giggled and said breathlessly, "Mr. Hathcock, I hate to disturb you…"

Rooster rounded the table in a flash, ushering her inside, looking very much like the Big Bad Wolf welcoming Little Red Riding Hood. "Oh, disturb me. Disturb me, darlin'. They've been telling me I'm disturbed for years now."

Rooster was a nice enough looking man, thought Grace, despite his mullet and copious tattoos. He had even more than Misty, but his weren't nearly as artistic. What she could see of them included a cross, some barbed wire, an American flag and – what a surprise – a cartoon rooster. They were all done in black ink.

The table was littered with empty beer bottles and overflowing ashtrays. A white plastic tub full of iced beer bottles was the centerpiece. Three other men sat around the table. A woman sat on the lap of one, and they were in such a passionate embrace, they didn't even notice the strangers.

"Bill, Larry, make room for these fine folk," Rooster said.

Grace recognized his band mates from their music videos, but she didn't know their names. She was grateful, however, when they moved down, as a wave of exhaustion hit her. She slumped clumsily into the nearest chair, trying without success to count how many hours she'd been awake.

"Where are my manners?" Rooster said with mock propriety. This here is Bill McGuire, my roadie and bodyguard. Next to him is Larry Trammell, my bassist. In the lip lock there is Rob Winchester, my lead guitarist and..." he turned to Bill and Larry, "what's that girl's name again?" They both shrugged. "Well, I don't guess it matters if we knew her name, cause I don't reckon she'd answer to it right now, anyway," added Rooster, who was casually scratching his chest, manners be damned. "And behind that curtain there is Bobby Melcher, my drummer." A little ripple went through the curtain that separated the bed area from the front of the grotto. A very feminine giggle wafted forward. "Don't pay him no mind." Rooster waved his hand at the curtain. "He's like a stray dog, humpin' everything that moves."

Misty took over the introductions. "Well, Mr. Hathcock..."

"Please," he interrupted with a hand to his heart like he had been wounded. "My friends call me Rooster. And I would certainly be delighted to claim you as a friend." That sentiment seemed meant for Misty, along with the smoldering gaze he had been giving her since the moment she walked up.

"Well… Rooster," Misty smiled coquettishly and Rooster beamed. "I'd like to introduce you to some friends of mine. This is Grace Howard and her husband Nick. They're fellow Southerners, from Alabama, I believe." Rooster tore his eyes away from Misty long enough to give a polite nod and a howdy to Nick and Grace. The unintoxicated portion of Grace's brain wondered vaguely how Misty knew their last name and where they were from.

"And this is…" Misty paused, looking up at Killian, waiting for him to fill in the blank. It was obvious by now she knew his true identity, but she was not about to divulge this information without his consent. Killian was clearly hesitating. Rooster seemed to be the last person who would narc on his fellow man, and also probably the last person to be impressed by a Hollywood sex symbol – a male one, at any rate. Killian smiled, stuck his hand out to shake Rooster's, and for the first time since she'd met him, Grace heard him say the words, "I'm Killian Ross. It's a pleasure to meet you."

Rooster blinked. For a second, Grace wondered if he even knew who Killian was. Then he grabbed Killian's hand and shook it with both of his. "No shit?" he said. "Well, hot damn! We're big fans of yours." He slapped Killian on the shoulder with such force he almost stumbled. "Are you kiddin' me? Why, we've watched *Tripwire* about a hundred times, haven't we, boys? We take it with us on the tour bus."

Larry and Bill seemed equally impressed and took turns shaking Killian's hand. "You know my favorite part of *Tripwire* is where you tell that one dude, 'If you don't know any prayers, you better make some up,'" hooted Larry. "Right before you bust in and blow 'em all to hell!"

Then another thought struck Rooster and his eyes lit up. "Hey, what was it like sleepin' with Anna Olafson? She's so hot she ought to have a warnin' label on her."

"Well, that was just for the movie," Killian said with a smile. "We didn't really have sex, Rooster."

Rooster looked crestfallen, as if someone had just told him that NASCAR season had been canceled. Killian hastened to add, "But she's an amazing kisser, and I did get to see her topless." That seemed to cheer the men a little. Of course, anyone who had seen the movie had also gotten to see her topless.

The beer tub, though large, slid easily, and it was like passing a bowl of peas at the dinner table. You just took a beer and kept it going. Grace had never heard of most of them. They had names like "Tall Tales Ale," "Party Line Lager," and "Three Dogs." She did see one she recognized, and pulled out a "Lazy Magnolia Southern Pecan." It was ice cold and tasted wonderful after all that dancing.

"Anna Olafson was on the bill with us last time we went to the Middle East," Larry said. "She was a real nice girl."

"Oh, that's right," said Grace, "I forgot you guys are always doing shows for the troops. Even going into some pretty hostile territory. I saw that on TV. I know they really appreciate it."

"Aw, that's the least we can do," said Rooster. "You know, there ain't nothin' pretty about war. So I figure if I can take some pretty dancers and actresses with me over there and play some good music and put on a good show, well... maybe they'll have somethin' good to remember in the middle of a whole bunch of bad."

"That's very noble of you, Mr. Hath..." Nick began.

"Rooster!" he pointed a warning finger at Nick. "I said my friends call me Rooster, and I'm markin' all of y'all as my friends."

"You can never have too many friends," Killian said with a broad smile. "Hey, why don't you all come by The Eye tomorrow evening? I'm going to have an un-engagement party of sorts and I would be honored if you'd be my guests. Say, ten o'clock?"

A bright flash filled their small room from the doorway. There were scuffling noises outside, like someone was throwing a bag of potatoes around. When her eyes adjusted again, Grace found that Bill was responsible for the scuffling. He was a big man, probably six-foot-four, 250 pounds, but he made it around Grace and Nick in a split second without even ruffling her hair.

In the next second, a short, pudgy man with fuzzy hair was face down on the table, his arms pinned behind his back by Bill. Two cameras lay on the table, and a third hung around the man's neck. Larry riffled through the man's pockets. "This is assault!" squealed the man. "I'll sue you! I'll have you arrested! You can't touch a photographer! It's assault." Bill didn't loosen his grip.

Rooster stepped around the table so he was right beside the pudgy man. "Walter," he said quietly, "I've had just about all I care to from you." He leaned down so he was sure the man would hear every word. "Lots of photographers out there just want to make an honest livin', but not you. No, sir. You'll get lower than a snake's belly to try and get dirty, sleazy shots of people. It's not enough for you to get pictures of people happy and smilin'. No, sir. You want to get 'em when they're cryin' or sick or doin' somethin' they ought not to be. You're like the little kid in school who was only happy when he could tattle on somebody and get them in trouble." Rooster shook his head in disgust. "Does that make you feel like a big man, Walter?"

Walter was still squirming, but had fallen silent. Now he started his tirade anew. "You'll hear from my lawyer!"

"You know what I think, Walter? I think that would be a very stupid idea. First of all, you know Mr. Koenig doesn't allow photographers in here. So he is gonna be mad as a wet hen when he finds out about you." Rooster chuckled to himself, picturing the scene to come. "Second of all, it's your word against all of ours." He waved his hand around, and Grace noticed that both Misty and Killian were missing. She looked down beside her. She could just see part of Killian's coat sticking out from under the table. Apparently, this was the last guy you want to be photographed by.

Larry flipped back through the last few pictures on each of the three cameras, all digital. He deleted a few and then wiped his fingerprints off the cameras with the hem of his tee-shirt.

"So you see my point, Walter," Rooster said. "I think you should leave and be happy you still can."

Misty hurried back in, this time with two die Nacht security guards behind her. They looked like professional wrestlers in nice black suits. They never said a word, just stepped inside. Each took one of Walter's arms, and escorted him out. Walter was silent for these guys, not a word about assault or lawyers. Bill stepped just outside the grotto and watched as they hauled the photographer down the stairs and out of sight.

Rooster took a deep breath. "I apologize for that," he said, as Killian crawled out from under the table. "Normally I don't mind photographers. You know, they say you should only worry when they stop wanting your picture, but some of this here stuff is private. I got fans who are kids, you know. I don't want them to see some of this stuff."

As if on cue, the drummer's companion for the evening, a petite girl with long curly black hair, fell out from under the curtain onto the floor in front of them. She was completely naked, but that didn't seem to bother her. She just giggled and said, "Oops!" The drummer threw back the curtain so she could climb back in, but he didn't seem to notice the three newcomers at all.

"See what I mean?" Rooster said. "But, I tell ya, Walter ain't the only one. I've never seen as many as were out front tonight." He gave Killian a pointed look.

"Yeah," Larry agreed. "There was almost as many photographers as there was people waitin' to get in. They must have been expectin' a lot of VIPs here tonight."

"Well, it wasn't us," Rooster said, still looking at Killian. "We gave 'em the slip. We put the word out we were headin' for the Canyon Club at the MGM."

"Hey, Rooster!" said Larry, surprised by his own insight. "Maybe they was expectin' Killian Ross! A big star like him would draw those photographers like a hen on a June bug."

"Larry, you're about as quick as molasses in January," Rooster said with a smile.

Nick, who had just popped open a cold one from the ice bucket, guffawed at this and sent a mouthful of beer spraying over the table. That started a chain reaction of buzzed laughter that even Larry joined in on.

Grace was holding her sides, trying to catch her breath. The laughter finally subsided and Larry said, "Um, I don't get it." That set everyone laughing again.

The drummer threw back the taffeta curtain that separated him from the rest of them and demanded, "What the hell is so funny out there?" But no one could catch their breath to tell him. Even Rob and his date had joined in the laughter, although Grace was pretty sure they hadn't heard the joke. The drummer looked around the room, scowling, then closed the curtain and went back to his own pursuit of happiness.

When the laughter was finally under control, Grace felt that wave of tiredness wash over her again. Rooster had turned to Killian and asked, "Hey, you know that chopper you rode in *My Way*? The one with the real big ape hangers...?" The conversation quickly dissolved into talk of chrome and pistons and V twins, and Grace found herself floating on that wave of exhaustion up and over, carried straight out into the ocean. She leaned her head over on Nick's shoulder, and he leaned back to put his arm around her. Now her head was on his chest and she could hear his heartbeat and the comforting rumble of his voice. Part of her brain could still hear words like "hard tail" and "suicide clutch," but she wasn't there anymore. The lack of sleep the night before, the busy day and the alcohol all seemed to be conspiring to lull her into a state of languor. She couldn't fight it anymore.

I could feel the waves, but when I opened my eyes, there was no water. Only smoke and fire everywhere. I was in hell. No, William the bellman was pushing a cart filled with suitcases past me. William wouldn't be here if this was hell. He seemed like such a nice guy.

I could see the Grand Canyon to my right, and the Pyramids of Giza in the distance. Tiny people were lining up at the far ridge of the canyon like plastic army men. I heard a distant noise, a muffled boom, and the earth exploded directly behind me. They were shelling me.

I covered my head and began to run. I tripped over something big and fell sprawling in the sand. It was the dead man from the airport. He had two red holes in his chest and one in his forehead. His eyes were open, staring at nothing, like a fish on ice at the market.

"Wake up, Grace. We've got to get out of here." Nick's voice was loud in her ear, calm but insistent.

She looked around at the flurry of movement that filled the little room. The drummer and his date were scrambling around pulling on their clothes, searching through the bedding for some of them.

Bill stood sentry just inside the doorway, one hand on either side, keeping his eye on the activity outside. Larry and Rooster sifted through the table's cluttered contents, picking up cell phones, lighters, keys, clips, filling their pockets and getting ready to dash. Rob, the guitarist, and his girlfriend were already gone.

"What's going on?" Grace asked.

"Some guys got in a fight downstairs," Nick said. "One took a swing, and the other pulled a gun and shot the first one. How he got a gun past security, I'd sure like to know."

"And when that happened," Rooster said, "flashes started goin' off everywhere, people trying to get pictures of the dead man.

It seems this place has got more photographers than a politician's got lies."

"Security's holding the ones they caught red handed, but there were so many flashes all at once, they don't really know who's who," said Nick. "The worst part is, they didn't get the shooter. Misty's gone to make sure we have a clear path to Koenig's office. We've gotta get outta here."

Killian hadn't said a word. He paced in the confined space like an expectant father.

Bill turned back to them. "Misty's motioning that the coast is clear. Look, we're going out as a unit, with Rooster and Killian in the center, flanked by the rest of us…" Bill was barking orders like a platoon leader, and everyone was listening.

A shiver ran through Grace. They were taking this very seriously. A shooter was on the loose, probably still in the building. They couldn't afford to hang around until the police showed up. And they couldn't afford to let the paparazzi in front of the hotel get shots of them emerging from the club. Not now. They had to move quickly.

Grace could see Misty's shiny halter top across the room. She'd rushed over to guard the fiery entrance to her boss's office, and had her finger poised on the switch that would halt the flames.

Grace's mouth felt dry. She realized that someone had turned off the music overhead. The lack of the thumping bass line was unnerving. The crowd downstairs sounded rowdy, like a hive of angry bees. Security wouldn't let anyone leave until the police arrived. People were shouting and someone with a bullhorn said,

"Everyone, please remain calm." Of course, no one ever remained calm when someone with a bullhorn told them to.

When they reached the fireplace, Killian, Rooster, Larry, Bobby and his date were the first ones in. Misty reached in and flipped the second switch that would rotate the whole platform. The rest of them waited impatiently for it to come to a halt thirty seconds later. Grace, Nick, Misty and Bill jumped on. As the fireplace turned, Bill had to duck to keep from hitting his head.

The sounds of the bullhorn and the frantic revelers dulled as they stepped into Mr. Koenig's office. The owner was not here, however. He was out front dealing with the mayhem.

Misty rushed across the room to the door that would lead them into the tunnel that connected the shops. Bill held the door open while everyone filed out after her. They hurried past garbage cans, wooden shipping pallets and mop buckets.

It felt like they'd covered half a mile when she finally called over her shoulder, "It's just up ahead." Her voice echoed off the cinderblock walls. "This will lead you out into the parking garage. We're going to go to the left and follow the back wall around to the door. My car's parked in the lot across Hanover." She looked the group over and pursed her lips, "It will take two trips, but I can get you all out of here."

Nick shook his head. "They don't know who Grace and I are. We can walk. We're just at The Isis."

"I'm going with them," Killian said. He stripped off his blue velvet tailcoat and tossed it in an open garbage can. Even at a time like this, Grace couldn't help but admire how his white silk shirt, now damp with perspiration, clung to his well-muscled frame. She quickly averted her eyes, not wanting to be as obvious as Bobby's tiny, dark haired date, who now stood only inches away from Killian, staring at his chest with her mouth open.

"It's just across the way, less than a block," he said. "Surely we can make it that far without incident."

"Are you sure you want to do that?" Bill asked, who, from his tone, clearly favored the all for one and one for all approach.

"The big news now is the shooting, isn't it? They'll all be hanging around the front door of die Nacht like vultures waiting for the coroner."

Rooster nodded. "It's true. If they can get a good shot of the body, they'll consider the night a victory."

Tomorrow's headlines flashed in front of Grace's eyes. "Panic at the Disco" or "Mad Man Murders Merry Maker over Macarena."

Misty said, "All right, you three turn right when you get through this door. The Isis is right across the street, about a block past the new construction."

Killian put out his hand to shake Misty's, but before she could move, he pulled her into a tight bear hug and kissed her on the forehead. "Thanks," he said.

She smiled up at him. "Don't mention it."

Rooster grinned and clapped Nick on the back. "See you tomorrow night at The Eye, amigos," he drawled.

They could hear noises, shouts, echoing behind them in the tunnel, incoherent but getting closer. Bill said in his deep bass voice, "I hate to break up the Summer of Love here, ladies, but we gotta shake a leg."

They followed Misty through the big, metal doorway. Then Nick, Grace and Killian made a sharp right. The rest of them followed Misty to the left. When they reached the ramp that went up and out of the parking garage, Grace paused to look over her shoulder. In front of an open doorway fifty yards away, Rooster Hathcock raised his John Deere baseball cap in a salute. She waved back at him, then he turned and disappeared through the door.

Nick was the first one up the ramp, peeking around the big stone columns that bordered the entrance. His whole body seemed to relax as he saw no signs of anyone waiting for them. "We're cool," he said.

Grace watched the empty doorway across the deck. Killian took her by the hand and pulled her into motion. She let herself be led up the ramp and out into the Las Vegas early morning. The sky was still dark, but she knew it wouldn't be long before the sun began to dull the neon and the night owls all went to bed for the day. Her head still felt heavy and sluggish from the shots and the unplanned nap. It must have shown on her face, because Killian put an arm around her shoulders as they walked and said, "Are you all right, Love?"

She nodded and stifled a yawn. "I guess I'm just kind of tired. It's been a long day."

She could see Nick on the sidewalk waiting for them, smiling. Just ten more minutes and she would be taking a shower in that huge bathroom and then crawling into that ridiculously comfortable bed with him. She could almost feel the softness of the pillows against her cheek.

And then everything began to fall apart.

Chapter 17 – Without a Barrel

The flashes were disorienting. Grace blinked, trying to focus on something, anything. Nick shouted angrily and Killian ran, dragging Grace behind him. She stumbled along in his wake, trying to keep her balance.

Nick grabbed her other arm, and between the two men, they half carried her as they sped across the six lanes of traffic, ignoring car horns and angry shouts from drivers.

How such a pudgy little man could be so stealthy was a mystery, but Walter had sprung out from the shadows like a camera-wielding ninja. He vanished like a cockroach as soon as he got the shots. Grace looked back when they reached the other side of Las Vegas Boulevard. There was no trace of him anywhere.

Killian grinned, shaking his head. "That slimy little bugger," he said. "Well, I guess we made his day. At least we're rid of him."

"Don't be so sure of that," Nick said. "Now that he knows you're here, do you really think he'll leave you alone?"

Killian shrugged. "Maybe I can pre-empt him with my party tomorrow night. I guess that would be tonight, since it's morning. I'll have Ruth call and tell The Eye we want press there. That way, I'll be *posing* for pictures instead of running from them." He ran his hands over his thick beard. "And I can't wait to get this itchy animal carcass off my face. I don't know what the hell I was thinking."

They were halfway across the construction entrance of the planned Hawaiian-themed mega-resort, gravel crunching under their feet, when headlights hit them. The suspension of the black SUV strained as it turned and hit the gravel entrance, going way too fast.

"Look out!" Nick yelled, pushing both Grace and Killian out of the path of the oncoming vehicle.

"What the hell?" Grace said. It took her a few seconds to realize this wasn't just a tourist who had one too many Mai Tais at Trader Vic's and missed the turn.

As the SUV slid to a halt spewing gravel, Nick and Killian were already dragging Grace deeper into the construction site.

The walls on the bottom three floors were built, but above that just a steel frame rose countless stories into the dark sky. Grace thought how odd it was that she couldn't see stars because of all the lights. Nick pulled her onto the concrete pad and through the vast, yawning opening that would one day be a grand entrance.

Emergency lights were strung up here and there, just bare bulbs and industrial wiring, enough to keep them from diving into total blackness. They sprinted through the first room, registration perhaps, and came out into a cavernous space that seemed to have no hint of a ceiling. It looked like it would eventually be an atrium. The concrete floor was molded into troughs and basins that would someday hold running water and tropical plants.

They raced across the open room, Grace tripping over everything in her path. The area was fairly clean of construction debris, but broken bits of sheet rock and scraps of cable and wiring still littered the ground. Grace noticed with a huff of disappointment that her buzz was now completely gone, but the lack of coordination stubbornly lingered on. Thank God for the combat boots.

They tried to head in a straight line, to come out on the other side of this main building and make a beeline for The Isis. But this hotel-to-be just kept going and going. They came out into another huge room, this one larger than the first. This one had a ceiling, three stories tall, and looked like it might be a casino. Grace could see it in her mind's eye, rows of glittering slot machines, bright, busy carpet with a tropical theme.

They raced through the room in the near darkness. Two narrow doors on the north side of the room had to be exits. They dashed through one and came to a screeching halt. It was a bathroom, with a dark green tiled floor all plumbed for two rows of toilets. The PVC stubs stuck six inches out of the floor. Some of the cabinetry for the sinks was already in along the front wall. A layer of sheetrock dust covered everything.

Grace leaned against one of the tiled walls, trying to catch her breath. Nick squatted down, his hands on his knees, chuckling.

"What's so funny?" she huffed.

"This whole thing," he said, looking up at her. "I mean, we're running from photographers, Grace. Did you ever think there would be a time in our lives when we would be *running from photographers?*"

She grinned back. It was pretty comical after all.

Killian slid down the wall until he was sitting on the dusty tile floor. Empty tubes of caulk and pieces of wire and paper littered the ground. He picked up one of the tubes and turned it over in his hands. "Believe it or not," he said, "I usually like photographers. Sure, they can be a little pushy at times, but they do keep you in the limelight and that's the idea, right?" He tossed the empty tube back on the trash pile. "It's just the principle of the thing now. I don't want anyone to know I was hiding. I don't want…her… to have the satisfaction." He sounded almost apologetic.

"You don't have to convince us, man," Nick said. "We're on your side."

A male voice boomed through the silence outside. It sounded like he was probably at the other end of the casino floor, but the echo was enough to make all three jump. "We know you're in here," the man called. "And we know you have what we want. So why don't you be nice boys and girls and come out now. There's no need for anyone to get hurt."

Grace whipped her head around to Killian. His face was a mask, his brows drawn together in a frown. "What does he mean, no need for anyone to get hurt?" Grace whispered. "How many photographic accidents are there in your line of work?"

Killian shook his head slightly to indicate this was a first for him.

The man spoke again, this time it seemed a little closer. "We can do this the easy way or we can do it the hard way. That's entirely up to you, but I must warn you, the hard way could prove quite unpleasant."

Something was very wrong with this picture. All three of them were on their feet now, three bundles of nerves.

The only light in the room came from above, shining weakly through the squares where a drop ceiling would eventually be. The light continued in the ceiling on three sides of the room, on the left, probably another bathroom, and on the other two sides which undoubtedly connected to the back of the house. In a big hotel like this, everything connected behind the scenes. The side that faced the casino was the only side that was stopped by a wall, making room for the main casino's high ceilings.

Nick went across the room to a dozen separate waist-high wooden cabinets that would eventually hold sinks. He waved Killian over and demonstrated his plan using hand signals. They picked up one of the cabinets and laid it on its side across three others. They laid another sideways in front of the group and Grace could finally see what they were doing. They'd formed steep stairs that someone with an extraordinary sense of balance could use to climb right up into the ceiling.

Nick lost no time springing up the cabinets and pulling himself up into the ceiling. With his legs on either side of an I-beam, and using his knees to hold on, he leaned over and waved to Grace to follow him. She raised her eyebrows at him in shock. Surely he didn't expect her to be able to do that. He'd known her for years and he knew she was no gymnast. Killian hurried over and took her by the hand. He put his mouth very close to her ear and whispered, "I'll help you." For the second time that night, she allowed herself to be led by Killian.

He grasped her right hand, his left hand at the small of her back, and steadied her as she climbed onto the first cabinet. It rocked slightly and she froze. Killian mouthed, "I've got you." She climbed onto the next cabinet as Killian followed her onto the lowest cabinet. He moved his hands to either side of her waist. She looked up into the ceiling at Nick. He stretched one arm down for her, but she had to get onto the next cabinet before she could reach his hand. She kept her eyes focused on him and took a deep breath. She stepped up onto the highest cabinet. Nick grabbed her wrist. He pulled her from above while Killian pushed from below. Somehow, she managed to get her arms up and over the I-beam, then she was lying along the length of it, her arms and legs wrapped around the steel beam so tight it hurt. Killian was up on the beam behind her before she opened her eyes. Nick put his head close to her ear and whispered, "Come on. We've got to get to the other side of this wall so we can find a way out." Grace nodded, but didn't move. He added, "See if you can sit up a little so you can slide along on your butt." He held on while she sat up and got her balance.

The man outside spoke again. He had a slight accent, but Grace couldn't place it. "Just tell us where the package is and you are free to go. We just want what is ours. There is no need for bloodshed." He was patronizingly patient, like the man was really enjoying this cat and mouse game.

"Hold on with your knees," Killian whispered from behind Grace. She nodded again.

Nick turned around and edged along the steel beam toward the rear of the bathroom. He was moving pretty fast. Grace tried to keep up while not looking down. Twenty feet, ten feet, and they were over the back wall into what appeared to be a passageway like the one leading to die Nacht.

Nick swung down, hanging from the beam by his fingers for a second, before landing almost soundlessly on the concrete floor. Grace made a mental note to tell him later how impressed she was with his acrobatics. She knew he was in shape, but she was surprised at how graceful he could be.

Killian followed almost as quietly, landing with a combat roll. That left Grace sitting alone on the I-beam fifteen feet in the air. Nick stood underneath her and held up his arms. She motioned for him to move out of the way. She would certainly break his legs if she fell on him. He shook his head and waved for her to hurry.

She lowered herself to her stomach so she was lying lengthwise on the beam. She gripped as tightly as she could with her arms, took a deep breath and slowly slid her right leg up and over so that both legs dangled in mid-air. The muscles in her arms screamed in protest. She couldn't lower herself far enough for Nick to reach her. She was just going to have to let go and drop. Grace looked down. Killian crouched facing Nick, his arms out in front like he was waiting to catch a football.

Grace could feel her hands slipping on the steel and she gasped as her grip gave way. Her legs collided with something hard, which turned out to be Killian. Nick managed to grab her under the arms and the three of them tumbled to the ground in a heap.

"I'm sorry," she whispered, hoping she hadn't hurt them, but Killian was already on his feet dusting himself off as Nick pulled her up.

The man in the casino was speaking again, but now his voice was muffled, so they couldn't make out his words. They took off down the cinderblock corridor at a jog. All six feet beat a soft rhythm on the concrete. The only other sound was the faint slap of Grace's vinyl skirt as the strips hit her thighs.

It seemed like ages before a dim light ahead promised an exit. They picked up the pace until they reached a single open door on the right of the passageway. They skipped down a flight of makeshift wooden steps at what would soon become an employee entrance and they were outside at last. At least one hundred yards separated them from the chain link fence that ran along the access road beside The Isis.

Grace was already out of breath. She promised herself she'd start going to the gym as soon as they got home. She leaned over, her hands gripping her sides. "Come on," Nick said. "We can't stop. We can't give them a chance to catch up with us."

They would stick close to the wall of a second building on their dash to the fence. It was presumably the parking deck. Steel rose into the sky six or eight stories, but the lowest two floors were already clad in thick concrete, with three-foot-high walls all around.

Crouched like a soldier in battle, Killian struck out for the parking deck. Nick grabbed Grace's hand and took off after him. He was bent so low in front of her that she felt like the Homo erectus behind the ape-man on those evolution tee-shirts. She would have laughed if she'd had enough breath.

As they reached the edge of the deck, something hit the waist-high wall in front of them. Grace heard voices in the distance, coming around the front corner of the hotel. Whoever was throwing rocks from there sure had a strong arm. Another rock hit the wall, this time taking a chunk out of it.

Grace froze. She had the sickening realization that those were not rocks hitting the concrete in front of her. These people had guns. These people were shooting at them. She wanted to wave her arms and say, "Wait a second! I'm sure you have me mixed up with someone else. I'm sure the bad guys you're looking for are somewhere getting away right this minute!"

But before she could articulate any of this, Nick pulled her up and over the three-foot concrete wall like a ragdoll. Killian was already there, poised to run like a sprinter at the blocks. And run they did. Grace kept as low as she could, which turned out to be lower than she would ever have believed possible. They ran the length of the parking deck, but the gunmen outside were getting closer. Grace could now pick out the strange, muted popping sound the bullets made as they passed through the suppressors.

They were nearing the end of the deck, almost to the home stretch, when the black Tahoe came speeding into view from the rear of the hotel, slinging gravel and dust in its path. Killian was thirty feet ahead of them, ready to leap over the low outer wall and head for the fence. He hadn't noticed the Chevy.

"Wait!" Nick shouted. But it was too late. Killian took the wall at a run and leaped right into the path of the oncoming SUV.

It looked like it had hit something on its mad dash to head them off. One of the headlights was broken and the metal surrounding it was crushed in an inch or two. The passenger door swung open even as it slid to a halt in front of Killian. A barrel-chested man with a bald head jumped from the truck. He had the look of a professional wrestler. He aimed a black .45 at Killian's chest. Killian stopped, then slowly raised his hands.

Nick and Grace had stopped ten yards from the wall. Nick's teeth were clenched. His eyes darted left and right along the ground, looking for something he might use as a weapon – a piece of rebar, a chunk of concrete – but the crew building the parking deck was much neater than the one building the hotel. Damn them. The floor was clean. Grace could see the frustration on his face. At home, he carried a pistol every day. He worked by himself, sometimes in dangerous areas, and he liked to play it safe. He was a good shot, a responsible gun owner, and a card-carrying member of the NRA. But, he obviously couldn't carry a gun on an airplane or across state lines, not as a law-abiding citizen at any rate, so his trusty .380 was back home, locked up tight in his gun safe. Grace knew he felt completely and utterly naked.

Another bullet flew past them, so close Grace could hear the *whoosh*. She would never forget that sound as long as she lived.

Nick lunged at her, pinning her to the ground. The impact knocked the air out of her – what little air she had left. Her lungs were desperate for oxygen and she couldn't pull it in fast enough. She saw stars spinning in front of her and felt like the whole building was swaying. Her left elbow took most of her weight when she fell, and the pain brought tears to her eyes. She tried hard to force them back. Her hand was tingling and partially numb, but it was air she needed more than anything else.

"Hold your fire!" called the man they had heard inside the casino. He sounded angry now, where before, he'd only sounded patronizing. He gave several harsh commands in some foreign language, perhaps Russian, directed at the gunmen.

After a pause, he sounded calmer as he called out, "You are surrounded and apparently unarmed. But, best of all, we have your friend here. So, I believe…what's that American expression I love so much? Ah, yes. You're screwed."

Grace heard a noise above her and opened her eyes. She hadn't even realized she'd squeezed them shut. Two gunmen stood outside the low wall, their pistols held tightly in both hands, aimed right at her and Nick. "Stand up," one of them barked, his accent much heavier than that of the man in the suit.

Very slowly, they got to their feet. Grace found herself wondering where the night watchmen were. Surely they had some sort of guard on a construction project this massive. She hoped they'd all get fired for their incompetence.

"Hands up," came the order from the taller of the two gunmen. He towered above them, probably six-foot-eight or more, even taller than their bellman.

Grace's elbow gave a stab of pain as she raised her arms and grimaced.

Nick stood up straight, trying to impart as much authority to his voice as possible with a gun pointed at him. "I think there's been some misunderstanding here. We don't have any package. We don't know what you're talking about."

The two men acted as if he hadn't spoken.

"Move." The tall man motioned toward the Tahoe with a nod of his head.

Nick tried again. "Seriously," he began. "I think that if you…"

"Shut up!" snarled the shorter man. He was looking at her even though he was talking to Nick. Grace's eyes darted to him. The look on his face made her sick. He wasn't a pretty man; in fact, it looked like there was some Pit Bull in his family tree somewhere. But the lascivious grin plastered across his sweaty face made him downright repulsive.

They turned and walked slowly toward the end of the deck, hands still raised. Instead of going over the wall, they turned and went through the opening between the skeletal, open stairwell and the shaft that would soon house the elevators.

Killian was on his knees in the gravel facing them, hands clasped on the back of his head. The bald man stood beside him, his gun touching Killian's head just above the ear.

When Grace caught sight of him with a gun to his head, she stopped. Her breath caught in her throat. This was not happening. This could not be happening. The tall man pushed her, and she stumbled forward.

The last of the four men, the leader, the man whose voice they'd heard for the past half-hour, was leaning against the front quarter panel of the Chevy, as casually as if he were waiting on some old pals to join him for drinks. He even smiled as they stepped out of the parking deck.

He looked younger than he sounded, early thirties, maybe. He looked like he was on his way to a cocktail party, dressed in a dark gray tailored sharkskin suit with a burgundy shirt and matching silk tie. His shoes were polished to a high shine, and his short black hair was smoothed back meticulously, like he had spent an hour primping in front of the mirror before coming out to shoot at tourists.

"Now," he said in a tone usually reserved for errant children, "I will ask you one very simple question and you will answer me truthfully. Where is my necklace?" He looked brightly from one to the other of them, eyebrows raised.

"As I told your *colleagues* here, I don't know what you're talking about," Nick said, an edge to his voice.

The man's face hardened and he said, "I hate a liar." He nodded to the tall man, who raised his enormous right hand and whipped the back of it across Nick's face. He stumbled from the force of the slap. Grace made a strangled noise and lunged for Nick, but the shorter man grabbed her by the arm and pushed her back. His hand was as sweaty as his face.

Fists clenched at his sides, Nick straightened up and glowered at the man who'd ordered the slap.

"Okay, okay," Grace said in a rush. "Let's everyone just take a deep breath, huh? Now, we would be happy to help you look for your necklace. No problem at all. You just point us in the right direction, maybe give us a description of this necklace." She was talking fast, trying to sound helpful and confident, but her words came out shaky and breathless.

The man in the suit sighed and shook his head with an exaggerated look of disappointment. "Tsk, tsk, tsk. Why do you say such things? Why do you act as if you have no knowledge of my necklace when in fact you were wearing it this very afternoon?"

Grace's mouth fell open. Her left hand flew instinctively to her throat, forgetting momentarily that it was supposed to be in the air. "That was my anniversary present," she said in a small voice.

Nick turned his head to stare at her, a look of complete confusion on his face. She answered his unasked question. "The hawk. The one you bought at the hotel and hid in your suitcase. I found it yesterday morning and I thought I'd have some fun with you and wear it to see if you'd say anything."

Nick shook his head. "I sure as hell wish I knew what you were talking about," he muttered.

The man in the suit began to laugh, a rich, hearty sound like he was genuinely amused at this fabulous misunderstanding. "You thought that was a *gift*?" he said incredulously. "You thought the priceless Amulet of Kavayet was a gift for you to wear around your filthy peasant neck?" He seemed to be enjoying the absurdity of it all, like he couldn't wait to get back to Villain HQ and tell all the other thugs around the water cooler about this one. "Let me see if I understand this correctly. You thought your sniveling husband here had bought you one of those cheap, garish trinkets they sell in the *gift shop* and you are such an imbecile that you couldn't tell the difference between it and a 3,300-year-old Egyptian artifact that once belonged to the mother of King Tutankhamen?"

Grace's mind flashed back to the necklace when she first held it in her hand, the odd, looped chain and the clasp she had such a hard time with. She thought they'd done a good job of making it look antique. She thought it looked better than the one in the case. She'd been right about that. Then she remembered the newspaper Nick was reading on the plane. The largest heist in the history of the Cairo museum. "Oh, my God," she breathed. "I wore it all day. I wore the Queen's Necklace to hike Red Rock."

"Now you're getting it," said the man in the suit, sounding as if he were talking to a child who'd learned to tie her shoelaces. "Although, to be accurate, Kavayet was never queen of anything. She was little more than a serving girl who managed to give Akhenaton a son. That's what they should call it. The serving girl's necklace."

Grace looked him in the eye for the first time. "How did it get in our suitcase?"

"Why, one of the men who stole it put it there, of course," he continued with a slight bow. "He got as far as Atlanta, but by then we discovered he was planning to double-cross us and sell it himself, so...my men killed him. But, not before he managed to slip the necklace into your suitcase. And since we were all heading to the same destination, it was a simple matter of retrieving it here."

His smile disappeared. Without it, his face was quite sinister. "But you, Nicholas and Grace Howard, have made it much more difficult than it should have been. So, I will ask you one last time, where...is...my necklace?"

Grace closed her eyes, her mind reeling. Where was it? With a start, she remembered it was at Vicious, protected by metal gates, multiple alarms and a mall security guard. "We can get it," she said, her words tumbling over each other in haste, "but it will take a couple of hours. We left it in the store where we bought these clothes. It's being delivered to our hotel this morning along with the rest of our stuff. I don't know exactly what time, but you can just...wait for it if you want."

The man in the suit looked disgusted. "Although it is painfully obvious that you three do not watch the news, I can't say the same for the rest of the city. So, no, I will not...*wait* for it. You will bring it to me. Instructions will be sent to your hotel room." For the first time, he stepped away from the Tahoe toward Killian. "Oh, and in case you are delusional enough to call the police, I'll just keep your friend here as insurance. He now has an expiration date, twenty-four hours from this second." He looked at his watch. "If I do not have the necklace in my possession by five-fifteen tomorrow morning, that will be the moment he draws his last breath. The same can be said if I suspect any foul play on your part, so if you aspire to be a hero, you should probably go ahead and say good-bye to each other right now. And, remember, I can dispose of his body and be out of the country before you can say *FBI.*"

Grace watched Killian's face. Instead of fear, she saw only outrage. His eyes flashed from hers to Nick's and he shouted, "Don't give in to this bastard. He's a *headcase*. Do you hear me?" His head was tilted from the pressure of the gun at his ear, but he still managed to spit on the leader's shiny, leather shoes.

The bald man pulled his gun up high and brought the butt down on the back of Killian's head in one swift motion. Killian toppled forward onto the gravel and lay motionless.

Poor Killian. Two days in a row someone had tried to knock him out, and this time they succeeded. If he didn't get out of Las Vegas soon, thought Grace, he was going to have brain damage.

The bald man put his boot under Killian's ribs and rolled him roughly over onto his back. He had bits of gravel and dust stuck in his beard. The man in the suit wiped his spit-covered shoe across Killian's shirt.

A tremor ran through Grace like an electric current. She could feel her whole body beginning to shake.

The leader moved to the rear of the Tahoe and lifted the gate. The bald gunman tucked his .45 into his waistband at the small of his back and leaned over. He scooped Killian off the ground like a baby and deposited him effortlessly into the rear of the truck. Killian's body was lifeless and his right leg fell out over the rear bumper. Baldy stuffed it back in and slammed the gate. It seemed incredibly loud somehow.

The man in the suit dusted off his manicured hands as if he had just done all the work instead of simply barking orders. "Run along to your room now, and await my instructions." He waved them away. They were being dismissed, just like that. This lunatic criminal, whose name they didn't even know, was now holding Killian hostage, and they had twenty-four hours to deliver a stolen Egyptian amulet if they wanted him back alive.

The two gunmen guarding them backed away toward the Tahoe. The sweaty one gave Grace a lecherous last look and blew her a kiss as he climbed into the backseat. She didn't even have the energy to be offended.

The big engine roared to life, and the man in the shiny gray suit spun the tires in the gravel for effect as he headed off to God-knows-where with his captive.

Grace and Nick stood motionless watching them go. As they rounded the corner of the hotel structure, Grace felt her legs give way. The ground had disappeared beneath her like a trap door.

Chapter 18 – Laurel and Hardy

Grace didn't realize she'd sunk to her knees in the gravel. She was surprised to feel the little rocks poking into her skin. It took her a minute to make out Nick's voice talking over the high-pitched whine that filled her ears. She looked up at him, blinked, and tears rolled down her face. She wasn't crying. She knew she wasn't, but tears were falling anyway.

Nick pulled her to her feet and steered her toward one of the construction entrances.

"…until we figure out what to do," Nick was saying. She'd missed the first part.

"Well, there's really nothing we can do until Vicious opens," Grace said, finding her voice at last. "I guess if we had some way of finding Misty, maybe she could open it early for us, but we'd have to find her first. We don't even know her last name."

Nick stopped. "You do realize we can't give them the necklace, don't you?" He looked surprised to see the tears that had rolled down her cheeks and he tried to wipe them away with his thumbs, but his hands were dusty from the ground and he only succeeded in streaking her face. He pulled up the hem of his WASP tee-shirt and used that instead.

She looked at him like she'd never seen him before. "What are you saying?"

"I'm just saying it's not that simple. This guy's a dangerous criminal. People like him don't make deals with people and keep their word."

"Why wouldn't he? I mean, he'd be getting the necklace. That's what he wants."

Nick shook his head. "Just think about it. You, me and Killian could identify all four of those guys." He paused to let it sink in. "They apparently stole this necklace from the Cairo Museum or somewhere. I have no idea what they'd do to you in Egypt for stealing something like that. They don't play around in Egypt. So a measly kidnapping is nothing to these guys. They don't intend to get caught. They'll have to get rid of all three of us, and they know that."

"That's ridiculous," Grace said.

"Look, his instructions are gonna be for you and me to deliver the necklace alone. Then he can have all three of us together and that's that."

"Well, then, we'll just have to go to the police," Grace said. "This isn't a job for us. I'm a secretary, for God's sake. What am I gonna do, staple them? This is a job for the police."

Nick shook his head again. He looked tired, at the brink of exhaustion. For the first time, Grace noticed the dark shadows under his eyes. "You heard what the man said, Grace. If they suspect anything, they'll get rid of Killian and be gone in a heartbeat. Well, the boss will be gone, anyway. I guarantee he won't be the one guarding Killian. Mr. GQ wouldn't put himself in danger like that. He'll be somewhere else, safe and sound. He doesn't care what happens to his thugs; I'm sure they're a dime a dozen. So, if they get killed by the police in the process, big deal. The thugs will shoot Killian and the police will shoot the thugs and the boss will get away. But, either way, Killian will still be dead."

"Well...well, what are we supposed to do?" Grace said. "You don't want to give them the necklace and you don't want to call the police. What's left? You just want to leave, go back home and to hell with Killian?" She could feel the blood rising to her cheeks. She was glad she was finally getting angry. Too bad it was at Nick.

"Easy," he said. "I'm on your side, remember?"

She took a couple of ragged breaths and nodded.

"All I'm saying is that we've got to put our heads together and think of a way out of this mess. But, I need you to be one hundred percent. I need you to focus. Can you do that?"

She said nothing. He put his arms around her, pulled her in close. He was so warm. She hadn't even realized she'd been shivering in the cool night air. She pulled her head back to look at him. He seemed so sincere, so focused. He'd always had an overdeveloped sense of fair play. He was always the responsible one. It was one of the things that first attracted her to him. But right now, she hated it. What did he think they could do that the police couldn't? She wanted to run, pack her things and dial 911 from the airport. She could sleep in her own bed tonight. She could forget this whole thing ever happened.

But, of course, she couldn't.

She had no clue what in the world they could possibly do, but she took a deep breath and nodded. Whatever Nick needed, she would do it somehow.

Oh, my God, Killian thought. *I'll never drink again. I mean it this time.*

His head was pounding like it was about to explode. The faint light he could see through almost closed eyelids was enough to make his stomach roll. Voices spoke softly in a foreign language over a television tuned to *The Andy Griffith Show*.

He tried to move, to stretch his aching body, but couldn't. Slowly, sickeningly, details began to swim closer into view in his throbbing head.

Killian kept his eyes closed and struggled to breathe normally. He stretched his fingers to touch the plastic zip-tie that held his wrists together behind his back. A second zip-tie looped through that one and bound him to a small wooden desk chair. *Don't panic. Don't panic*, he told himself.

He opened his eyes a fraction of an inch. He could see he still wore the faux alligator pants. A stained orange carpet covered the floor. Another fraction of an inch revealed the corner of a bed covered by a garish, paisley bedspread, frayed at the edges from years of use.

It was evident he was somewhere in a no-star motel. The only light in the room came from Andy Griffith, thank God. Killian knew his head wouldn't be able to handle anything brighter right now. His guards — there appeared to be two — were playing cards on the small round table in front of the window near the door, the only exit.

He didn't have to speak Russian to figure out that one of the men was accusing the other of cheating. They were so preoccupied, he opened his eyes a little wider. The giant and the short, sweaty one had been assigned guard duty. Only one chair at the small table — presumably he was tied to the second one — so the tall man perched on the far edge of the twin bed to play cards.

The orange curtains covering the window were like most other curtains in Las Vegas – they blocked the incoming light completely. Killian couldn't tell if it was night or day. He had no way of determining how long he'd been unconscious or how much time was left before his "expiration date."

The tall man's cell phone rang, an absurd disco beat. He snapped to his feet to answer, as if he were standing at attention. It was a short conversation, with a lot of crisp "da's" on his end, one of the few Russian words Killian understood. He spoke fluent French, acceptable Italian, and fair Spanish. He even spoke a little German. Unfortunately, he'd never played a Russian in a movie. He promised himself he'd learn it if he ever got out of there, back to his normal, crazy life.

The two twin beds had not been slept in. A nightstand between them held a lamp and an alarm clock, which was turned away from him. A press-board dresser held a nineteen-inch analog television that turned all of Mayberry green. The small round table and one remaining chair made up the rest of the dingy décor. Killian assumed the bathroom was behind him. The moment he thought bathroom, he regretted it. He had to go. He shifted slightly in his chair, trying to get in a more comfortable position. It was no use. He may as well get it over with.

"Pardon me, comrades…," he said. His mouth was as dry as the desert outside, and his voice came out raspy and cracked. The two men turned to look at him as if they were surprised he was there. "...but I really need to pee."

The men turned back to face each other. Killian wondered how much English they knew. "You know, splash the boots... drain the lizard... shake the snake."

The short man stood and pulled a pistol out of the holster on his belt. Killian's heart sank. The tall man snapped a small switchblade open. Killian held his breath while the giant moved behind him and cut the zip-tie that bound his hands together. When he felt the snap, he pulled them slowly around in front of him, careful not to make any sudden moves. He rubbed his wrists to get the feeling back in his fingers. He kept his eyes on the gun until the man motioned for him to stand up.

"Go pee," he said in a thick accent. "But no try to escape, or I shoot."

A dingy sink and counter took up the space behind his chair, with a big plate glass mirror mounted on the wall above it. To the right was a small room that housed the toilet and shower. The tall gunman stepped back from the door to let him enter, but put his hand out to stop the door when Killian tried to close it.

"Oh, come on. There's not even a window in here. There's nowhere for me to go."

The tall man just stared at him, his huge hand still on the door.

"Fine," Killian said, and turned his back on the giant. He surveyed the tiny room as he unzipped his alligator pants, looking for anything to use as a weapon. The room was empty. Nothing but a roll of toilet paper sitting on the tank lid and a cheap framed print of a sandcastle hanging on the wall above the toilet.

"So, what's your name?" he called over his shoulder. "I feel like I need to call you something if we're going to be alone in this room all day. Manners cost nothing, you know." His captor made no effort to answer. "Don't want to be friends, eh? Well, that's okay; you're not exactly at the top of my Christmas list, either." These guys weren't big on courtesy.

"I think I'll call you Laurel," he said, zipping up his pants, "and your comrade in there, I'm going to call him Hardy. What do you think of that?"

As he leaned forward to flush the toilet, he caught Laurel's reflection in the plastic covering the sandcastle print. Something Barney Fyfe said on TV had caught his attention, and he momentarily looked away. In one smooth motion, Killian grabbed the rectangular toilet tank lid, swung around and slammed it into the stomach of his captor like a battering ram.

He let out a shocked, "Oof!" and doubled over. Killian swung the porcelain around and landed it on the man's skull with all his strength. It cracked in two as the giant crumbled to the ground.

Without a moment's hesitation, Killian launched himself across the room at Hardy, armed with the remaining piece of jagged porcelain. He'd surprised Hardy with a mouthful of potato chips, sour cream and onion dust still clinging to his sweaty hands. He put them in front of his face to shield himself from the tank lid. Killian brought the weapon down like a baseball bat, hitting the side of his head. The man shouted Russian obscenities as he grabbed for his bleeding ear. Killian pulled his weapon back for a second blow. One more should do it, and he was out the door.

Instead, the tank lid was ripped from his hands mid-air. He managed to turn just in time to see Laurel, blood running down his forehead, towering above him. The piece of porcelain looked small in his enormous hand.

Killian knew he was about to be bludgeoned to death by part of a toilet, and for a second he wished he could see tomorrow's headlines. He thought instantly of Walter. That little pig would have the last known photograph of Killian Ross. He hoped Walter choked on it.

Hardy was still yelling, but his tone had changed. He was yelling at Laurel this time, and it sounded like a command. Laurel's hand froze mid-air, even though Killian knew he wanted nothing more at this moment than to pound him into a bloody pulp. His yellowed teeth were bared and his nostrils flared. He looked like a monster. Killian knew it was taking every ounce of self control the big Russian had to let his arm fall to his side. The porcelain dropped to the orange carpet with a dull thud. It was clear who gave the orders in this duo.

Hardy pointed his gun at Killian's stomach. "Back in the chair," he said. Laurel grabbed a handful of his hair and slung him back across the room. That only served to accentuate the pounding in his head.

At gunpoint, Killian sat in the chair and put his hands behind his back. Right back where he started from, only worse, since the zip-ties were much tighter this time, cutting off the circulation in his hands and forcing his shoulders into an awkward, cramped position.

He gritted his teeth and hoped he hadn't just blown his only chance for escape.

Chapter 19 – Leaps of Faith

Grace and Nick walked in a daze back to their hotel room. Grace collapsed across the bed and slept in her clothes, patent leather combat boots and all, for almost an hour and a half. She woke with a start a little after seven a.m. Something in a dream had roused her, but she couldn't remember any of it. All things considered, it was probably better that way.

The only light in the room was the lamp on the desk where Nick sat. He scribbled on one of the papers that littered the work surface. An open phone book, sections of a newspaper, and an unfolded roadmap were scattered around him. His hair was wet and he'd changed clothes. He'd taken a shower while Grace slept. That's what she needed – a shower. A shower would make everything better.

She padded over to him. She could see the papers he'd been working on, but his notes made no sense whatsoever. Before she could inquire, Nick pushed his chair back and pulled her into his lap. She put her arms around him, and he laid his head on her shoulder. She could feel his heart beating and hear the steady sound of his breathing. She stroked his wet hair. It smelled like coconut shampoo. Somehow, she still felt safe in his arms, even though the world was in turmoil around them.

The thought of losing this – of losing Nick – was something that had never really crossed her mind before. But the last twelve hours had changed all the rules. She'd never had anyone point a gun at her before. And she'd never seen her husband forced to stand helplessly while someone backhanded him.

Grace headed for the shower before she could get all weepy again. She was tired of crying, tired of feeling like a victim.

The vast bathroom seemed less impressive now. She unhooked the vinyl skirt and let it fall with a slap to the stone floor, then turned on the shower and the water steamed up the mirrors as she peeled off the rest of her clothes and unlaced the boots. The makeup was almost gone from the left side of her face, probably all on her pillow now. She looked almost comical with one false eyelash still clinging on. She examined her scraped elbow. It didn't look as bad as it felt.

Nick ordered room service while she was in the shower. She didn't realize how hungry she was until the smell of the bacon and coffee hit her. Wrapped in an Isis robe, she sat at the foot of the bed and began eating without a word. It only took a couple of minutes before she felt a stab of guilt. Nick had stopped eating with a bit of toast and jelly still poised in his hand. She knew he was thinking the same thing she was, wondering if Killian's kidnappers would give him anything to eat.

Nick dropped the toast on the plate and turned back to the desk. Grace heard him draw a sharp breath. "We have a message," he said, indicating the red light on the telephone. He picked up the receiver as Grace dove for the extension by the bed.

But, it was only the front desk notifying them they had a package. The staff must be at work bright and early over at Vicious. Nick dialed the bell desk and asked if William was available to bring the package to their room.

It took almost fifteen minutes for William to arrive and during that time Nick filled Grace in on the skeleton of a plan he'd been constructing. She listened and nodded and asked all the appropriate questions. It was like being briefed for battle. She kept sipping the coffee because her mouth was so dry, but it was like trying to water the desert.

He showed her a section of the newspaper he'd been reading, folded and then folded again. It wasn't the front page; that was behind him, propped up against the wall under the lamp. The front page read, "Queen's Necklace Stolen from Cairo Museum," in one-inch letters.

This smaller article was from today's *Atlanta Herald*, purchased in the gift shop while Grace slept. It was just a few paragraphs buried in Section E. "Body Found in Atlanta Airport Identified."

Atlanta, Ga -- Authorities say the body found at the Hartsfield-Jackson Atlanta International Airport has been identified as that of 33-year-old Russian national Makar Solovyov.

An airport employee found the body around eleven p.m. Friday in a stairwell behind the main terminal.

Solovyov was known to have close ties to Moscow's infamous Krasnyee Coalition, the powerful syndicate led by crime czar Boris Vasily Kuznetsov until his disappearance in 2006. Since that time, his protégée, Alexander Kirill Volkov, a graduate of New York's prestigious Grosvenor College, has led the Coalition. Volkov is known for his flamboyant personal style and is today considered to be not only more ruthless, but also more reckless than his predecessor.

Lieutenant Veronica Brooks, a spokesperson for the Atlanta Police Department, said she is unable to comment on the case, as it is part of an ongoing investigation.

Yeah, Grace thought, an ongoing investigation of the museum heist. This was the man who had slipped the necklace into their suitcase. And he was tied to a Russian crime syndicate. And that Russian crime syndicate had kidnapped Killian. The hole they were in seemed to get deeper and deeper.

William arrived with a cardboard box in his arms and a broad smile on his face that only faltered a little when he caught sight of Nick's grim expression. "Come on in," Nick said. "We have a favor to ask of you."

William set the box on the black wooden dresser while his eyes flitted around the room uncomfortably, belying his charming smile. "What can I do for you?"

"This is not in your capacity as a bellman," Nick said. "This is strictly personal."

William raised his eyebrows a little, and Grace wondered what was going on in his mind right now, being called into a couple's dark hotel room for a personal favor. "It's not what it sounds like," she added. "It's just that we need some information and don't know who else to ask."

"It's like this," said Nick. "Do you remember the guy who was with us Friday night when you told us about the Barrelhouse? About my height, sandy hair and a beard?"

William nodded. "Sure."

"Well, he's …" Nick took a deep breath. "He's…lost. And we need to find him as soon as possible."

"Today," Grace added. "We have to find him today."

William looked a little confused, but still the picture of politeness. "So…have you called the police?"

Nick shook his head. "We can't call the police."

"It's … umm … complicated," Grace said, wishing she could think of a better word to use there. Complicated was such a cop-out.

"I see," William said, looking very much like he did not see.

"The thing is, we were hoping you could tell us how to get in touch with Skye," Nick said.

William's polite smile faded.

"Well, it's not really Skye we want, per se," Grace assured him. "We were hoping she could help us find some of the guys we met at her bar the other night."

"Okay," William began. "This guy, this friend of yours. Is he a guest here?"

Nick nodded.

"By any chance is he … staying in the penthouse?"

Nick nodded again.

William let out a deep breath, like he'd just been deflated. He sat on the edge of the dresser, his long legs stretched out at an angle in front of him. It looked like an involuntary motion, as if the dresser hadn't been there, he could have gone all the way to the floor.

"Are they asking for ransom?" he asked.

"Yes, but not like you think," Nick said.

"They don't know who he is," Grace said. "At least not yet."

"Then what do they want?"

Grace and Nick glanced at each other again. Not knowing how much they'd have to reveal to him, they decided to play it by ear. Without many options at their disposal, they didn't have time to worry about it. They would have to take a leap of faith.

Nick cleared his throat. "The Amulet of Kavayet."

Grace half expected William to laugh. After all, it *was* pretty absurd. But, he didn't. Instead, he looked like someone had thrown cold water in his face.

"I guess you heard someone stole it from a museum in Cairo," said Nick. "It's in the paper and I'm sure it's been on the news. They call it the Queen's Necklace."

William nodded. "I don't think they've shown anything else all weekend."

They were silent a few moments, letting it all sink in.

"So, um, how do they expect you two to get your hands on the amulet?"

Nick wasn't about to tell William he was leaning on it, that he'd delivered it to their door only minutes before. After all, they didn't know him that well. He could just grab it and run. But he had no option but to tell him the truth. "We have it."

William looked stunned.

"Of course, we didn't realize that until about four-thirty this morning, when the guys who stole it and stashed it in our luggage came looking for it," Nick said by way of a blurry explanation.

"Wow. This is … unbelievable." William didn't look nearly as panicky as Grace expected. On the contrary, he looked downright excited. "You're not going to give it to them, are you?"

"No. No way," Nick assured him. "It would be suicide. We can identify all four of them and they know it."

William nodded in solemn agreement. "Good. So, who are you looking for from the Barrelhouse?"

"Well, Sunshine or Shady. Anyone we can get, really," Nick said. "We just need people who know the area to help us locate the car used to take our friend. We have a good description and most of the license plate. But we have less than twenty-four hours, so we're gonna have to split up. We need all the help we can get."

"Twenty-four hours? They gave you a deadline?"

"They know we've got the necklace," Grace said, "so they figure if we take any longer than that, we must be involving the police or something."

"And they swore they'd kill him if they caught a whiff of the cops," Nick added. "And I believe them."

"Yeah," William shook his head. "The cops always screw up everything anyway." It was easy to see this new turn of events was fascinating to him. You could see it in his face. Grace was glad he wasn't afraid to get involved, that he wasn't washing his hands of this. It would have been nice to sit and mull this over for a while, to discuss their options, or lack thereof, but they didn't have that luxury. She was just about to mention the time when William stood.

"Okay, well, I can get in touch with Sunshine, and he'll get a contingent together. And I've got another friend, too, a guy who would be perfect for this." He clapped his hands together like he was getting ready to dig into Thanksgiving dinner.

"Wait a minute," Grace said. "Now make sure these guys aren't seen. We just want them to report back to us. That's all. We don't want anyone getting hurt."

"All right," he assured her. But Grace couldn't help noticing he looked a little disappointed. Maybe he was expecting some real excitement, maybe even an ambush. Maybe that would happen anyway, before the day was over, but it would be just her and Nick. They couldn't put anyone else in danger.

They exchanged cell phone numbers, and William wrote down a description of the Tahoe, including the damage to the right front quarter panel and headlight, and other pertinent information they could remember. He seemed very interested in descriptions of the four men, but Grace didn't see how that mattered, and told him so. "We just need you to find the truck; that's all. These guys are dangerous. Don't try to get close to them."

He promised not to do anything stupid, and as he started to leave he put the back of his hand to his forehead. "I think I'm coming down with a fever," he said weakly. For a second, Grace felt her heart sink. Their only help was getting the flu. Then he turned with a grin and said, "Oh, well, I guess I should take a sick day. Gotta go tell the boss."

When William walked out the door, the first part of the plan was in motion, like it or not.

Nick took the butter knife from their breakfast and opened the box William had delivered. Their clothes were folded neatly inside. He pulled everything out looking for the necklace, careful not to drop anything. He finally found it stuffed deep in a pocket of the baggy denim shorts Grace had been wearing. He pulled it out like it was nitroglycerine. "So, this is what all the fuss is about," he mumbled. "I remember seeing it yesterday, but you've got a lot of necklaces. I didn't think anything about it. It's pretty, I guess." He shrugged. Grace knew he didn't care about jewelry. His wedding ring was the only jewelry he'd ever owned.

He held the necklace up to the light. The chain was actually made of tiny gold loops, and the clasp was an elaborate hook and eye. Yesterday, when Grace thought it had come from the gift shop, it hadn't seemed that fragile. But now the necklace looked like the slightest touch might shatter it. A chill ran up her arms when she thought about the fact that she was probably the first person to wear this necklace since King Tut's mother, more than 3,000 years ago. And she had worn it *hiking*.

Nick locked the necklace in the little in-room safe in the closet, then went back to the desk and stared at the papers without seeing them.

"Do you think we should try to contact Ruth?" Grace said from among the pillows.

"I don't know." He sighed. "I thought about that, too, but I think it would just worry her. There's nothing she can do. Not to mention the fact that she doesn't know us from Adam. She might just call the police and have us arrested."

"Maybe, but don't you think she has the right to know what's going on? She's probably worried sick."

Nick shook his head in disbelief. "And you think Killian's current reality is somehow better than her imagination? No way. In this case, I guess ignorance is bliss."

She thought about that for a moment, then tried a different tactic. "Okay, look at it this way. If she doesn't hear from him by the end of the day, she's probably going to call the police anyway."

"It won't matter by the end of the day," he muttered.

"What if she calls before that? It would blow everything. We can't take that chance. We have to tell her something, even if it's a lie."

Nick couldn't deny this logic, but Grace had forgotten one major roadblock. "Even if we wanted to, we don't know how to get in touch with her. Do you even remember her last name?"

Grace pondered that for a moment. She was sure she'd heard someone say it, but it wasn't like she would be in the phone book anyway.

If Killian's cell phone wasn't in the middle of the Bellagio fountain, they could have used it. But even if they could fish it out, she knew the SIM card would be toast, or in this case, mush. She brightened for a moment, thinking they might somehow get the number from the hotel, then remembered the circumstances surrounding Killian's spur-of-the-moment arrival. Ruth had not made these reservations.

Who else could they contact who even knew Ruth existed?

A smile began to twist the corners of her mouth before the thought was fully formed in her head. She grabbed the phone book and found what she was looking for almost immediately. The quarter-page ad proclaimed "We Rule the Night," and pictured a skull with fire in its eye sockets.

She used her cell phone since they were still waiting for instructions via their room phone. Grace knew she would get an answering machine. What she didn't expect was for Herr Koenig himself to pick up the phone halfway through her rambling message.

"Guten tag, Mr. and Mrs. Howard," he said cheerily. "To what do I owe the pleasure?"

"We're sorry to disturb you at this early hour."

"Nonsense, my dear." His voice sounded warm and sincere, like someone's grandfather.

Grace hit the speaker button so Nick could hear too and dove right in. No time to waste, after all. "We need to get in touch with the woman who made our reservations last night, Ruth, and we don't have her number."

After a moment of silence, Mr. Koenig said, "Is something wrong with Mr. Ross?"

Grace made an exaggerated sour face. She and Nick had really not thought through exactly what they were going to tell people. "Hmmm…The truth is, I don't think you would believe me if I told you." She made a feeble attempt at a laugh.

Mr. Koenig chuckled. "Oh, I believe you underestimate me, my dear. I am an old man, true, but by virtue of that fact, I have witnessed many, many things, some of which might shock you. And I have learned over the years that truth is almost always stranger than fiction."

Nick sighed. Grace knew he was a terrible liar and could tell by the sigh that he was about to take his second leap of faith of the morning. "He has been … He is being held by some men who want to exchange him for something we have, something they stole."

After a pause, Mr. Koenig said, "And the problem is…?"

Kelly Adamson

"The problem is, we can identify them, and if we gave them this...item, they would just kill us, all of us. So we have to find Killian and break him out of wherever he is, all without police involvement." It sounded really pathetic when they had so little information to go on.

"Then by all means, we shall find him," Mr. Koenig said with complete assurance. He didn't sound troubled or surprised in the slightest. "I will assist you in any way I can. My people and I are at your disposal."

"Thank you," Grace breathed. "For starters, would you mind just calling Ruth and filling her in? Tell her whatever you think is best, but mainly just ask her not to call the police today. Okay? We're afraid she'll worry if she can't get in touch with him."

"But, of course. I shall do so immediately."

After Grace hung up, they went back to their interminable study in patience, waiting for a call they didn't want.

Nick retreated to his papers, his pen making light scratching sounds every now and then. After several minutes, Grace couldn't take the silence anymore and turned on the television. She sat on the bed flipping through channels until she found one showing the news. Nothing interesting. The weather forecast for the week. Sun. What a surprise. Sunny in Las Vegas.

Just as she was about to change the channel, there it was, inside a huge, glass case in a museum more than 7,000 miles away. The necklace that was currently resting not ten feet from her in her room safe. The piece of history that proved a heretofore unknown woman named Kavayet was the mother of the Boy King.

She turned up the volume, but could have left it muted. They were just reporting that they had no leads and no new information. They didn't even know exactly how the necklace was stolen, since all four security guards on duty at the time had been killed. They only knew that the state-of-the-art alarm systems had been disabled, including the security cameras. There were no fingerprints, no eyewitnesses, and nothing to go on.

Grace felt a chill on the back of her neck. Four people killed to steal it the first time. They wouldn't think twice about killing three more to steal it back.

When the phone rang, Grace jumped like she'd just been tased. Her heart pounded painfully in her chest. They'd been waiting for this, dreading it, all morning. She and Nick picked up both receivers at the same time.

"Hello," Nick said, his voice deeper than usual.

The gravelly voice on the other end said, "The Pleasure Palace Inn. By the airport. Now what?"

Chapter 20 – Shooting Fish in a Barrel

"Who is this?" Nick demanded.

"This is Shady. Who the hell did you think it was, your fairy godmother?" came the terse reply. "Your black Tahoe's at the Pleasure Palace Inn. Old dump of a joint just past the Las Vegas sign. William said we weren't supposed to do anything until we talked to you."

"You found it already?" Grace said. "That's amazing."

"There's nothing amazing about it," Shady said. "These dumbasses stash the guy not two miles from where they grab him, and they don't even know how to hide the damn car. They're either stupid or cocky...or both."

"Can you tell which room they're in?" Nick asked.

"Nah," Shady said. "There's at least fifty rooms here. The curtains are drawn on most all of 'em. It's not like they got a sign on the door sayin' *Kidnappers in here.*"

"I guess not," Nick muttered. "Look, I really appreciate you finding the car. If you could keep an eye on it until I get there, that would be great. I'll be there as soon as I can."

Nick got to his feet as he hung up the phone. He took three quick steps towards the door and stopped. He couldn't go anywhere until the Russian called.

He exhaled. Grace watched as he ran his hands roughly through his hair and came back to sit beside her on the bed.

"He's doing this on purpose, you know," he said, more to himself than to her. "He's playing with us. He wants us to remember who has the upper hand here. I wouldn't be surprised if he made us wait all day before he calls."

"Oh, no," Grace groaned. "Surely not. I don't think I can take it. Why? Why would he do that?"

"A power trip. He knows we're stuck in this room until he says so, and I'm sure he knows we're chomping at the bit to get out and look for Killian, to do *something*."

The Russian knew exactly what he was doing if he was trying to drive her crazy, thought Grace, and it was obviously working on Nick, too. He got to his feet again and began pacing, stopping every few laps to peruse his illegible notes.

Grace found herself biting her nails and wishing she had a cigarette, two things she hadn't done in years. When her cell phone rang, she jumped again. Her mother always said that was a sign of a guilty conscience, but in this instance it was just an aggravated case of the jitters. She looked at the number – a local one with no name. Her ring tone, "Hoochie Coochie Man," started over and Nick said, "Answer it before it goes to voice mail."

Her hand shook as she pressed the button. Her "hello" was a little shaky, too.

A bright cheerful voice answered her. "Hey. It's Misty. Rachel and I are downstairs. Herr Koenig sent us. What room are you guys in?"

Nick was waiting at the door when they knocked. Rachel hugged them both and Misty came in ready for action. Grace felt oddly comforted by their presence, as though she and Nick were lost in a foreign country and she finally ran across a couple of people who spoke English.

Both girls were dressed as if they were on their way to the gym. Maybe they had been. Tank tops, yoga pants and running shoes. They even had gym bags slung over their shoulders. Misty's white-blonde hair was smoothed down to her head now, not in the spiky 'do she sported the night before. A tiny streak of emerald green dye ran through it here and there. On anyone else, it would have looked like a polar bear with algae in his fur, but somehow on Misty, it looked exotic and playful.

"Now give us the lowdown," she said, perching on the edge of the bed. "Herr Koenig gave us the *Cliff's Notes* version, but I want to hear it from you. Tell us everything."

The two girls listened quietly while Grace and Nick told the story, beginning with Walter ambushing them outside the parking deck and ending with Shady's call.

"So our next step is to find out which room they're holding him in," Nick said.

Rachel giggled. "Leave that to us." She patted her gym bag with a manicured hand. "We can take care of that in a flash, can't we, Boo?"

Misty nodded, a smile lighting up her pretty pixie face. She might have looked like Tinkerbell if it hadn't been for all the tattoos.

The girls took their bags and went into the big bathroom together. Nick looked inquiringly at Grace. She shrugged, lay back across the bed and closed her eyes. She was so tired.

"Do you think this room is bugged?" she asked after a few minutes, eyes still closed.

"I doubt it," Nick said. "He's too full of himself to think we would do anything but cower and cooperate. And anyway, he doesn't care what we say, only what we do."

Misty and Rachel stepped back into the room.

"Well, I'm interested to know what you two…" Nick began, but when he caught sight of the girls and his voice faltered, "…um…have in mind."

They were dressed in matching red jumpsuits, made from some sort of plastic that was so shiny it looked wet and creaked lightly when they moved. The suits looked like they had been vacuum-sealed in place. A zipper ran all the way up the front, but was only zipped up as far as decency laws demanded. They were each spilling out the top in a very premeditated way.

Their makeup was wild -- lots of sparkles, false eyelashes, and blood-red lipstick. Pointed boots with stiletto heels made them four inches taller. Misty's hair was spiked again and Rachel's was in a high, tight ponytail.

They made a dazzling duo. Whatever they had in mind, it was going to be like shooting fish in a barrel.

"All right," Misty said, "we're going to head on over to the Pleasure Palace. We'll call as soon as we find out what room they're in. And if the Russian calls you first, let us know, okay? Here's my number." Her handwriting was neat and tiny on the Isis notepad.

"So, what exactly is your plan, if you don't mind me asking?" Nick said, finding his voice again.

"We're going to pose as strippers trying to find our bachelor party," Rachel said sweetly, twirling the end of her ponytail between

Kelly Adamson

her fingers. "We forgot to write down the room number. Oops!" she shrugged her shoulders innocently.

Nick grinned. "That should work. They might even invite you in."

Grace rolled her eyes. Las Vegas was one of the few places on earth you could dress like this and not look suspicious. "Okay, girls, I guess you need to be scooting along."

As Nick ushered them to the door, Grace called over his shoulder, "Hey, have either of you ever seen a movie called *Headcase*? One of Killian's, I think. An indie flick from his early days. For some reason I'm drawing a blank on it. It might not mean a thing, but he called the Russian a headcase, and it just dawned on me that was the name of one of his movies. It's probably nothing."

"Oh, sure," Misty said with a wave of her hand. "That movie's awesome. I love the part where he starts singing and you can tell the bad guys don't know if he's crazy or not, and he knows they don't *care* because all they want is his money, so he just piles it on, seeing how crazy he can act…"

"Whoa," Grace said, clearly not expecting this. "Let me get something to write on. You need to sit right back down here and start at the beginning."

It didn't take long to get the gist of the plot, a sting operation orchestrated by Killian's character, an undercover British agent. The bad guys in the movie were Colombian drug lords, not Egyptian antiquities thieves, but the premise could work. Then Nick pointed out one major problem – they were missing their leading man.

At that point, Misty became positively ecstatic. "I've got just the guy. Rooster Hathcock." She pulled her cell phone from the gym bag — there was nowhere on her person she could currently have concealed it — and began dialing.

"Rooster Hathcock?" Nick said. "What makes you think he'll do it?"

"Trust me." Misty gave him a sly wink. "Rooster's always game for a good adventure."

They could hear his voice as he picked up on his end, obviously happy to hear from Misty. "Cock-a-doodle-doo!" he crowed.

Grace raised her eyebrows and stole a glance at Nick. His face was grim. She knew he was wondering just how the hell they were going to pull this off.

But Misty had been right on the money. Rooster was thrilled at the prospect of danger and intrigue. He, too, had seen *Headcase* and kept peppering their conversation with quotes drawn straight from the movie's dialogue. The more he did, the less certain Grace became with their choice of leading man. Misty, however, was unwavering, and even Nick seemed convinced after talking with him on speaker phone. When they hung up, the wheels were in motion.

"He's got the swagger," Nick told Grace after Misty and Rachel left for the Pleasure Palace Inn. "He's got the money. He's got the name. I mean, who would suspect him? He's known for being eccentric anyway. He'll be completely believable."

Grace wished she shared his confidence.

It was precisely eleven minutes after eleven when the phone rang again. Grace knew this because she'd been lying on her stomach, crossways on the bed, staring at the clock. She jumped anyway. This was definitely turning into a heart-check weekend.

She put her hand on the extension and nodded to Nick. They picked up simultaneously. He said "hello" in the same deep voice he'd used earlier.

"Write this down," said the dreadfully familiar voice on the other end, "because I don't like having to repeat myself." Grace scrambled for the pen and notepad by the phone. "Drive east on Harmon Avenue," continued the Russian, "until you reach Swenson Street. Then north until you pass the UNLV practice field. Beyond that, you will see an abandoned convenience store with plywood on the windows. The two of you will bring my necklace there in one hour. Pull around behind the building, get out of the car and wait for us. Do not be late."

"No," Nick said.

Grace looked at him. He didn't meet her eyes. This wasn't part of the plan.

"Not both of us. Just me."

"Oh, yes, Mr. Howard, I'm afraid I must insist that your wife accompany you."

"She's not coming," Nick replied calmly. "And if that's a deal breaker for you, then so be it. You can go ahead and slit his throat right now, because I'm not bringing her with me."

Grace watched his face. She was sure he was bluffing, but his voice was rock steady. Apparently the Russian believed him, because after a pause he said, "Very well." The words sent a shiver up her spine. She knew that meant he would just send someone to kill her later.

"Listen," said Nick, as if he'd been debating whether or not to mention it. "I know you know we were with Rooster Hathcock last night at Die Nacht." He looked at Grace. She nodded. "Well, all he could talk about was that damn necklace and how he wished he could get his hands on it. He said he wished he knew who had it because he would pay them twice what they were getting for it. And God knows he's got the money. If I'd known I had it at the time, I'd be a very rich man right now, and you and I wouldn't be having this conversation."

When the Russian didn't answer, Grace felt her throat tighten. He finally said, "I don't believe you. You're trying to set me up."

Nick chuckled. "Yeah, *we're* setting *you* up. That's rich. Listen, he's not the police; he's a redneck country singer with a shitload of money and nothing to spend it on but Jack Daniels and cowboy boots. It's just a coincidence that he happens to be obsessed with King Tut. He calls himself an *Egyptophile.* He says he's having a pyramid built on his ranch in Mississippi."

"A pyramid?"

"Yes, a pyramid. You know what they say about a fool and his money."

"No. What do they say?" He might have been educated in the States, but his knowledge of idioms was still lacking.

"They're soon parted."

"Ah, yes. That is often true. However, I don't believe someone named *Rooster* would be willing to part with the kind of capital needed to acquire this necklace."

Kelly Adamson

"His bass player told us that he spent over three million dollars last year on a statue of a cat that was supposed to be from King Tut's tomb. He wasn't even sure if it was genuine."

There was another pause, a good fifteen seconds of total silence, before Nick sighed. "Look, I was just trying to hook up Rooster; I don't give a damn what you do with the necklace. You can shove it up your ass for all I care. I just want it out of my hands. Personally, I hope you choke on it and die."

"You forget yourself, Mr. Howard." For the first time, the Russian lost a little of his condescending tone. He sounded like someone barely controlling his fury.

"Hey, I'm just passing along the information. If you don't want his money, you don't have to take it. Forget I mentioned it."

The Russian finally asked, "How do I get in touch with him?"

Grace smiled.

Nick rattled off Rooster's number. "Do you still want us to meet you in an hour?"

"No. Wait in your room until after I talk to this Rooster."

"Call me on my cell phone," Nick said, enjoying at least momentarily how the balance of power had wobbled. "We're going to get some lunch."

Chapter 21 – Daytime

Killian had somehow managed to drift off to sleep again, despite the plastic biting into his wrists. Now he cursed himself for it, since he couldn't tell if he'd been asleep five minutes or five hours. The TV was still on. It was *I Love Lucy*, the one where Lucy falls over the garden wall at Richard Widmark's. These big Russians sure loved their TV Land.

One of the men, Hardy, was reclining on the bed, eating almonds from a can. When Widmark's St. Bernard found Lucy hiding under the bearskin rug, the Russian shook with silent laughter.

They'd finally let Killian up to relieve himself about an hour after his failed escape attempt, or the "tank lid incident," as he preferred to think of it. Both men had stood with guns drawn at his back while he peed. Oh, yes, very relaxing. But by that time, he had to go so bad they didn't even bother him.

What they had *not* done, however, was offer him anything to eat, despite the fact that Hardy had been stuffing his own face nonstop since they got there. Junk food wrappers were scattered all over the bedspread, spilling over onto the floor. Killian knew they were probably thinking he wouldn't be their problem much longer, one way or the other, so why feed him? Not to mention the fact that he hadn't exactly ingratiated himself to either man by hitting them with a big chunk of porcelain.

He'd asked for water earlier, and they'd given him some from the sink, pouring most of it down his face onto his shirt. It tasted like a tin can. He considered himself lucky it wasn't from the toilet.

He wondered what Nick and Grace were doing. He hoped they were safe. He also hoped they were looking for him. No one else on earth had a clue what happened to him. He suddenly felt very, very sorry he chucked his mobile phone. Astrid would assume he'd been so overcome with grief at seeing her with another man that he committed suicide. What a bitch.

The tall one, Laurel, noticed he was awake and eyed him from across the room.

"Pardon me, chaps," Killian ventured, "but do either of you have the time?"

They both ignored him as if the frequency of his voice didn't register in their world.

He tried again, a little louder. "Could I trouble you gents to tell me what time it is?

Laurel reached for the edge of the heavy orange curtain and pulled it back.

"*Day*time," he grunted in a thick accent then laughed at his own joke. At least *someone* found him amusing. He let the curtain fall back in place, but not before Killian caught a glimpse of movement outside. He couldn't tell what it was or how far away. It could be a person, a car, or a bird, but it was definitely the shadow of something.

The big Russian stood, still chuckling at his own dazzling wit. He took a cigarette from a pack of Camels and lit it with a

Zippo. He clicked the cover closed and reached for the door. He was going to step outside to smoke. Maybe he thought the smell would offend Hardy, though Killian didn't see how it could possibly make the stale, musty air in the room any less appealing.

Laurel turned the knob, and the bright Nevada sunshine and searing heat came rushing in through the open doorway.

Killian didn't think about it. He didn't plan it out or wonder if it would work. And he certainly didn't ponder what the consequences might be if it didn't. He just yelled. The most ear-splitting scream he could manage. Certainly anyone in the vicinity would hear him.

"Help! Help me! Help!"

Hardy tossed the can of almonds in the air in shock. A couple of nuts hit Killian in the shoulder and chest.

Then Laurel hit him in the face. He saw it coming, the fist as big as a ham, but there was nothing he could do about it. He couldn't dodge. He couldn't throw up an arm to block it. He just had to sit there and take it.

He'd been hit before, but school yard brawls and the occasional slip of a stuntman in a fight scene could not prepare him for the force of this punch. His head exploded with pain. His neck snapped hideously. Stars flashed before his eyes. He wasn't sure how many times the big man hit him — he thought three — but knew one would have been enough.

His captors began to argue heatedly in Russian. Laurel's knife flashed momentarily. He closed his eyes — one was already beginning to swell — and braced for the impending pain. They'd probably get in a lot of trouble with their boss if they killed him, but that didn't mean they had to deliver him unharmed. He just had to be breathing.

He heard, more than felt, his shirt rip. With the help of the knife, Laurel took off his right sleeve at the shoulder. The shiny material proved sturdier than it looked, and the blade nicked Killian's skin just above his tattoo. A thin trail of blood rolled down his family crest.

Laurel twisted the sleeve between his big hands, and for a second Killian thought the man planned to choke him with it. His lungs tightened at the thought of it. But when Laurel stuffed it in Killian's mouth and tied the ends tightly behind his neck, it was painfully obvious it was just to ensure he didn't make any more noise.

Hardy was still breathing heavily from the excitement. He pointed at Killian's arm and began talking in slow, measured Russian. It sounded to Killian like a record being played backwards. Maybe he was giving Laurel pointers on his knot-tying. Killian wasn't paying much attention to the words – he couldn't understand any of them anyway. Then something happened that sent a chill down his spine. He felt like someone had doused him with a bucket of ice water. Because in the midst of these words that meant nothing to him, he heard two that meant quite a lot to him – his own name.

In addition to classic American sitcoms, it seemed Hardy also enjoyed a good Hollywood blockbuster. He recognized Killian's tattoo, just as Grace had, and his pudgy lips split into a wide grin. His evil little brain was whirring away at the possibilities. Killian realized he liked Hardy a lot better when he was scowling.

Two well-ridden Harley Davidsons were parked together at Big's Java Hut, the coffee house that shared an alley with the Pleasure Palace Inn. Nick parked the Subaru on the far side of the little restaurant's dumpster, where it wouldn't be so visible to the occupants at the motel. Shady and Little Frank loitered in the thin slice of shade the dumpster offered. A stub of a filterless cigarette hung from Frank's mouth at a precarious angle.

Shady inclined his head to Nick and Grace as they climbed out of the car. "Chevy's around back," he said.

"Where's everybody else?" Grace asked. Despite her dark sunglasses, she still had to squint in the early afternoon sun as she scanned the parking lot. There was something anticlimactic about Las Vegas in the broad daylight. All the bright colors looked faded and worn. It was like finding out how a magician performs his tricks.

"Sunshine and Skye are parked around back, behind the fence, so they can see the other rooms. William and his buddy had to go get something. Should be back any minute, I reckon."

Frank flicked what was left of his cigarette onto the asphalt and crushed it out with the toe of his boot. "Your girlfriends are *nice*." He grinned boyishly, which might have been endearing if he hadn't been missing one of his front teeth.

"Where are they?" Nick asked.

"Around back, goin' door to door," Shady said.

"They're *nice*," Frank repeated, nodding his head. Frank had an accent, Greek maybe. It didn't sound nearly as sinister as the man in the shiny suit, Volkov, if that was his name.

Grace shaded her eyes from the glare of the sun. She ducked into the backseat and pulled out the cap with the dice on it that

Killian had been wearing the day before. It helped block the sun considerably.

"Skye wanted to talk to you guys when you got here. She was looking for somethin'; said she needed somethin' that belonged to Killian."

"Like what?"

Shady shrugged. "Oh, I dunno. She's into all that voodoo stuff. She wanted it for some kinda spell, I think."

"Voodoo?" Nick said. "Well, that's…interesting."

It dawned on Grace that Shady had said "Killian," not "Bubba." William must have spilled the beans about his true identity. But it didn't seem to bother him any. That was a shocker.

"So…you know who he is, huh?"

Shady nodded, eyes on the motel.

"And you're okay with that? You're still willing to help?"

He nodded again then said, "Killian Ross is a friend of the Vipers. We'll do whatever we need to do to make sure he's safe."

Grace must have looked stunned, because she certainly felt it. Two nights ago Shady was ready to kill him. Now that he'd found out Killian lied to him about his identity, it should have made him even angrier. Instead it sounded like he was talking about a fellow gang member.

Frank looked at Grace with a grin. "He taught us about women."

Grace looked at Shady. His arms were folded across his chest and his eyes never wavered from the Pleasure Palace Inn, but she could make out a hint of a smile on his weathered face.

"Well, that's great," Grace said. "We'll go see if we can help Skye with her voodoo."

"They're around behind the fence," Frank said. "They had to get where you couldn't see 'em. Sunshine's car runs like a bat outta hell, but she don't blend in too well on a stake-out."

Grace and Nick pulled back onto the main road to avoid driving through the motel's parking lot. They turned right onto McCorsten Street and around behind the chain link fence that ran along the back of the Pleasure Palace Inn's parking lot. The green plastic strips that had been woven through the fence as a privacy screen were cracked and faded, even missing in some places.

Concealed behind it sat a 1969 Plymouth Road Runner painted the color of a radioactive lime. Sunshine and Skye were leaning against the front quarter panel, each stationed behind several of their own cracks to look through in the fence. Skye smiled and waved as they pulled in close beside the Road Runner and stepped out to join them.

"Anything yet?"

"Nope," said Sunshine, his big moustache moving slightly in the desert breeze. "I keep thinkin' they'll come out for some food. This place ain't exactly got room service. But no sign of 'em yet."

Grace could see the back of the Tahoe, parked on the other side of the fence in the far corner of the motel's parking lot. It was partially concealed by empty wooden pallets someone had discarded.

Everyone watched the motel in silence for a few minutes, then Nick nodded at the Plymouth. "What you got under the hood?"

Sunshine beamed, happy to show off his sublime green baby. He leaned in the driver's window and popped the hood. Skye stepped away from the car, glided over to Grace and leaned against the Subaru. As the two men stood, arms folded across their chests, discussing the superiority of the 440 six-pack, the girls watched the rear of the motel.

Misty and Rachel walked the second floor balcony towards the far end. If the curtains in a room were open, they simply peeked in to see if it was occupied. If the curtains were closed, they were forced to knock and go through their "lost strippers" routine.

"So," said Grace, trying to sound casual, her eyes never leaving the motel, "Shady says you're into voodoo."

Skye laughed, a clear, beautiful sound. "Is that what he said?" She shook her head, dark hair falling around her face. "Voodoo is a religion, and it's mainly practiced in the West Indies. I'm a Catholic, and I've never even *met* anyone from the West Indies." She chuckled again, just thinking about it. "That Shady. What a card he is."

"He said you needed something of Killian's...for a spell."

"Oh, yeah," she said. "You wouldn't happen to have anything, would you?"

"Maybe. So...you're gonna do a spell?"

"I'm certainly going to try."

Grace pondered that a moment. "Are you like a shaman?"

Skye smiled again. Grace thought she looked a little like the Mona Lisa, like she knew a lot of secrets she wasn't telling.

"No. Shamanism is a Siberian mystic tradition. It doesn't have anything to do with Native Americans. That's a common misconception, though."

"Oh."

They watched as Misty and Rachel found a room with at least one occupant who wanted their company very much. The man who answered the door was in his fifties. His beer belly protruded over the top of his one article of clothing, a checked pair of boxer shorts. He was in high gear and doing his best smooth talk trying to get the girls inside his room. He attempted to put his arm around Rachel. She sidestepped so quickly, he stumbled. Misty pinned his arm behind his hairy back and marched him into the room. She pulled the door closed. Whatever she said to him must have made an impression, because it didn't open again.

"So," began Grace once more, "what exactly is it you do? Is it some sort of...magic?" She was hesitant to use that word. It sounded silly.

"It has some elements of magic, that's true, but it's difficult to pigeonhole. My Grandma Chenoa was a Cherokee medicine woman, a direct descendent of *Tsi s qua A ge yv*, very well-respected for her knowledge and abilities. I learned a lot from her, and not just about herbs and berries. She taught me so much about looking beyond what the eye sees. She taught me to be open to new ways, while respecting the old. I suppose that's what I've done."

Right, thought Grace. Clear as mud. She wasn't sure how Skye reconciled her magic with her Catholicism, but that wasn't her cross to bear. Besides, she was the first to admit there were things that existed far beyond human understanding, and maybe that was something both magic and Catholicism shared. At any rate, she wasn't about to doubt Skye's conviction, so she just nodded.

Then she pulled the red cap off her head and held it out to Skye. "Here. This is Killian's. Use it well."

Misty knocked sharply on the door of room 219 and winced. These heavy doors were murder on the knuckles after a while. The curtain moved a little and a few seconds later, the door opened no more than an inch. The room beyond was dark.

A man's voice said, "What do you want?" The heavy accent made it sound more like "Vutt do you vont?" Misty's pulse quickened. Pay dirt.

Chapter 22 – Safe

"Oh, hey, sugar. I hope we're not too late." Misty put on her best sly kitten act. She put her left hand against the door and stepped forward as if it was a given that she and Rachel were walking right in.

"Late for what?" asked the man in a deep Russian voice. Boy, this guy really was a few fries short of a Happy Meal.

"Why, the party, of course," Rachel purred. "You did call for a couple of dates, didn't you? This *is* room 219, isn't it?"

The man actually opened the door wider so he could peek out at the room number to make sure. What a whopper he was. He had to be close to seven feet tall.

Quick as a cat, Misty ducked under his outstretched arm and peeked around him into the room. It was dark except for the green glow of the television screen, but the shaft of daylight coming in through the door fell across the stretch of ratty orange carpet and illuminated the very thing they'd been looking for.

She caught her breath and plastered a fake smile on her face as the tall man caught her by the shoulder and pushed her back outside. "You can't come in," he growled.

"You like to get freaky, huh?" Misty ran a finger down the front of his shirt. "Well, a little bondage is okay with us, but it'll cost you extra."

The man grinned down at her, which was more than a little creepy. They heard the toilet flush. The man's smile vanished and he pushed them out of the room and closed the door.

The two girls turned to each other, eyes wide. Misty nodded. They ran as fast as their spike heels could carry them to the stairs at the end of the balcony.

Shady and Little Frank were waiting by the dumpster.

"Well?"

"Room 219," sputtered Misty. "Looks like they have him tied to a chair. He's gagged, too, and he looks like they roughed him up a little."

"Is he conscious?"

"I don't know," she admitted. "I couldn't tell. I just saw him for a split second."

"We only saw one of the kidnappers," Rachel added. "He's built like a tree and just as smart. The other one was in the bathroom. He didn't see us. I doubt the brain surgeon is going to admit his mistake in opening the door, so I think we're safe."

Shady nodded. "Okay. You girls did good. Now get on outta here just in case they come lookin' for you."

Misty couldn't wait to get out of her plastic jumpsuit. She felt like a baked potato wrapped in aluminum foil. The crap she had to wear at work was bad enough, but this heat was unbearable. The girls jumped in Misty's Honda and took off, turning the air conditioner on high.

As soon as she saw the girls bolt, Skye was ready to begin her contribution to the rescue mission, although Grace still wasn't sure exactly what that was. She pulled a plastic Wal-Mart bag out of the back seat of the Road Runner, then headed off along the fence line at a jog, stopping directly in front of room 219. She was probably thirty yards from the door at this point, and well-hidden by the fence.

She pulled a whisk broom out of the bag and cleared a space on the asphalt about four feet in diameter.

Grace, Nick and Sunshine followed her, but stopped about ten feet away. Skye sat cross legged behind the spot she had swept and emptied the contents of her Wal-Mart bag to one side. Grace could see playing cards, a padlock, assorted candles and two plastic baggies filled with what looked like dried herbs, one pale green, the other almost black. A third, larger bag looked like it contained sand.

The two Harleys roared to life. Shady and Little Frank would be joining them momentarily, wanting marching orders, wanting to know what to do next. Were they supposed to wait on this spell to be cast? On impulse, Grace scurried the last few steps over to Skye and crouched beside her. "Can I just ask you one quick question before you get started?"

"Of course." Skye pulled a butane wand lighter out of its blister pack and put it with the rest of her supplies.

Grace tried to choose her words carefully. "What exactly is this spell supposed to accomplish? I mean, is it supposed to *free* Killian?"

Skye shook her head. "Oh, no, I'm not that powerful. My Grandmother Chenoa, she might could have done that, but not me. This will just keep him safe."

"Oh, that sounds good."

"...for as long as he stays in that room," she finished.

Shady and Little Frank parked their bikes next to the Plymouth and walked the twenty yards to Nick and Sunshine. Grace doubted any of them really believed in magic, but it was clear by their reverence that none of them wanted to be on Skye's bad side either.

In hushed tones, Shady filled them in on what Misty and Rachel had learned, that Killian was bound and gagged and possibly injured, and there were two guards, just as they suspected.

Nick clenched and unclenched his fists. Shady reached out a beefy hand and patted him roughly on the shoulder. "We'll get him, brother, never you worry," he said in his gravelly voice.

This was unfathomable. This world of armed robbery and kidnapping and murder. These people were insane. They had to be stopped. Grace still believed they were wrong for not calling the police to start with, but she had a feeling it was too late for that now. She just hoped that mistake hadn't doomed them all.

She stepped back to join the guys as they focused their attention on Skye. She began by taking two handfuls of sand from the larger bag and let it sift through her fingers to form a three-foot circle. Each hand started at the back and made a semi-circle that met at the point closest to room 219.

Grace was caught off guard by the music. She almost turned to see where it was coming from before realizing it was Skye. It wasn't a chant, more of a lullaby, and seemed to cover the whole area in a blanket of calm. It was just her imagination, of course, but Grace felt more relaxed than she had in days.

Next Skye placed four votive candles just within the circle of sand and lit them. The North and South candles were white, while the East and West were red. She took one of the playing cards, laid it on the ground, then carefully covered it with Killian's baseball cap. Next, still singing, she sprinkled the bill of the cap first with the dark herb and then the light one. She took the wand lighter and set fire to the herbs. Grace knew the cap was about to go up in smoky, smelly flames, but it appeared unharmed. Only the herbs were burning.

Then Skye took the other two playing cards and lit each of them from the little flame rising from the bill of the cap. Her singing came a little faster. She held the burning cards in her hands until the last possible moment, and when she released them, the ashes flew away over the fence.

Soon, the flame of the herbs died away, too. They looked clean and untouched, as if they hadn't burned at all. Skye's singing slowed back to the lullaby. She picked up the candles and let a drop of wax from each one fall on the crown of the hat.

Her onlookers were quiet as church mice, hesitant to even shift from one foot to another, but they were all wondering how long this would take.

Skye then took a small leather pouch tied with a long black drawstring from around her neck. A pinch of sand and two pinches of herbs from the bill of the cap were dropped into the pouch. Next she added a drop of wax from each candle, then cinched the bag and laid it carefully on top of the cap. Her eyes were closed. She rocked back and forth gently as she sang.

As if on cue, a quick gust of wind swirled through the parking lot and blew out all four candles. Skye's song appeared to be over as well. She put both her palms on the bag that rested on the crown of the cap and sat quietly for a few moments, head bowed.

She picked up the cap to reveal the card, the King of Hearts. But on top of the card lay an opened padlock, the one Skye had taken out of the bag earlier. Grace hadn't seen her place it on the card. She could have sworn she was paying close attention, but surely she'd just missed that. She felt the hair on the back of her neck bristle a little at the thought.

Skye stood and approached her spellbound audience. She handed the cap back to Grace with a smile and turned to Nick. She hung the small pouch around his neck. It hung right over his heart. Skye patted it with one hand and looked up at him with her big, brown eyes. There was no trace of a smile on her pretty face now. "It will guide you," she said. "And you'll need it more than the rest of us."

Nick looked down at the pouch, but didn't touch it. He met Skye's gaze and nodded, but didn't say a word.

Instead of feeling alarmed that Skye thought her husband needed extra guidance, Grace found herself feeling relieved that he now had a bag of sand and leaves around his neck. She tried hard not to analyze that too closely.

Minutes later, while Skye was still bagging up candles and sweeping away sand, Nick's cell phone rang. Unknown caller. He motioned for Grace to lean in close so she could hear the conversation too. He put a finger to his lips, took a deep breath and answered the phone. "Yes."

"Are you trying to play with me, Mr. Howard?" came the biting voice of the well-dressed thug. "Did you really think I wouldn't find out? Just who do you think you are dealing with?"

Nick wasn't quite sure what the man had found out, but knew he was waiting on some sort of answer. "Well…I think I'm dealing with Alexander Volkov."

The hysterical laughter that followed was a surprise. When he found his voice again, the Russian said, "You are not worthy to speak the name of Volkov. Do not utter it again. As for me, I am merely Volkov's humble servant. If you must have a name, call me *Clark*. I always liked that name."

"As in Griswold?" Nick asked.

"No, as in Gable," came the smooth reply.

"All right, *Clark*. Have you been in touch with Rooster Hathcock yet?"

"Yes, but that is a separate matter. We will deal with that shortly. Right now, I want to know why you tried to pass off an international movie star as your backwoods cousin and thought I wouldn't find out."

Grace closed her eyes. Damn. This was really not what she wanted to hear.

"Well?"

"What do you want?" Nick asked.

"What I want, in addition to the money I will get from the sale of my necklace to your silly musician friend, is a bonus for housing such an iconic and beloved star of the silver screen as Mr. Killian Ross." The Russian voice was cheerful again, as if he'd forgotten all about Nick's disrespectful use of Volkov's name.

"A bonus? You mean you want ransom money."

"Ransom is such a crass word. I prefer bonus. It sounds so much more civilized."

Nick's free hand was balling into a fist again. He shoved it into his pocket and tried to keep his voice composed. "Well, *Clark*, just what kind of bonus are you looking for?"

"I think a nice round million in cash will suffice. I'll even do you a favor. I'll take it in U.S. currency. Just think of the bargain you're getting, considering the current exchange rate. You should thank me."

Grace could see a vein sticking out in Nick's neck. His face was turning red. She figured he was trying to count to ten, but she bet he wouldn't make it past four. "A million dollars? Just how do you expect me to come up with a million dollars?"

"Oh, I don't expect *you* to come up with a million dollars. What is it you do for a living again? Something with a hammer and nails? No, I don't expect *you* could come up with a hundred. I was speaking of Mr. Ross's people."

"I don't know Mr. Ross's people, or how to get in touch with them," Nick said through gritted teeth. "I just met him two days ago. He has nothing to do with any of this. Why don't you just let him go?"

Clark chuckled. "You know, Mr. Howard, I'm really becoming quite fond of you. You have such an outstanding sense of humor. Now let's see, it's almost two. That makes it ten in England. I'll call you back in two hours. That should give you plenty of time. The banks are closed, of course, but you can make the arrangements to have my money to me tomorrow. It looks like lucky Mr. Ross will be safe for another day, thanks to banking hours." He hung up.

Grace and Nick stood motionless, the silent phone still held between them. They were in so far over their heads. How had this happened?

At some point, the crowd had grown. William and his friend had shown up. Everyone was closing in, waiting to hear the other end of the conversation.

Nick told them what Clark said. It was their turn to be stunned. The bikers cursed. William and his friend mumbled to each other. To Grace, it was mostly unintelligible, like a language twins use with each other. The bikers had one language and William and his friend had another.

Grace turned away from them all. Nick followed and put his arm around her, but he didn't say, "It'll be all right," because he never made promises he couldn't keep.

Chapter 23 – Anywhere But Here

Grace stood with her head on Nick's chest for a long minute. Whatever fool's courage she'd gained in the past hour was gone. Clark had seen to that.

She took a deep breath and said, "We have to call Mr. Koenig to get in touch with Ruth." When Nick didn't respond, she pulled away and looked up at him. "What other choice do we have?"

They climbed into the Subaru so both could hear the conversation on speaker phone. Nick dialed from memory.

"Hello, my friends. What news?" Koenig listened, but didn't seem the least bit surprised by these new demands. "I only wonder why it took them so long," was all he said. He promised to call Ruth to make arrangements for the money transfer as soon as they hung up, but first he had news of his own.

"I have agreed to act as the intermediary between the Russians and Mr. Hathcock. They will make their deal here at my office, since they both feel it's neutral ground. They have agreed to this evening at nine, before the club gets crowded."

"I want to be there," Nick said.

"I'm sorry, Nick, but that's out of the question. That's the main stipulation from both sides. Just the three of us will be in the room."

"You can bet the Russians won't keep to that," Nick snarled.

"I have my own security here. I assure you I'm very well protected, and I'm not afraid of them."

Nick sighed, frustrated but resigned. "All right. The main thing is to keep the necklace in play. Stall for time. I may have to give it back to him eventually in order to get Killian, but if it disappears into his original buyer's hands, then it's gone for good."

"Agreed. It's imperative that we keep it from reaching its original destination."

While they continued their talk of tactics and espionage, Grace felt a wave of nausea hit her. The closed car was sweltering. She got out and sat with her back against one of the chain link fence posts, thankful for the bit of shade the plastic strips offered. She felt removed from the action as she watched the flicker of activity in the parking lot annex.

Skye had packed her things and Sunshine drove her back home. When he turned the key in the Road Runner's ignition, the commanding roar of the engine made all the men turn their heads, even the ones who seemed perpetually glued to their cell phones, like Nick and William.

Grace took the opportunity to give William's friend the once over. A well-built, black man with perfect teeth, Anthony wasn't a bit taller than Grace's five-foot-six. But as she watched him leaning against the back of William's Jeep Cherokee, calmly watching everything around him, she got the feeling he could be a force to be reckoned with. William said they'd been in "the service" together, but that was all. She could picture Anthony dressed in desert camouflage, an M4 rifle on his shoulder, or maybe a grenade launcher. Since his arrival, he'd said little, but had taken in everything around him. Grace felt sure he could close his eyes and give a description of everyone he'd seen go into the motel, not to mention their license plate numbers. He caught her looking at him and smiled. He had a nice smile.

Fifty yards away, a battered beige pickup truck turned off the side street into this forgotten stretch of parking lot. It moved slowly, rolling all the way down to their little group before it stopped. When Misty and Rachel's coworker, Brett, stepped out, everyone relaxed. When he began pulling bags of fast food out of the passenger seat, everyone got really friendly and went to help.

The logo on the side of the bags was a green sombrero with the words "Mi Taco es Su Taco." Brett also had a Styrofoam cooler full of drinks in the bed of the truck. Bottled water and sodas, no beer, and again Grace was struck by how young he looked. He probably wasn't old enough to buy it.

He definitely looked different than the glam-meets-pretty-boy he evoked the last time she'd seen him. Instead of chainmail, he was wearing baggy jeans, flip-flops and a faded tee shirt with the UNLV logo on the front and bleach spots on the right shoulder. His long black curls were pulled back in a ponytail at the nape of his neck.

Everyone dug into the tacos. Brett settled beside Grace, his back against the fence. He opened a bottle of water and drank half of it in one gulp, then took off his dark sunglasses and wiped his forehead with the hem of his shirt. Grace found that an odd gesture. The air here was so dry it was impossible to sweat, no matter how hot it got. She was used to eighty to ninety percent humidity back in Alabama. She was used to condensation on the outside of a Coke can.

Nick, Shady, Little Frank and Anthony were huddled in the shadow of the pickup, eating the cheap, spicy tacos like they had never had anything so good. They watched as William used his finger to draw in the thin layer of sand that covered the asphalt. Sometimes he pointed at the motel, or Nick, or himself. His voice didn't carry to where Grace sat, and she was glad. She should be paying attention, she should be trying to help them figure a way out of this mess, but it was all just too overwhelming to deal with. From her vantage point, she could see the airplanes taking off at McCarran and found herself wishing she was on one of them. It didn't matter where it was going, just anywhere but here. She and Nick had come to Las Vegas for excitement. The old saying was right — "Be careful what you wish for."

Brett cleared his throat. Grace turned. He was offering her a taco. She almost said no, but her empty stomach won out. She forced a smile and took the taco. "Thanks."

"Don't mention it."

They sat in silence while they ate, then Brett said, as if it were an afterthought, "Misty and Rachel are gonna pick up Rooster and take him to die Nacht this afternoon so he and Herr Koenig can practice. They've gotta get their stories straight."

Grace stared out at the airplanes. "I wish they wouldn't do that," she muttered. "It's too dangerous."

"What?"

"This isn't a movie," she said. "These are people's lives." She was annoyed that everyone was acting so calm. Was she the only one who felt like screaming? She looked at Brett. He was smiling. It was infuriating. He reached out like he was going to pat her on the knee, but thought better of it. The glare in her eyes said she might hit him.

"Look, you have every right to be worried, Grace, but I'll be honest with you. I trust Wilhelm Koenig with my life. And if he says it's covered, then it's covered. Don't be scared. Remember that old Ambrose Redmoon quote, 'Courage is not the absence of fear, but rather the judgment that something else is more important than fear.'" He tipped his water bottle to her in a toast and downed the rest of it.

Before Grace could ask who the hell Ambrose Redmoon was, Brett continued, "Besides, being afraid is no excuse for not taking action."

"Who said that?" she asked.

"I did. Just now."

Nick walked over and squatted down in front of them like a catcher, balancing easily on the balls of his feet. "We're gonna try to get Killian out at the same time they're making the deal at die Nacht. Nine o'clock. It'll be dark by then, and that's good because this involves getting up on the roof. The fewer people who see us, the better off we'll be."

For such a small, low-rent motel, there were a surprising number of occupants. Young couples, families with kids, some middle aged women who came to see Celine Dion, some young guys who came to see the strippers, and gamblers intent on losing every last dime in the hopes of striking it rich. There was also a woman who looked much too classy for a joint like this who was staying right next door to 219. She was tall, with straight black hair that hung almost to her waist. She wore dark glasses and an expensive-looking wide-brimmed sunhat, and she was pulling the largest Pullman case Grace had ever seen. Got to have somewhere to keep all those hats, she guessed. The woman looked like a high-end prostitute. Hopefully, she'd be working at nine p.m. Hopefully, she didn't plan to work in her room.

"What in the world are you gonna do on the roof?" she said, but Nick's phone rang. She was sure he was delighted to answer it instead of explain his plans to her. Part of her didn't want to know anyway.

If they managed to free Killian, the next logical step would be to go straight to the police, but there was no point in doing that if the Russians still had him as a hostage. Tomorrow morning, Ruth Averhart was going to be out a million dollars. And if they couldn't free Killian before the exchange with Rooster, that meant someone was going to have to come up with several million more. Otherwise, it would all be for nothing. Maybe Rooster could change his mind, say he didn't want the necklace after all, but then they'd just be right back where they started from. And that might also put Rooster in a very dangerous position. She'd been right; she didn't want the answers anyway.

It took Grace a few seconds to realize her cell phone was ringing. She didn't recognize the number and thought half-heartedly of ignoring it, but pushed the button anyway. At first, all she heard was a woman sobbing.

"Hello," said a trembling voice. "Is anyone there?"

"Who is this?" But Grace thought she knew.

"This is Ruth Averhart. I'm trying to contact Grace Howard. Do I have the correct number?"

"Yes."

Ruth's sobs started again.

Grace knew it was a double standard — especially considering how much of it she had been doing herself this weekend — but she hated being around people who were crying. She felt totally awkward and completely inadequate to console this woman she'd never met and knew practically nothing about.

But Ruth Averhart continued as if she'd found a long-lost friend. "Oh, Grace! Is it true? They have Killian?" Her voice was ragged.

"Yes."

"Oh."

It was just one syllable, but Grace had never heard a word packed with so much anguish.

"I've arranged for the money to be wired to Wilhelm," Ruth managed to say. "He'll have it tomorrow morning. And if they want more, I'll send it. Whatever they want."

Grace nodded, as if a nod were visible through the phone. She didn't know what to say.

"Please, please, promise me you'll get him back." Ruth's voice was barely above a whisper. "Promise me he'll come back to me. He has my heart."

Or maybe she said, "he *is* my heart." Between the British accent and the tears, Grace couldn't tell. There wasn't much difference anyway. Grace didn't answer.

She could see the door of room 219 through a crack in the fence. It had remained closed since Misty and Rachel were there.

She was desperate to know what was going on behind that faded orange curtain.

"I'm on my way," Ruth finally said. "I want to be there. I *have* to be there. I can't get a flight until morning, but I'll be there by three tomorrow afternoon."

Grace stood and brushed herself off. She didn't bother to tell Ruth not to come, that there was nothing she could do, or that by three tomorrow afternoon, it might be all over anyway.

Chapter 24 – 8.6

At six-thirty, Nick, William, and Anthony made a trip to the local home improvement store. They came back with rope, flashlights, and a bunch of odds and ends that didn't look like much of anything to Grace. Judging by their bags, they were preparing to hang a tire swing, not spring a man from captivity.

By seven-thirty, they were as ready as they were ever going to be. They'd gone over the plan a dozen times. In a round booth at Big's Java Hut, Grace, Nick, William, Anthony, and Sunshine had gone through every possible scenario. Shady and Little Frank opted to stay outside where they could watch the room in return for a western omelet and a double cheeseburger.

On the Formica table top, the syrup pitcher had served as Killian and the salt and pepper shakers were William and Anthony. Nick was a bottle of hot sauce and Grace was a container of half-and-half, while Sunshine was a packet of grape jelly. The two henchmen were squeeze bottles of ketchup and mustard. No one in the Java Hut paid the slightest bit of attention to them.

Meanwhile, at die Nacht, Rooster and Koenig had made their own preparations. Brett had to work at Vicious that night, but promised he would pick up Ruth from the airport the next afternoon. Rachel and Misty were on hand at die Nacht, taking turns playing the role of the Russian in the rehearsal. And when nine came, they would be dressed in their silver lamé halter tops and black satin hot pants, blending into the background in the best possible camouflage.

At seven-thirty, Rooster, Bill, and Larry went back to their rooms at New York, New York, mainly so they could be seen arriving at die Nacht closer to nine. They didn't want to appear too anxious.

At five minutes after nine, they were back, sauntering up to the VIP entrance as if this were any other night. Rooster even stopped to sign a few autographs for the people waiting in line. He was dressed in jeans, an old Lynyrd Skynyrd tee shirt and a heavy brown duster that hung to mid-calf, ending just a few inches before the heel of his weathered cowboy boots.

He wore no hat, and his light brown curls hung loose around his clean-shaven face. When the light hit him just right, he actually looked ruggedly handsome. One of the girls who got his autograph remarked breathlessly that he looked like an angel brought back from the Wild West.

Of course, the Russians saw all of this, as planned. Clark and his bald sidekick, who turned out to be more Stretch Armstrong than Pillsbury Doughboy, were waiting rather impatiently just inside the VIP entrance, having arrived at eight-fifty-five on the nose.

No sooner had Rooster stepped over the threshold than Rachel and Misty seemed to materialize from the shadows. Misty looped her arm through Rooster's, and Rachel made a little curtsy in front of the Russians. "Good evening, gentlemen," she said. "If you would be so kind as to follow us this way. Herr Koenig is expecting you."

Without acknowledging each other's presence, the two groups made their way down a narrow, semi-concealed hallway that ran the length of the club. Framed photos of celebrities enjoying themselves at die Nacht lined the wall. One was of Rooster, smiling broadly, his arm around a pretty brunette. He chuckled devilishly as he passed it. "That was Miss Arizona. Remember her?" he asked Bill and Larry. "That was a good night."

They trooped up a short flight of steps, and Rachel knocked on the plain wooden door at the top. Zoe, the pretty, young waitress with the long red hair, opened the door and stepped back for them to enter.

"Welcome. Please come in, gentlemen," Herr Koenig said warmly, rising from behind his desk and walking around to shake each one's hand in turn. He was dressed in a black suit, with a black shirt and sapphire blue tie. The faint spicy smell of cigars lingered in the room. A small round table was set with coffee and sparkling water for three. He moved toward it. "Now, as we discussed, if it's just going to be the three of us, I'll ask these lovely ladies to escort your associates to the VIP lounge until our business is concluded."

"Of course. Just one thing before they go." Clark nodded to his burly sidekick. With surprising speed, the big man stepped behind Rooster and attempted to frisk him. He had his hands around Rooster's waist when the singer yelled, an incoherent sound. He threw back his arms, knocking the sidekick off balance, then whirled around and centered the heel of his boot in the man's chest. Stretch fell back into the wall with a deflated thud, managing to stay on his feet only because the wall held him up. The next instant, Bill and Larry stepped in front of Rooster, blocking any chance at retaliation.

Rooster yelled at Clark, "What the hell is this? What the hell is this shit?"

"Vasiley was simply making sure you are not armed," Clark answered in a near bored tone. "For my protection, you understand."

"Well, you can tell that son of a bitch that if he tries to grab my junk again, he's gonna lose those hands. The last fairy who tried to give me the reach around walks with a permanent limp now."

Vasiley crouched low, scowling, clearly itching for a fight. He looked eager to take on all three of them. But a few words in Russian from his boss and he straightened up, chastened, hands falling to his sides.

"Don't take it so personally," Clark said. "It's simply a precaution."

"Oh, yeah?" Rooster's voice still vibrated with anger. "What about you, buddy? How do I know *you're* not carryin'?"

Clark smiled, the picture of calm. "Me? I don't *have* to carry. I have people for that." He motioned lazily toward Vasiley, who still glowered at Rooster, staring through Bill and Larry as if they were made of glass.

"I want him out of here," Rooster said. "Get that big, commie piece of shit outta here. Now!"

A few more words from Clark, and Vasiley turned on his heel toward the stairs. Rachel intercepted him, directing him instead to the tall, circular fireplace that served as the portal to the VIP lounge.

As the platform turned, Vasiley, flanked by Rachel and Zoe, never took his eyes off Rooster.

Koenig watched him go. "Be advised, I will tolerate no disturbance in my club. If your men are armed and the police are called for any reason, they *will* go to jail. I will not vouch for them. Do you understand?"

Rooster nodded.

"You'll have no trouble from my man," Clark said.

Misty crossed to stand in front of the now empty fireplace and smiled encouragingly at Bill and Larry.

Bill said, "You gonna be okay, Rooster?"

"Yeah, you guys go on." He patted the cell phone clipped to his belt. "I'll call if I need you."

Bill and Larry followed Misty onto the fireplace platform, and as it began to turn, they gave Clark one last menacing look. He ignored them. He chose a cigar from the humidor on Koenig's big mahogany desk, turned it over in his hands, inhaled its honeyed, nutty aroma. The entire incident was behind him now.

"So, I hear you are building a pyramid at your home. Do you plan to be buried there?" He snipped the ends of the cigar with Koenig's desktop guillotine cutter and popped it between his lips.

Rooster had been warned about Nick's little ad lib. "How'd you know that? That's not public knowledge."

"Our mutual friend, Mr. Howard, told me."

In the uneven silence that followed, Koenig gestured toward the round table again. "Please, gentlemen, do make yourselves comfortable."

Rooster moved a little closer, but it was clear neither man wanted to be the first to sit. "Got anything stronger than coffee?"

"But, of course, my friend." Koenig opened a pair of bat wing doors to the left of his desk. The light inside revealed a sparkling, well-stocked bar, lined, no doubt, with a selection even more extensive than the public bar out front. "What's your pleasure?"

"Jack Daniels on the rocks."

Koenig put two clear chunks of ice in a high ball glass, pulled a square bottle down from one of the shelves and poured a double shot. He handed the glass to Rooster, then said to the Russian, "Anything for you...ah? Forgive me; I understand the desire for anonymity, but surely there is a name we can call you, for convenience sake?"

"My friends call me Clark." He grinned at this as if he found it very amusing.

"Clark. Of course. Anything from the bar, Clark?"

"Still water for me, thank you. I like to keep my wits about me when transacting business."

Rooster ignored the jab by turning up his glass and downing the rest of his whiskey. "Ah! That hit the spot," he said. "Now let's have a look at that necklace."

That wiped the smirk right off Clark's face. He stepped out of the halo of cigar smoke that surrounded him and took the glass of water from Koenig's outstretched hand.

"Surely you didn't expect me to bring it with me?"

Rooster did his best to look shocked and offended, not difficult to carry over from the frisking incident. He looked from Clark to Koenig, then back again. "You're kidding, right? This is a joke?"

Clark's only response was to blow out another plume of smoke.

Rooster slammed his glass on the table. "What the hell kind of trick is this? You gonna try to sell me the Brooklyn Bridge next? You get me in here on good faith to spend God-knows-how-much money on something you don't even *have*? What am I doing here? Do I look like a punk to you? You're just wasting my time."

Now it was Clark's turn to be indignant. His face turned dark in an instant, His voice was full of disdain. "We are talking about the Amulet of Kavayet, not some dime store novelty. It's not something I carry around in my *pocket*. Or, perhaps you expected me to wear it around my neck. If you don't know what it looks like, then you are either an idiot or blind. You couldn't walk past a television in the last week without seeing it."

The two men glared at each other, their mutual distrust filling the room with menacing electricity.

Koenig cleared his throat. "If you will allow me, gentlemen, I'll be more than happy to present the terms as I understand them. Each of you are to interject as you see fit. Will that be acceptable?"

Both men nodded. Koenig motioned one more time toward the table and, finally, hesitantly, they took their seats.

Their host pulled a sheet of paper from a manila folder on his desk. On it was a color photo of the amulet, taken in its display case at the museum in Cairo. Something he had downloaded from the Internet, no doubt, but it was a clear, high quality photo and Clark became immediately reverent.

"This is the item in question, is it not?" Koenig asked.

"Yes," breathed Clark, reaching out to brush the photo with his fingertips.

Koenig continued from memory. "Discovered by the legendary team of Taylor and Ennis in 2006, the Amulet of Kavayet is largely considered the greatest single archaeological find in almost 100 years. Found in her burial chamber along with her mummy, the necklace – more precisely the markings on the necklace – prove irrefutably that Kavayet is the mother of King Tutankhamen. The identity of Tut's mother has heretofore been one of the ancient world's greatest topics of debate. And so, if for no other reason than that fact alone, this treasure is considered priceless." Koenig smiled at Clark then and added, "But, of course, every man has his price. Am I right?"

Clark remained stoic, ignoring the dig.

Koenig continued, "Now, I am given to understand that there is another buyer, someone who…commissioned the acquisition of the amulet. Is this person's offer still on the table?"

"Yes."

"Then perhaps it would be helpful if you gave us some sort of baseline price, a ball park figure, if you will, since we know Mr. Hathcock will have to best that offer. Also, in the interest of Mr. Hathcock, if you could tell us when he might expect to take delivery of the item…if terms are accepted, of course."

"I can have it to you day after tomorrow. And since I require cash payment, I assume it will take that long to put together this sum. If it takes any longer than that, the deal is off and I deliver to my first buyer."

Rooster nodded. "Agreed. How much?"

"One more thing. It goes without saying that if anyone ever finds out you're in possession of the amulet, the Egyptian government will not only take it back immediately, but you will certainly be prosecuted for numerous offenses, the least of which would be receiving stolen property."

"I'm not an idiot," Rooster said. "How much do you want?"

Clark laced his fingers behind his head and leaned back in his chair until it was on two legs. He looked up at the ceiling as if figuring the number in his head. "Well, I will certainly be alienating my original buyer and will have to leave the country for a while. Then there are all the people I must pay off..."

Rooster thought about tipping Clark's chair over and watching him flail. Instead, he said, "How much?"

"To make it worth my time and effort, I couldn't take a penny less than 8.6 US." He sounded like a used car salesman.

"Eight point six," Rooster repeated. He stared down at his empty glass, then pushed back from the table and crossed to the bar. He poured another double shot and brought the bottle back to the table. "I'll be honest. I don't think I can come up with that in forty-eight hours."

Clark exhaled loudly and brought his chair back to all four legs. Rooster wanted to laugh at how easy it had been to frustrate him. He knew Clark thought of him as a backwoods yokel with no credibility. He probably thought Rooster didn't have a pot to piss in, but had just wanted a peek at the necklace.

Rooster took a sip of his Jack and said, "I'm probably going to need more like seventy-two hours. Most of my liquid capital is offshore. A sum this large will raise a red flag if I don't go about it just right. I have to be careful. Give me until close of business on Wednesday. If you can do that, I'm in."

And that was it. No quibbling. No haggling. Not an eyebrow raised about 8.6 million dollars. But Rooster could see the change in the Russian's eyes. A couple of quick blinks while he thought of how much extra money he was about to make, then a soft, unfocused look, followed by rapid pupil dilation. Then there was the smile Clark fought to suppress when he thought he was pulling a fast one on this long-haired country boy.

"Seventy-two hours. That's acceptable."

"And Mr. Koenig here should get something for his trouble. Say… ten grand?"

"But, of course."

"And you'll pay that?"

The smile never left Clark's face as he nodded in agreement.

"That's kind of you," Koenig said, "and very much appreciated. Of course, you are welcome to make the exchange here if you like."

They agreed to the same time, same place on Wednesday night, two of the three men knowing it would never happen.

Rooster saw Clark eyeing his cowboy boots and saw the elitist sneer return to his face. "You must be quite the Egytophile, Mr. Hathcock. A lover of all things ancient. And yet, you barely spared a glance for the photo of the amulet."

"Like you said, I know what it looks like."

"Of course. But you never changed expression when Mr. Koenig spoke of the Taylor and Ennis find. I suppose I am used to seeing more enthusiasm from collectors."

Rooster said nothing, just returned Clark's stare.

"If you don't mind me asking, Mr. Hathcock, I'm terribly interested in this pyramid of yours. Tell me, are you going with Ionic or Corinthian for the structure?"

Rooster's brow furrowed. He looked confused and Clark smiled.

"The structure? Well, I suppose I could do something out front, maybe sort of a gateway." Rooster laid the southern drawl on thick. "But certainly nothin' Greek. I might get away with Doric, but definitely not Ionic or Corinthian. And it sure wouldn't be structural. If I'm puttin' columns inside a pyramid, then I'm doin' somethin' wrong; a good 51.8 degree angle doesn't need any support. Why, you oughtta know that, Clark." Rooster chuckled to himself. Who did this guy take him for? Rooster Hathcock's mama didn't raise no fool. He could Google as well as the next guy. "And if I didn't look excited when Mr. Koenig mentioned Taylor and Ennis, it's probably because he said the find was in 2006 and that's not entirely true. It was actually 2005. It just wasn't authenticated until 2006. I guess that kinda threw me off."

He downed the rest of his whiskey and stood. "Well, it's been real, gentlemen, but I gotta scoot. I got places to go, people to see, women to woo. Plus, I gotta go call my accountant. I hope I wake his ass up," he grinned impishly. "Well, see you folks in…" he looked down at his watch "about seventy-one hours."

Koenig followed him to the fireplace and shook his hand before pressing the button that would send him into the VIP section.

Rooster could hear the bass from the club thumping louder as the platform turned. It took his eyes a few seconds to adjust to the dark interior and the flashing lights that shone down on the dance floor. A foggy mist encircled his ankles. He looked up. Misty stood in front of him, smiling. "How did you...?" he began, but she pointed to a glint of silver in her ear. A tiny receiver, no doubt.

"I've been listening the whole time," she said.

His face broke into a wolfish grin and he put his arm around her shoulders as they walked toward one of the grottoes. "You ever been to Mississippi?"

She shook her head.

"Hmm... I think you might like it there. I'm thinkin' about buildin' me a pyramid..."

Kelly Adamson

Chapter 25 – Monkey Wrench

Grace kept her mouth shut tight to keep her teeth from chattering. She finally remembered why she hadn't liked *Headcase*, why it didn't spring to mind when Killian yelled the words in the parking lot. She'd seen every movie he had ever made, but in *Headcase*, Killian's character dies at the end, double-crossed by his own man, shot in the back of the head.

She didn't bother to pass this information on to Nick. It wouldn't change his mind and she didn't want him to know how scared she was. He was counting on her. After all, it was Nick who would be in danger, not her. Both William and Anthony had volunteered to go instead, and she tried hard to talk him into letting them, but Nick said it wasn't their place, not their responsibility. Even though she hated to admit it, he was right. William, Anthony and the others could all walk away right now and suffer no consequences. They could forget they'd ever met this unlucky couple from Alabama. They could wash their hands of the whole mess. Only Nick and Grace seemed to have no way out. She decided the others were all a bunch of adrenalin junkies. Why else would they agree to this?

She wondered for the hundredth time if they would have been better off calling the police or the FBI or whoever and high-tailing it home.

All she could do now was keep her mouth shut, smile and nod at all the appropriate spots in the conversation, just try to look stalwart and encouraging, instead of meek and fragile, like she felt. She tried to listen, to pay attention, but she'd heard it all at least a dozen times in the last few hours. Her mind kept wandering, unbidden, to crazy things like their dogs back home and how much they would miss Nick if something happened to him. He was their alpha. Grace could see them wandering around the house, listening for the sound of his truck in the driveway. She shook herself out of this morbid thought. No more of this. She had a job to do. She was a lookout. She took the phone out of her pocket and checked it again. Battery fully charged and four bars of reception. Check.

They'd pulled back into their now familiar spot behind the worn fence at the Pleasure Palace Inn, headlights off, and waited for nine p.m. It was finally dark. William's Cherokee was half hidden by a stack of empty cardboard boxes and packing crates near the dumpster. Nick steered the rental car behind the fence, rolling the length of the old motel under cover of darkness. He cut the engine. William and Anthony joined them, squeezing into the backseat of the little Subaru. William had to lean forward to keep from hitting his head on the ceiling.

"Where's your gear?"

At Grace's feet was a coil of white nylon rope, a small LED flashlight, a pair of pliers and a screwdriver. It seemed like a pathetic excuse for gear.

They sat in silence until the alarm on Anthony's phone beeped. It was nine p.m. Less than a mile away, Rooster Hathcock would be meeting with the Russian boss, known to them only as Clark, and arranging to buy priceless stolen artifacts, the kind of thing that could land a person in federal prison.

Their foursome's goal, during this guaranteed hour of diversion, was to slip into room 219 by way of the roof, get Killian's attention without drawing the attention of his two captors, get him to come into the bathroom alone and climb silently up into the crawlspace, following Nick to safety. Piece of cake, right?

The closer it got to nine o'clock, the more ridiculous the plan sounded. But Grace smiled as she kissed her husband goodbye and wished him luck. It was too late to back out now. Besides, it wasn't as if she had a better idea.

He pocketed the tools and flashlight and threw the coil of rope over his shoulder.

Anthony used bolt cutters on the metal clamps that held the fence to the posts. He took out the lowest three on one post and pulled the chain link up from the ground. Nick slipped under. William followed him, then held the fence on the other side for Anthony.

Then it was just Grace, straining to see the men in the darkened lot. One block behind her, airplanes took off and landed at McCarran. One block in front of her, the cars and taxi cabs rumbled up the Strip as Las Vegas began to wake up, everyone looking forward to what they just knew would be their lucky night. But here, the quiet seemed oppressive. Grace could hear her own heart beat. Her jaws hurt from clenching her teeth. She slipped back into the car, locked the doors and positioned herself where she could see through a crack in the fence. She took the phone out of her pocket and checked it again. Then she waited.

The three men walked across the narrow parking lot, avoiding the few weak patches of light cast by the ancient security lamps. They crouched behind a car parked illegally at the very end of the building. Nick looked up, following the line of the cast iron drain pipe he was about to climb. From a distance, the old, two-story building seemed small, especially in comparison to the mega-monsters just a few blocks away. But up close like this, it was more than a little daunting.

He took a couple of deep breaths. This was nothing. He could do this. He climbed on top of houses all the time, although usually via a ladder, and usually at the property owner's request. Never mind. This was just another day at work. Just another day at work.

Anthony lay on his back, partially concealed by the car. He pulled a suppressed .22 caliber pistol out of his pocket and took aim at the security light that illuminated this end of the motel. With a pop and a spray of glass, the light went out. Comforting darkness washed over them.

William walked casually around the corner of the building. He scanned the lot, then looked at his watch as if he were waiting for a ride. He sauntered back to the corner and bent down to tie his shoe, their pre-determined all-clear signal.

With one last look over his shoulder, Nick stood and grabbed the metal pipe. He pulled on it to make sure it was secured firmly to the wall. With a leg up from the trunk of the old car, he began pulling himself up the wall like Spiderman. Hand over hand, knuckles white from the strain. The rubber soles of his sneakers gripped the sides of the pole and his knees were jammed against the wall as he worked himself upward. He was careful to keep his eyes on his hands and not on the pavement below.

At the top, he grasped the roof's edge. Something sharp cut into the palm of his left hand. He swore under his breath. He swung his leg over the edge of the roof and pulled himself up, breathing hard. The three-foot-high parapet that surrounded the old motel offered cover as he landed on the graveled roof with a crunch.

A trickle of blood ran down the side of his hand. Not too bad. He wiped it on his pants and pulled the slim flashlight from his pocket. It was too dark to see the entire length of the roof, but the shadows made it look like a barren, sci-fi landscape. Directly ahead, in front of the first low fire wall, were two of the large metal turbines he was looking for.

He scrambled to the rear edge of the roof and peeked over. The top of the Subaru shone dimly in the moonlight. He took out his phone and pressed redial. Grace answered immediately, breathlessly.

"Right or left?" he turned the display of the phone outward for a second, shining its light toward the car.

"Right," Grace said, "my right, about six feet."

He edged over six feet and flashed the phone again.

"Perfect. You're right on top of their window. The bathroom should be right behind you."

"All right, thanks."

Before he could hang up, she called him back. "Hey!"

"Yeah?"

"I love you," she whispered, trying to keep the fear out of her voice.

He smiled in the dark and whispered back, "I love you too."

They'd estimated one turbine for every eight rooms, but this looked more like one for every six rooms. Better odds than he'd hoped. Nick stared at a spot directly across the roof from where he stood. He walked toward it in a straight line, stopping at the nearest point to the turbine. He did a direct left-face, then counted the steps, heel to toe, to the plate that held the galvanized turbine to the roof. Twenty-three steps.

Nick opened the door of the service disconnect box and switched off the breaker. The fan underneath slowed. He pulled out the wrench and knelt to remove the four bolts that ran up through the plate. Not an easy task. God only knew when these things had been installed, meaning God only knew how many Nevada summers they'd baked on this roof. He rammed the tip of the screwdriver against the base of the stubborn bolts and gave them a few solid taps with the edge of the pliers. It took every ounce of his strength before he felt them slowly begin to give.

With the bolts finally off, Nick slammed his heel against the base of the turbine to loosen it, holding the cage to keep it from rattling. He worked it free and set it aside. The beam of the flashlight reflected off the now silent fan blades. He removed four more bolts and lifted the fan out of the vent pipe.

The opening looked to be about eighteen inches in diameter. He had been hoping these turbines weren't hooked up to ductwork and he was right. Thank goodness for shoddy workmanship. Three feet, straight down, his light reflected off a series of two-inch metal pipes, stretched out side by side to form a flat surface, a kind of balance beam that ran the length of the building. They carried every wire in the place and would serve as his bridge to room 219.

He pocketed his tools and held the little flashlight between his teeth. If he jumped down and missed the landing, he'd go right through someone's ceiling. He lowered himself through the hole until he felt his toes touch the pipes, then his knees. It was a tight squeeze. When his fingers reached the metal, he let his knees slide off the sides, careful to keep the toes of his shoes up on the pipe behind him. Inch by inch he slid back until his head and shoulders were free of the pipe. On his belly on the pipes, he turned his head, fanning the light beam. It took a second to remember which direction he was supposed to be heading.

One...two...three...he crawled forward like an inchworm, silently counting off the twenty-three steps. His size ten Chuck Taylors were exactly a foot long, which made for exact measurement on the roof. But that wasn't a lot of help now, as he slid along on his belly, guessing a foot at a time.

At the count of twenty-one, some of the pipes branched off to the left and the right. He pointed the flashlight to his right, scanning the beams, the pipes, the insulation.

He could see the tops of the interior walls and the checkerboard pattern of the drop ceiling. Within an eight foot by ten foot square formed by the interior walls, he spotted a tile with a dark hole in the center. The bathroom vent. So far, so good.

He slid closer and positioned himself where he would be able to see back out into the room. If Killian was in the same place where Misty and Rachel had seen him, he'd be easily visible.

He put his ear to the vent and listened. Nothing. He used the screwdriver to pry up an edge of one of the yellowed ceiling tiles, just an inch, just enough to make sure the room was really vacant.

Lying flat on the pipes, he raised the tile a little more. The chair sat in front of the sink just as Misty and Rachel said it would be. It was there, but it was empty.

He released the breath he didn't know he'd been holding. Plan, meet monkey wrench.

Nick could see the reflection of the farthest bed in the plate glass mirror behind the sink. Two huge feet, definitely not Killian's, hung off the end. He held his breath and listened. The big man was snoring. No. *Two* men snoring. But which two?

He slid onto the top of the wall that separated the two rooms, fighting to keep his balance. Slowly, quietly, he lifted a corner of the nearest tile with the screwdriver. Both of Killian's guards were sacked out, one on each bed, sawing logs like they were building a house. On the television, in greenish black and white, Herman Munster had managed to get himself trapped inside an Egyptian sarcophagus in a museum.

Killian was nowhere. Nick could see every bit of floor space from his perch. There was no closet, no cabinet where they could have stashed him. The only place he could possibly be was under one of the beds, but that seemed highly unlikely.

Listening to Herman Munster call for help, Nick clung to the top of the wall, trying to figure out what he should do next. None of the rescue scenarios they had practiced involved being unable to locate the kidnapped party. It was hot and stuffy. Nick realized he was sweating for the first time since arriving in the desert.

There was nothing to do but retreat. He'd have to crawl back out empty-handed, the same way he crawled in. He lowered the tile in place and pushed himself backward along the top of the wall.

One foot was caught. His shoelace was hung up on something he couldn't see. He twisted around to reach it. He felt something shift. He'd slid the screwdriver back in the pocket of his jeans, but obviously not well enough. In what felt like slow motion, it slipped back out again. He watched helplessly as it fell, hit the aluminum metal grid that held the drop ceiling with a clatter, then landed with a heavy thud on one of the tiles.

It was impossible to hear if the two men were still snoring. He grabbed the screwdriver and used it to unhook his shoestring from the piece of jagged sheetrock that had caused the problem.

He moved into high gear.

He slid back onto the pipes and made short work of the twenty-one steps back to fresh air and freedom. He pulled himself up through the narrow vent pipe and quickly replaced the fan and turbine. He made it about five steps away before the urge to put the bolts back on made him stop. He put each one on finger tight, cursing a conscience that wouldn't let him leave something broken, and flipped the breaker back on.

At the edge of the roof, he sat in the gravel, back against the wall, and caught his breath. He pulled out his cell phone to call William. It was vibrating in his hand. No, it wasn't the phone. It was his arms, shaking from the strain of holding onto the balance beam of pipes. Those same arms were about to have to lower him off this roof, so they may as well get over it, he told himself.

He pressed the button for William's cell.

"Is it clear?"

William hesitated. Nick heard a car rumble by beneath him. "Clear," William said.

Nick grabbed the nylon rope and peeked over the top of the wall. The drainpipe was secured to the side of the building with wide metal bands, sturdy enough to take his weight, but if he looped the rope around the pipe, he wasn't sure if it would slide well enough across the edges of the metal bands. Leaving the rope to dangle off the side of the building wasn't an option, so he had little choice. He fed the rope behind the drain pipe just above the highest clamp and tied a quick bowline knot at one end, pulled it tight and prayed it would hold in the nylon. The other end fell down the wall and stopped six feet off the ground. He wrapped the end of the rope around his left hand and wedged his right foot into the loop at the other end.

Nick sat on the edge of the parapet, legs dangling over the parking lot. Anthony, almost thirty feet below, looked up at him. A fall from this height would probably cost two broken legs. He took up the slack in the rope, wedged his foot against the side of the drainpipe and slid over the edge.

He walked down the wall with one foot while the other stayed rigid in the loop. The rope snagged more than once on the metal clamp, but he was able to pull it loose, reaching the ground faster than he would have thought possible. He gave one quick tug on the looped end of the rope, and it whizzed around the pipe and fell back to the ground with a soft slap.

William came back around the corner to gather up the rope. "Where's Killian?"

"I wish to hell I knew," Nick hissed. He was breathing heavy from the strain of lowering himself off the roof. He looked down at his shaking hands. The left one was bleeding in a steady stream, thanks to the rope. He stuck it in his pocket so Grace wouldn't see.

The three men made their way back across the darkened parking lot and under the chain link fence. Grace was waiting for them. Nick didn't give her a chance to speak, just said, "He wasn't there. I looked all over the room. He wasn't there. The two guards were there, dead asleep. The chair was in front of the mirror, just like the girls said, but it was empty. He's gone."

Grace shook her head. "That can't be. Someone's been watching this place ever since Misty and Rachel saw him. No one has gone through that door."

The four of them stood behind mountains of packing crates, stunned, speechless. What the hell could they do now?

"Oh, my God," Grace muttered.

Nick's head snapped up. "What?"

"It's so simple. So perfect."

"What?"

"While you were hanging from the ceiling, did you happen to see a second door, you know, one you could open between adjoining rooms?"

"I don't know. Yeah, I guess so. Yeah."

Grace flipped open her phone and scrolled to Shady's number. She had acquired a lot of new numbers this weekend. After a quick recap, she said, "Shady, did the woman with the big hat and the high heels leave her room while you were watching today? The lady in the room next door to Killian?"

Without a moment's hesitation, Shady said, "Yep, she left while you guys were at Big's Java Hut. I remember 'cause she had on blue jeans and sneakers this time. Real casual like. I thought it was a funny thing to wear for a workin' girl, not sexy at all. Couple of guys came to pick her up. They helped her with her suitcase."

Grace groaned and squeezed her eyes shut. "She took her suitcase with her? The big Pullman?"

"Yep, and you know she must be pretty strong for a woman, because she didn't have nearly the struggle with it bringin' it in all by herself as those two guys had takin' it out." Shady chuckled. "I guess you can't judge a book by its cover, huh?"

Grace felt sick all the way to her toes. Killian was gone. They'd taken him right out from under their noses. Where was he now? Was he still alive? It seemed like it would be a lot easier to stuff a dead body into a suitcase than a live, struggling one. She sat down on one of the empty crates and put her head in her hands. This was going to be a long night.

Chapter 26 – The Courier

Over the sound of her own rapid heartbeat and shallow breathing, Grace heard Nick answer his cell phone. She wanted to yell at him, "Why are you answering your phone at a time like this?" It hadn't occurred to her that the caller might be Misty, relaying news of the meeting at die Nacht, or Rooster's acting debut, as she called it.

Nick put her on speaker phone, and they all huddled together behind the empty crates to listen. They could hear Rooster in the background, full of piss and vinegar, reminding her to tell them this bit or that. Misty passed the phone to him. "Tell them yourself, Bogart," she said with a laugh.

"Hot damn!" Rooster yelled into the phone. "That was more fun than humpin' a Playboy Bunny on a pile of cash!" He was still wound up from the adrenalin, and it took him a minute to calm down enough to tell the story. Finally, they were able to grasp that he had agreed to buy the necklace from Clark for 8.6 million dollars. The only one who didn't seem stunned by that exorbitant amount was William, who, thanks to his job at The Isis, was not unfamiliar with Egyptian artifacts and the ridiculous sums of money they could fetch.

"He only gave me seventy-two hours to get the cash," Rooster said, "but I know that part didn't matter none. I knew you'd have Killian back any minute, and then you'd set the cops on their asses."

No one spoke.

"Hey!" Rooster called. "You still there?"

"Yeah," Nick said. "We're still here. Just a little screwed, that's all." He told Rooster what happened, that Killian was missing from room 219, and that their best and only guess was that the sexy woman next door had spirited him away in a suitcase.

"You gotta be shittin' me," said Rooster.

"I wish I was, man," Nick said. "So, now we don't know where he is or what to do next. Clark's going to want the necklace back tomorrow. We won't be able to stall him anymore. I think we're going to have to turn it over to the law after all. Poor Killian. The Russian swore they'd kill him if they got a whiff of the cops. He'll be lucky if he makes it out of this alive."

Everyone was quiet while that reality sank in. Then Nick cleared his throat and continued. "But, hey, man, I can't tell you how much we appreciate what you've done for us. You really stuck your neck out when you didn't have to. I wish there was something I could do to repay you."

"Well, there is one thing," Rooster said in his slow Southern drawl. "You got 8.6 million bucks on you?"

That almost got a grin from Nick, until he heard his call waiting beep. "I gotta take this. I think it's Clark."

It was, and his voice was seething with a fiery rage that made everyone in the circle shift from one foot to the other uneasily. He began with a string of obscenities, many of which were in Russian, most of them incomprehensible. Clark spoke spotless English, and the fact that he was angry enough to revert to his native tongue was unnerving, to say the least.

They let him vent, not even attempting to interrupt. When at last he seemed to run out of furious epithets, regardless of the language, they could hear him breathing heavily into the phone, waiting for a response.

Calmly, Nick replied, "I could be mistaken, Clark, but I sense you may be unhappy about something. Am I right?"

"You're a very funny man, Mr. Howard." Clark spat the words out. "A real comedian. Well, let's see how funny you think this is. I want my necklace back, and I want it tonight."

"Well…"

"Shut up!" Clark shouted so loud his voice was distorted over the phone's little speaker. "When my boss saw your little band of misfits staking out the motel…" He broke off, too angry to finish. "Let's just say you made me look like an incompetent amateur in the eyes of my superior. And that will not happen again. I assure you."

Grace closed her eyes. She'd been wrong when she thought this day couldn't get any worse. Incredibly wrong.

"I want my necklace delivered to the corner of Swenson and Mesa at exactly eleven p.m. I don't want any excuses. I don't want any delays. If I don't have my necklace by eleven-fifteen, or if I even *think* I see anything untoward, your friend will be dead before midnight. Oh, and one more thing, your lovely wife will be the courier. She will come alone, and when she arrives, she will get out of the car and stand in front of it, keeping both hands visible."

"No," Nick said, talking over him. "I'll bring it, not her. Keep her out of this."

"That's not for you to say, now is it?" Clark said cloyingly. "We could have done this the easy way, Mr. Howard, like gentlemen, but you abused my good nature. You took me for a fool and now I don't trust you."

"There's got to be some other way…"

"Oh, there are plenty of other ways. But this is the one I choose. Eleven o'clock, and not a moment later. Oh, and tell her to wear the necklace. I want to see how it looks on her. I'll bet it's stunning." Clark hung up, leaving them all staring at "Call Ended, 10:04 p.m." on the phone's display.

When the screen went black, it seemed to spur Nick into action. He dialed quickly. "Las Vegas," he said and after a pause, "Yes, can I have the number for the FBI office in Las Vegas?"

In a flash, the phone was lifted from his hand. William shook his head as he ended the call. "I'm sorry, but I can't let you do that, Nick."

Grace felt her pulse quicken, making her a little light-headed, considering it had almost stopped a few moments before.

"Oh, you shouldn't have done that," Nick said, his tone full of menace. He took a step forward as William, a good five inches taller, backed up, his hands in the air.

"Look, just hear me out," he said. "I'm on your side. You gotta believe me. Just give me five minutes to explain."

"Give me back my phone."

William held out the phone. Nick snatched it from his hand.

"You have two minutes to explain. And it had better be good."

William glanced at Anthony, whose expression hadn't changed throughout the whole conversation, then back to Nick. He said, "All right, but it might be easier if I show you." Slowly, as if he were trying not to make any sudden moves, he unbuttoned his shirt pocket and pulled out a thin leather wallet. Only, it wasn't a wallet. He opened it and offered it to Nick. On one side was a bronze metal shield with an eagle across the top, and on the other side was a passport sized photo of William, grim and unsmiling, along with information that proclaimed him to be an agent of the Federal Bureau of Investigation.

Nick and Grace stared at it, then at William. Anthony held up a similar badge. "You, too?" asked Grace in a small voice. Anthony nodded.

"Look, I'm sorry," William said. "Part of me wanted to tell you right from the beginning. But you were so adamant about not wanting the law involved. I figured you would have bolted right off if you knew. I needed your full cooperation."

He was right, thought Grace. They would have bolted. They *should* have bolted.

"We've been working this case for months. I had to do what I had to do to make you guys trust me. This was a huge break for us. I couldn't lose it. And, of course, the fewer people know about us, the less chance our covers would be blown."

Nick looked unconvinced.

"Besides, if we were *with* you, we could protect you."

"Yeah? With what?" Nick said. "Those .22's against the Krasnyee Coalition? Why don't you just tickle them to death?"

William managed a sheepish grin. "Well, that's not all we've got."

Anthony chuckled, a deep wolfish sound. "Not by a long shot."

"You wanna see?" William inclined his head toward the old Jeep Cherokee.

Grace knew that no matter how angry Nick was at being deceived, he would never pass up a chance to see the arsenal of two FBI agents.

William lifted the rear door to reveal nothing but stained beige carpet. It all looked painfully ordinary until he threw back the carpet. Underneath was a specially built framework that concealed a treasure trove of weapons. Two H-S Precision sniper rifles, complete with bipods and scopes, six clear plastic boxes of ammunition, an AR-15, a shotgun, a dozen flashbang stun grenades, riot cuffs, Tasers, Kevlar vests, and even two pairs of night vision goggles.

Nick stepped closer, his eyes wide like a kid in a candy store, his anger at William quickly dissolving. "Holy shit," he mumbled.

Grace, not nearly as awed by the firepower, looked uncertain. "There's something I don't get," she said. "The necklace arrived in Las Vegas the same time we did. So, how could you have been working the case for months?"

William smiled broadly, as if he were a teacher and she were his prize pupil. "Good question. The fact is, the crime originated here, a case of demand dictating supply. Remember I told you about the owner of The Isis, Neil Clifton, and what a glutton he is for anything from Ancient Egypt? What I neglected to mention is how filthy stinking rich he is from all of his hotels and casinos. With money like that, you can buy pretty much anything you want. And what he wanted more than anything was the Amulet of Kavayet. A couple of months ago, we received a tip that he was actually putting out feelers among the international art thief crowd, trying to see if he could find someone to steal it for him. It didn't take long to find someone greedy enough to bite. Although I have to admit we were all a little surprised to find out it was the Krasnyee Coalition."

"Wait a minute," Grace said. "You knew ahead of time that they were going to steal the necklace? You could have prevented all this? Why didn't you just stop them?"

William shrugged. "Easier said than done. After all, we didn't know any of the specifics, plus the museum's curator was convinced that his security systems couldn't be breached. He just refused to believe it could happen. And anyway," he continued a little apologetically, "I guess this is turning out to be a blessing in disguise. Instead of just taking down Clifton, we'll be taking down some major Coalition players. The guy who calls himself Clark is actually Pavel Alkaev, the second in command since their founder, Kuznetsov, disappeared a few years ago, and quite possibly the only person alive who knows the whereabouts of their current leader, Alexander Volkov. If we can bring them down...well, it's impossible to know how many lives we'll have saved."

For a minute, no one spoke. Somewhere in the distance a car alarm was going off unheeded. Nick said, "Well, all I can say is I'm glad I can officially wash my hands of the whole thing. I'll get you the necklace. You can take over from here. We're getting the hell out of Vegas as soon as possible."

Grace nodded, feeling relieved, if a little guilty.

William shook his head. In a tone that left no room for argument, he said, "You know you can't do that."

Nick pulled himself up to his full height and sucked in a breath through clenched teeth. "Grace isn't going to meet him. She is *not* going to be a pawn in this. I won't allow it."

William didn't answer, but the tired, sympathetic look on his face told Grace one thing for certain: She was definitely going.

She stepped in front of Nick. His fists were clenched at his side. She took one of his hands in hers and brought it up to her lips. Dried blood crusted his fingers. He pulled his hand away and stuck it in his pocket. She looked into his eyes, and hesitated. He looked ten years older than he had when they left Alabama. He had dark circles under his eyes and thin lines she had never noticed in his forehead. She reached for his other hand and brought it to her lips. He didn't stop her.

"You know I love you more than anything," she said, so quietly only he could hear her, "but you know I have to do this. I'll never forgive myself if I don't. And I could really use your support. Besides," she added, raising her voice so the others could hear, "my good friends, the FBI agents, will have my back. Protect and Serve, right guys?"

"Actually, that's the police," said William. "The FBI's motto is Fidelity, Bravery, and Integrity."

Grace shrugged. "Eh. Tomayto, tomahto. The point is you will protect me with your lives, right guys?"

"We'll do everything humanly possible," William said, "and then some."

Anthony nodded. "You have our word."

Grace felt a knot in her stomach as she looked into her husband's bloodshot eyes. Helpless was not a position he was used

Kelly Adamson

to playing. "Are you sure you want to do this?" he asked in a strained voice. Grace nodded. He blew out a deep breath, defeated and exhausted. He kissed her on the forehead and walked over to the Subaru. He reached into the glove compartment and pulled out a small plastic bag with the Isis logo on it. Inside this unassuming little bag was the Amulet of Kavayet.

William inhaled sharply when he saw it. "Don't tell me you had it in your car all this time. You were just driving it around?"

Nick shrugged. "What did you expect me to do with it, leave it in the room safe? You know they've probably checked that every day."

Grace lifted the hair off her neck and Nick fastened the clasp of the necklace. It felt cool and smooth against her skin.

No one knew why Kavayet had lived in anonymity, far removed from the palaces and riches that should have been hers, but Grace got the feeling she understood. Maybe Kavayet hid on purpose, to protect her unborn pharaoh son, the person she loved more than anything, the person who, despite her best efforts, only lived to rule for a few short years.

When Grace turned to face William and Anthony, her voice didn't waver. "I'm ready."

William, Nick and Grace piled into the Cherokee and made the short drive past the UNLV campus. With Anthony following in the Subaru, they circled around on Juniper, and parked behind yet another dumpster. It was the Las Vegas dumpster tour, Grace thought, and almost laughed out loud with a burst of nervous energy. This dumpster was behind a KFC a block away from the empty convenience store. The boarded-up windows sported spray painted gang symbols that meant nothing to ninety-nine percent of the people who saw them on a daily basis. But to the other one percent, they meant unity and ownership of territory. Luckily, for now, it was completely deserted. The gang members would do well to stay away tonight.

On the drive over, William had confirmed Grace's fears. Yes, Clark would make her get in the car with him. And, yes, she would have to go. He wanted a second hostage, but more than that, he wanted to remind everyone involved that he was in charge. Of course, William assured her that Clark had his facts woefully wrong. The FBI was indeed in charge. He promised her they would follow wherever Clark took her. "We'll be right behind you, even though you won't be able to see us. And don't worry; she may not look like much, but this Jeep has a supercharged 350 and she can go zero to sixty in six seconds."

He seemed very sure of himself. Grace tried to convince herself, but her mouth was dry and her palms were wet. She smiled anyway, pleased that at least she wasn't shaking.

"They'll lead us to wherever they're keeping Killian, and while they're all in one place, we'll make our move."

"How do you know they're going to take her to the same place they have Killian?" Nick asked through gritted teeth. He had been silent until then, as motionless as a statue in the back seat.

"They won't split up hostages; that's poor personnel management."

"Yeah, Nick," Grace tried to sound light-hearted. "That's Spy 101 stuff. You must not have paid attention in class." She was trying to coax a smile out of him, but when she looked at his face, so pale and strained, it looked like he'd forgotten how.

William told her not to argue, not to fight, and by all means to stay calm. "If you lose your cool, you'll just give him the upper hand. If you're panicked, you're not focused and if you're not focused, you're d..." He stopped, but they all knew he was going to say "dead."

Nick pulled the drawstring bag from around his neck and slipped it over Grace's head. It hung almost to her waist. She opened her mouth to protest, but he put a finger to her lips. He shook his head. He didn't say a word. She knew he couldn't.

She traded places with Anthony, who had parked in the shadows a few yards away. "Don't worry," he said. He handed her the keys. "We've got you."

Grace didn't look back as she drove down the alleyway and onto Swenson Street. She wound her way through the empty practice fields and in a few minutes was back at the vacant lot in front of the old convenience store. She cut the engine, relieved to find she couldn't see the Jeep from this vantage point.

The second hand on her watch worked its way slowly around to eleven o'clock. She took a deep breath and stepped out of the car.

She took a good look at her surroundings for the first time. This neighborhood was pretty depressed to be only a stone's throw from the excess of the Strip. The convenience store wasn't the only abandoned building. Across the street, a coin laundry stood silent and dark, no washers or dryers visible through its grimy windows. A gas station had been next door, but the pumps had been removed and capped and the canopy sagged sadly. A faded sign next to that read

Ace Aquarium Supply, but the lot below it was empty. Even the building was gone.

Lights appeared from the east. A black Chevy Tahoe with a dented fender rumbled up the street. It pulled slowly into the lot, right beside Grace. She forced herself to stand up straight, head high. The tinted window of the passenger door rolled down with a mechanical whir. Clark, hands on the wheel, stared at her across an empty seat. His cold eyes glittered, locked greedily on the amulet that hung around her neck. He smiled, which somehow seemed even more frightening, and said, "Get in."

She wanted to say no. She wanted to throw the necklace through the open window at him and run, but she remembered what William had said – don't argue; don't fight; stay calm. She got in.

Stretch Armstrong was in the back seat. She avoided looking directly at him; she didn't think she could handle his leer just now. She hated the thought that he was behind her, watching her, but she felt safer in the front seat than back there with him.

"I'm delighted you could join us, my dear," Clark said, pulling the Chevy immediately back onto the road. He wasn't about to linger. "And I'm glad your husband came to his senses and decided not to try and play the hero. The graveyards of the world are full of heroes, after all. Who needs another?"

She didn't respond, just stared straight ahead, anxious to get this over with.

Clark wheeled the big car around and headed south toward the airport tunnel.

"Show me your cell phone."

Grace shifted in her seat, slipped the phone out of her pocket and held it up. The window was still down, air rushing in, whipping her hair across her face.

"Throw it out."

Grace said nothing, just sat perfectly still until he repeated himself, this time with more force. "Are you deaf? I said throw it out."

She tossed the little phone out the window and watched the night swallow it up. It felt like she was being swallowed up too.

Clark chuckled, rolled up the window, and turned on the radio. It was tuned to a '50's station and he started singing along to "Peggy Sue."

They headed east on 215. The car wound through Henderson, past Paradise Hills and on towards Boulder City. She wondered vaguely if he was planning to throw her off the Hoover Dam, but decided it was probably too heavily monitored.

She stared out the window unseeing while Clark butchered "North to Alaska" and "My Boyfriend's Back." She'd heard of using music as a weapon before, but thought it was supposed to be speed metal or something. It turned out doo wop worked just as effectively if the right person was singing it.

They exited the freeway before Boulder City and followed a smaller highway for a mile or so, then took a right onto a pockmarked two-lane. "Earth Angel" played on the radio. A few miles south, they took another right, this time onto an unmarked dirt road. They hadn't seen another car since leaving the highway. Grace figured this was what was meant by "the back of beyond."

Their headlights showed nothing but more sand stretching out in front of them, with the exception of an occasional scrubby bush, mesquite or creosote or whatever the hell they were. Grace didn't know or care. She was sick of the desert. She missed pine trees and dogwoods and grass.

The dust cloud they were stirring up was visible in the side mirror, illuminated by their tail lights. But nothing else. No buildings, no signs, no headlights as far as Grace could see. She hoped William hadn't taken a wrong turn, followed the wrong person by mistake. Maybe she was on her own now with two crazy men in the desert. She squirmed in her seat and wondered how much farther they had to drive.

Clark slowed the Tahoe and eased it off the road. There was no shoulder, just a faint edge to the beaten path. He turned off the engine and headlights. For a moment, the darkness and the silence threatened to engulf her. Then Grace took a breath, and then another. *Don't argue. Don't fight. Stay calm.*

"What are we doing here? Why are we stopping?" she said.

"I have to take care of a little business here," Clark said. To Stretch he said, "Bring the shovel, Vasiley." He didn't even bother to say it in Russian.

The air seized in Grace's lungs. Of course. It was so clear now. They'd never planned to make a trade with her. Their plan was to drive her into the desert, take the necklace and dispose of her body. Maybe Killian was out here, too, somewhere. Of course, he was already dead.

She scrabbled for the door handle and threw it open. Running blindly through the darkened desert had to be better than getting buried in it. If she could evade them long enough, maybe Nick and William would find her first. They couldn't be that far behind.

But before she could launch herself from the car, there was a menacing crackle, an electrical spark by her left ear. The pain was instant and extreme. Her neck was on fire, like someone had thrown boiling water on her. She tried to reach up, to brush it away, but her arms wouldn't work. None of her muscles worked. She crumpled forward out of the car like a crash test dummy. Stretch caught her before she hit the ground. He scooped her up like a baby, the same way he'd carried Killian, and headed off into the desert without missing a step.

Grace's head lolled and fell back onto Vasiley's shoulder. There seemed to be a million stars in the sky overhead. To Grace, they were all swirling like water going down a drain.

Clark walked along beside them, the shovel in one hand and the Taser in the other. He held it up so Grace could see it and pressed the button again. The blue-white light was almost blinding when it sparked, arcing in the air between the two terminals. The sound it made was chilling. "My new toy," said Clark. "One million volts."

They walked about thirty yards off the road before they stopped. Grace watched by the light of the moon as Clark stabbed the shovel into the sandy ground and traded the Taser for a pistol with a suppressor screwed to the end of it. It made the gun four inches longer than normal and somehow cartoonish.

Vasiley lowered her to her feet, but her legs still felt like jelly. She could feel his breath in her hair and knew he was enjoying the chance to hold her pressed tight against him. His big hands squeezed her sides and one of them managed to slip under the hem of her shirt.

"How do you like the gravesite?" Clark asked. "Vasiley dug it only an hour ago." Clark pointed the gun at them both. "Let go of her. She won't run. And if she does, she won't get far." Vasiley let her go. She stumbled sideways, away from the grave, but managed to stay on her feet. He watched her with a grin.

When Grace looked back at Clark, his gun was pointed at Vasiley, not at her. Vasiley saw it too. He stopped grinning.

"You were supposed to be watching them," Clark said. "You were supposed to be following them. You had very specific orders, did you not? Yet I had to hear it from my boss that the two people you were supposed to be watching were, in fact, in the parking lot of the Pleasure Palace Inn watching us."

Vasiley stammered, something breathless in Russian, his hands up in supplication.

"You are my oldest friend, Vasiley, but you know I can't let you go. What kind of example would that set for the others? Besides, a chain is only as strong as its weakest link."

Clark looked at Grace. "Vasiley did a fine job digging the grave, don't you think? He was not aware it would be his." Vasiley turned and began to run. He made it about ten feet.

Clark shot him in the back. One pop, quieter than the sound of the Taser. He fell hard, but was still moving, his hands clawing weakly at the ground. Clark walked to him while tucking his pistol into the holster at the small of his back. It stuck out awkwardly with the added length of the suppressor. He rolled Vasiley over, grabbed him by the feet and dragged the big man across the dirt and sand until he was parallel with the hole he'd dug.

Grace should have run then. She could have run up behind Clark, grabbed his gun and pushed him in the grave. She saw it all in her mind's eye. But her legs were only now beginning to feel like legs again. The chance was gone before she could react.

Clark stood over Vasiley for a moment, watching him writhe and gurgle. Then he put his foot under the big man's back and rolled him into the grave. Vasiley cried out, but it was muffled by the blood filling his lungs. Clark pulled the pistol out, pointed it into the hole, and put two more bullets into his oldest friend.

Then he turned to Grace and told her to fill in the grave.

Half an hour later, sweating and crusted in a layer of sand and grit, Grace slumped in the passenger seat of the Tahoe. She flexed her hands in her lap, feeling where the shovel had rubbed fat blisters. Every muscle was shaking from the shock of the Taser, the physical exertion of filling the grave, and the impact of witnessing her captor shoot his best friend in the back as if he were swatting a mosquito.

Clark, on the other hand, seemed to be in fine spirits. Cruising east on 215 again, he turned off the radio and said, "Now, I want you to be on your best behavior when you meet my boss. Do you understand?"

Grace forced herself to nod.

"She is more than just my boss," he said. A smile crept over his face, a genuine one this time, not the smirk Grace had seen before.

She? The boss of the Krasnyee Coalition was a woman? And apparently Clark was hot for her. Well, this was a surprise. How did a woman hold a bunch of Neanderthals like this in check? Grace almost felt a twinge of sisterly pride for her, before she remembered the woman might shortly order her death.

The upscale neighborhood they were in now had sprawling stucco homes with terra cotta roofs. The lots were angled, and the hills that surrounded Lake Mead jutted up in the background.

They pulled into a short driveway that ended at an ornate wrought iron gate with the letter M displayed in the center. A stacked stone fence surrounded the property, and through the gate Grace saw a beautifully lit, modern style house, rising three stories with the hills as a backdrop. It was ten times the size of her house back home and the front of it was nothing but glass. So, this is what crime pays, she thought sourly.

Clark rolled down his window and pressed buttons on a keypad that stuck out from the stone wall. There was a beep, and a camera mounted on top of one of the fence posts followed their car through the gate.

Grace wasn't sure what she expected to see inside the fence — a contingent of armed guards, a Panzer tank, at least a pack of German shepherds — but it was quiet, not a soul in sight. They pulled around to the side of the garage and parked.

"Remember, no funny business," Clark said. He stroked Grace's cheek with the back of his hand, then grabbed her chin and turned her face toward him. "You are a lovely woman, but I have killed lovelier."

He walked around the car, opened her door, and caught her right arm in a vice-like grip. If she told him he was hurting her, it would just make him happy, so she bit her lip and walked toward the house. A flight of flagstone steps led up the hill to a patio at the rear of the house. The back yard sloped up sharply, disappearing into the dark hills. A warm, golden light shone through the French doors and bathed the patio in a warm glow. A fountain bubbled in the center of the courtyard, a true sign of affluence here in the desert where water consumption was so closely monitored. Only the best for the crazy, cold-blooded mobsters.

Clark pulled her behind him up the back steps. But as she followed in his wake, Grace couldn't fight the feeling that she was climbing the steps to the gallows.

Chapter 27 – People in Glass Houses

Laurel stood at the top of the stone steps, gun in hand this time. Grace wondered if they had found him sleeping in the motel room and, if so, how much trouble he got in for it. She hoped a lot. But as much as she hated the sight of him, he was still preferable to his comrade, Hardy, who Grace was sure was a pervert, in addition to being a thief and a murderer.

Laurel stepped away from the door to let Grace and her escort enter. He grinned down at her as she passed, his long yellow teeth reminding her of a wolf. And she was Little Red Riding Hood.

Clark rushed through the door, prattling breathlessly in Russian as soon as he stepped over the threshold. Even though Grace couldn't make out the words, the tone was unmistakable. The man who had just killed his oldest friend and left him in a shallow grave in the desert now sounded like a love-struck teenager. His body blocked Grace's view of whatever glorious creature was worthy of all this adoration, but then he went down on one knee, absolutely groveling. Whoever this woman was, Clark was actually kissing her hand.

Grace expected to see the sleek black hair of the woman with the Pullman. Instead, what greeted her eyes were the cascading blonde curls and bountiful cleavage of the woman she'd first seen gambling in the Caesar's Palace casino. Grace thought she was arm candy for a rich, old man and nothing more. Then she saw her again dancing with Killian at die Nacht.

Grace stifled a gasp. These hadn't been coincidences. The old man must be the elusive Alexander Volkov, and this leggy blonde wasn't his girlfriend. She was his second in command.

With Clark still fawning, Grace wondered what their boss thought of this fraternization. Surely, Volkov knew of Clark's infatuation; he certainly wasn't trying to hide it. And the woman definitely seemed to be enjoying his attention, but pushed him away as soon as she saw Grace — or rather, as soon as she saw the necklace Grace was wearing.

"The amulet." Her face began to break into a smile, but she caught herself. She turned to Clark, who was still on one knee. "It's about time you bumbling idiots did something right. I was beginning to wonder if I had put my faith in the wrong man." Her English was perfect, with no accent at all, and her voice was husky, like someone who had smoked too much and for too long. Nothing like the squeaky voice she had used at the casino.

"If I failed you, I would gladly give my life." Clark sounded so earnest it was almost laughable.

The blonde was dressed to kill again, having abandoned the jeans. She wore heavy evening makeup with red lips and fingernails, silver palazzo pants and a black off-the-shoulder sweater. She was dressed as if she were hosting a dinner party. Her stiletto heels made her almost as tall as Laurel and her perfume smelled like lilies.

She made a striking figure, it was true, but close up there was something about her, something rough, that kept her from being truly pretty. Grace knew no amount of makeup and fine clothes could change that.

Hardy stepped in from the hallway and cleared his throat. He said something in Russian, but when he saw Grace, his fat lips broke into a lecherous grin. She tried to pretend she didn't see him, but her stomach felt queasy.

The blonde, eyes still on Clark, said, "*Who* is coming? And you'd better answer me in English. You know I hate it when you speak Russian. We are Americans now. We speak English."

"It is the hotel owner, Clifton, I think."

"I don't pay you to think. Go and make sure," she snapped.

Grace heard the door opening and then the sound of Hardy's considerable bulk descending a staircase.

"Good help is so hard to find these days," the woman said over her shoulder to Grace as if she were sharing a complaint with a colleague.

She began to turn away from Clark and he reached out for her like a drowning man reaches for a life preserver. "Alexsandra, I have good news…"

The blonde whirled around and her open hand connected with the side of Clark's face, catching him in mid-sentence and completely off guard. It sounded like the crack of a whip. Grace jumped back, startled by the sudden change in her mood. These people all needed a good dose of lithium.

Apparently, Clark knew what he'd done to deserve this treatment. Instead of looking surprised, he just looked contrite. He bowed his head and spoke in hushed tones. He was already on his knees and now he was cowering. He looked pathetic. "I'm sorry. I'm sorry. Please forgive me, my darling. But I must tell you before Clifton arrives. I did it for you."

The blonde rested her manicured hand against Clark's cheek again, but this time she was gentle, as if she were stroking the face of her lover. "Oh, my pet," she said, her voice as soft as her touch. "I could never stay angry with you. Tell me your news. What have you done for me?"

That is one big, crazy bitch, thought Grace. The blonde, Alexsandra, was Jekyll and Hyde, and Clark was eating it up.

"I got more money for the necklace," he whispered hurriedly. "*Much* more."

Alexsandra froze. "What are you talking about?"

"I made a deal with a musician, a rich American country music star. He will pay 8.6 million dollars for the necklace." Clark was so pleased with himself that his face practically glowed.

Grace couldn't see Alexsandra's face, but it was clear she was anything but pleased. Her body went rigid. The air around her seemed to crackle. When she spoke again, it was little more than a hiss. "You fool! You careless, ridiculous fool!"

"But…my angel…I thought you would be happy…"

Grace heard the sound of feet coming up the stairs now, two pair.

"Get out of my sight. Take the girl down the hall and stay hidden while I talk to Clifton. I'll have to smooth it over with him."

Clark reached for her again and she slapped his hand away. "Go!"

Anthony had taken up position in a house across the street that was still under construction. He could see anyone entering or leaving the property through the gate.

Moving as quickly as possible, it took William and Nick almost ten minutes to get into position in the hills behind the house. Carrying heavy equipment and trying to remain hidden wasn't easy on the loose rock. Every few feet, one of them would lose their footing, which sent little showers of pebbles down the thirty-degree slope and over the retaining wall into the courtyard. The tiny sliver of the new moon kept them invisible, but also made it almost impossible for them to see what they were about to stumble over next. Nick had wanted to bring the night vision goggles, but William promised him they'd be more trouble than they were worth. Nick currently doubted that.

They were doing little more than crawling from the cover of one boulder to the next. Nick marveled at the stupidity of contractors who would build such nice homes in the shadow of a mountain that apparently had frequent rock slides. Still, he was grateful the larger boulders were there to hide behind.

Nick tugged at the collar of the long-sleeved black tee-shirt William insisted he wear. He had pulled it from the back of the Jeep along with ski masks and black Kevlar gloves. The end of the sleeves hung past Nick's fingertips. He had to roll them up.

They found a spot with a view into the main floor but that kept them mostly hidden by one of the bigger rocks. Luckily, the rear of the house, like the front, was largely glass. Lights were on inside, and the den, kitchen and two bedrooms were easily visible.

William began setting up the rifle on the bipod, checking the scope, loading the ammo, not needing light to do something he'd done so many times before.

In one of the rooms, the foot of an ornate, white wrought-iron bed was visible, the head obscured by long, white curtains no one had bothered to close, despite having a hostage in the room. Pride goeth before a fall, thought Nick, with grim satisfaction.

The bedspread was a pearly white satin, with a delicate, powder blue design that looked rather like snowflakes at this distance. Stretched out on the bed was a pair of legs, obviously Killian's, judging by the fake alligator pants. Nick really wished he could see the rest of him and do a little damage assessment, but settled for the moment when he moved his feet. At least he was alive.

When Clark stood, all the syrupy sweetness he'd reserved for Alexsandra drained right out of him. He grabbed Grace by the wrist and dragged her down the hallway. He shoved her through the first doorway he came to, hard enough to make her stumble, and slammed the door behind them.

In the pecking order of the house, Grace was at the bottom. This would be the trickle-down theory of abuse. Clark would never raise his hand to defy Alexsandra, but Grace knew she was about to pay for that slap. She threw her arms up in front of her face instinctively, bracing herself for retribution. But none came.

She opened her eyes, expecting to see Clark's angry face bearing down on her. Instead, he was at the door, his back to her. Thankfully, he was more concerned about what was going on between Alexsandra and Clifton. He eased the door open enough to hear their conversation. They weren't exactly keeping their voices down.

Grace caught her breath and looked around. They were in a woman's bedroom, too feminine and fussy for her taste. Almost everything in it was white — walls, carpet, drapes, furniture, bedding — with accents of pale blue here and there. Crystal perfume decanters and big pillar candles sat on the dresser. Everything smelled like lilies. It was a scent Grace had always liked, until now.

The bed was too large for the room, made of elaborately scrolled wrought iron, painted glossy white, and there, on top of the pristine satin spread, sat Killian. His back was against the headboard, his arms stretched out on either side of him, bound at the wrists to the wrought iron with plastic zip ties. A pillow was stuffed behind his back — someone had been that kind — but his left eye was purple and swollen shut, and his beard was caked with dried blood. He was gagged with what looked like part of his own shirt, now in tatters. Torn and blood-spattered, it was barely recognizable as the airy white silk he had worn out of Vicious less than two days before. But he was awake and alert, and that was better than Grace had hoped for.

Clark stood at the door, eavesdropping on the conversation down the hall. Grace could hear it too. They certainly weren't keeping their voices down. Alexsandra was telling Clifton about the deal for more money, acting like it was her idea and that she'd done it for him. She said they would wait six months, then steal the necklace back from the American musician. It would be much easier than breaking into a heavily guarded museum had been and would only cost Clifton a fraction of what he would have paid. She was good. She almost had him convinced, her voice purring like a cat, relying on his greed. But, when she told him she loved him, something inside Clark snapped.

He spun around in a frenzy, leaped across the room and, gun in hand, gave Grace the backhand she'd expected earlier.

She fell sideways into the dresser, knocking the crystal decanters into each other, then onto the plush carpet. She was disoriented. Her cheek felt hot, like he'd hit her with an iron. A whooshing sound, like the ocean, filled her ear. The smell of the spilled perfume was nauseating.

She reached up to touch her face, but Clark grabbed her arm and pulled her to the door. He hooked his left arm around her neck, holding her tight in front of him. The gun was still in his right hand, but it wasn't pointed at her. He was going to use her as a human shield. As they stumbled down the hallway, she reached up with both hands to pry his forearm from around her neck. She was gasping for breath when they reached the den.

Nick and William were close enough to the house to witness all of this without binoculars. William, who had Alexsandra dead center in his scope, now had to set his sights on Clark. He had to move only an inch or two, but when he shifted positions, the loose rock beneath his knees gave way. He scrambled to catch hold of something stable, but everything he touched was loose and followed him down the side of the hill.

By the time Nick reached out, he was gone, down the rocky slope and over the ten-foot-high retaining wall. Nick saw him disappear over the edge and heard the sickening crunch as he made contact with the flagstones below.

When the shower of pebbles stopped, Nick whispered, "William! Are you okay? Say something."

There was a pause, then William whispered back, "I'm okay." He let out a faint groan, followed by, "I think I broke my leg."

"Are you sure?"

"Well, it's bent in a place it's not supposed to bend, so, yeah, I'm pretty sure."

A few whispered obscenities later, Nick was back at the scope. William would have to stay where he was for the time being. There was no way Nick could just saunter down to the courtyard and carry him out. He would definitely be seen.

Nick couldn't hear what the crazies in the house were saying, but he could see the gun Clark was waving, and he could see his wife at Clark's mercy, terrified and gasping for air.

The crosshairs of the scope were lined up right between Clark's eyes. Nick had to trust that William had the gun zeroed in. There was no wind, no shadows, nothing to adjust for except the pane of glass that separated them. But he didn't know what to do about that anyway. He had shot hundreds of times before, maybe thousands, but always at paper targets, not at human ones. He tried to imagine Clark's right eye as the center of the bull's-eye. *Just another day at the range*, he told himself.

He steadied his hands, breathed in, breathed out, and squeezed the trigger.

Grace pulled at Clark's arm with all her strength, clawed at his skin with her nails, but he was oblivious to her, almost like he'd forgotten she was there. He was busy shouting at Alexsandra, things that might have shocked Grace, if she hadn't been on the verge of blacking out. Tiny stars floated and popped in front of her eyes. Her legs felt heavy, weak.

Then she heard the sound of glass breaking. Someone had thrown something through the window. Glass was everywhere. Clark fell backwards onto the terra cotta floor, and Grace fell back with him. She flung his arm from around her neck and gasped for air. She tried to stand, but her hand slipped in something wet and warm on the floor. She looked down at the growing pool of dark liquid that surrounded Clark's head like a sinister halo. There was a hole in his forehead, right above his left eye.

Behind her, Alexsandra screamed. Grace turned in time to see Clifton bolt for the door. She heard him taking the steps two at a time. Then he was gone.

Alexsandra began switching off the lights in the house. She yelled orders in Russian to the remaining henchmen. Grace scrambled toward the back door, but saw Hardy there just in time. She ducked behind the island in the kitchen, crouching low. The island had a column of shallow drawers. Maybe she could find a butcher knife, something to use as a weapon. She pulled one drawer open slowly, quietly. It was full of dishtowels. She took one and tried to wipe Clark's blood off her hand. It was smeared on her clothes, drying already. Transfixed, she stared at her bloody handprint on the side of the island.

Then she saw a fire extinguisher hanging on a hook under the bar. She grabbed it and discarded the pin.

Alexsandra was shouting again, this time in English. This time at her. "My men are guarding the doors," she called. "There is no way out. Make it easy on yourself and come out where I can see you. If you make me look for you, I will just be frustrated and angry when I find you. Is that what you want?"

Grace didn't move. She wondered how many doors were in the house. There couldn't be someone guarding every one of them.

"I will give you one minute to surrender or I start taking it out on your friend. How many fingers does he really need, anyway? He is an actor, not a violinist."

Grace heard Alexsandra's voice retreating down the hallway, heading for Killian.

Crouching low, Grace made her way back to Clark's body. She didn't want to get too close to him, even though he was definitely dead. There was a single bullet hole about an inch above his left eye. The pool of blood around his head was black in the faint light. Like oil. Grace thought what a shame it was that it was ruining the beautiful bamboo floor.

His gun was gone. Alexsandra must have come back for it. Grace stood up, shifting the fire extinguisher behind her back. It was heavy. Ten pounds, she guessed. She tiptoed around the blood, and into the hallway.

By the time she reached the bedroom door, her eyes had adjusted to the low light, and she was able to see Alexsandra standing at the head of the bed by Killian. The curtains kept her hidden from the gunman outside. One hand was wound tightly in

Killian's hair, pulling his head sideways. Her pistol was pointed right at Grace.

"Come. Bring the necklace to me. Take it off and lay it on the bed. Slowly. I can't believe you had the audacity to wear it in the first place."

"Your dead boyfriend told me to."

Alexsandra snorted. "My boyfriend. What a joke. Pavel's problem was he tried to own me. I am no one's property."

"Did you love him?" Grace asked.

"Love him? That's none of your business, you filthy little mongrel. Give me my necklace and don't speak of him again."

Well, that had certainly touched a nerve.

Grace didn't move. The thought of Clark on his knees, kissing Alexsandra's hand came back to her. It made her feel sick. "Pavel," she said. "His name was Pavel? That rhymes with grovel, you know. Coincidence?"

"I said don't speak of him!" Alexsandra yelled. Her voice boomed in the small space. She released Killian's hair and grabbed his little finger. He balled his hands into fists and jerked at his restraints. Alexsandra snapped his finger backwards in one swift motion. Killian's head jerked back, slamming into the iron headboard. His scream was muffled by the gag, but that somehow made it sound even worse.

Grace lunged toward the bed. She took aim with the fire extinguisher and blasted Alexsandra full in the face with it. The chemical smell of the foam was harsh, but it finally blotted out the scent of the lilies.

Then she took the final few steps wielding the fire extinguisher by its nozzle, and swung it like an ax. She brought it around with all her strength into the side of Alexsandra's blonde head. It made a sound like an aluminum bat hitting a baseball, and she was aiming for the cheap seats. White foam and blood spattered the wall. Alexsandra's body crumpled in slow motion and fell across the bed, landing on Killian's legs. He kicked and pushed until her limp body rolled against the graceful wrought iron at the foot.

Grace didn't know if she was dead and didn't care. They still had to contend with three others in the house. Killian was trying to talk. She pulled the gag out of his mouth. It hung around his neck like a dirty bandana. She could barely understand him as he panted, "There are scissors in that desk drawer. I've seen them."

She cut him loose as quickly as her shaking hands would allow. Hardy was coming down the hallway, calling something in Russian. Grace picked up Clark's gun from the floor, spun around and shot towards the door just as he was about to enter the room.

The gun kicked in her hand. She didn't know if she'd hit the big Russian or not. He ducked back into the hallway. "Come on in," she yelled. "You know, it's just like Scarlett O'Hara said. I can shoot straight if I don't have to shoot too far."

She held the gun in both hands, pointed straight ahead. The suppressor added about a pound to the weight of the pistol, and made it hard to handle. She seriously doubted she could hit anyone with it unless she got lucky.

Killian followed so close he was almost touching her as they made their way down the dark hallway, around the black pool of blood that surrounded Clark's head, and across to the door that led downstairs to the garage.

Alexsandra hadn't made it downstairs to turn the lights off. No one was on guard here. The single door was dead bolted, with no key in sight, and the two garage doors would require an opener. They tried to lift them but they wouldn't budge. There was no emergency rope in sight.

"I really appreciate the rescue and all," Killian said, "but would you please watch where you're pointing that thing?" It was as if Grace just now noticed what she was holding in her hand. She tossed the gun to Killian like a hot potato. He caught it one handed.

Maybe they could find the garage door opener in one of the cars. The Cadillac was locked, but the BMW wasn't. Grace flipped down the sun visor, and something even better than the garage door opener hit her hand. The car keys.

Relief washed over her. "Get in!"

Killian hurried around to climb into the passenger seat. As he did, he almost sat on the garage door opener. He started pushing buttons and the door began to rise slowly, too slowly.

The door at the top of the stairs flew open, and Laurel and Hardy appeared in the opening, guns in hand. The windshield of the little car shattered.

Grace threw the car into reverse and floored it. The rear of the BMW slammed into the aluminum garage door, only half opened, and pulled it right out of the roof. The whole mechanism crashed down on the hood of the car. She turned blindly and slammed on the brakes. The tires squealed and the metal slid back off the car with an eerie screech.

Grace threw it in gear and took off again, this time through the half-open wrought iron gate. One of the other buttons Killian had pushed must have operated it. The little car slammed into the gate, sending sparks flying, then ricocheted into the stacked stone wall. Grace didn't take her foot off the gas as they careened out into the street. Less than 300 yards and they would be out of the neighborhood, away from this horrible place forever.

Both headlights had been smashed on the way through the gate. So it was only at the last moment that they saw the blockade at the bottom of the hill.

Chapter 28 – Good People

Grace stomped on the brake pedal with both feet. The little car's tires squealed as it skidded to a halt just inches away from a big Ford sedan and a navy SUV, parked bumper to bumper across the road.

She looked at Killian, his forearms braced against the dashboard. He held the pistol in his right hand and his left hand was already beginning to swell from the broken finger. "You all right?"

Before he could answer, the doors were thrown open and they were facing more than a dozen guns. This just kept getting better and better.

"Hands where I can see 'em," boomed one voice. "Drop the gun. Slowly. No sudden moves or you're dead."

Then another voice called out, "It's okay. It's okay. It's the hostages."

They were pulled out of the BMW and taken to the Ford. One of the men talked on a two-way radio, reporting on their safety, while the other man showed them a badge and told them they were a sight for sore eyes. He was a dark-skinned man with a Texas drawl and he said his name was Agent Rodriguez. They were the good guys.

Grace heard a deep voice on the radio. It was Anthony. "We've got a man down, here. Behind the house. He's gonna need an ambulance."

A chill ran through her. The shooter, of course. She hadn't stopped to wonder who it was. William was somewhere out there. He could be the man down. And where was Nick? What if he was the man down? They could see the wrought iron gate standing open. They could see everyone who went in or out. There were cars and people swarming all around. Since this was the only entrance to the road, they must have been hidden in plain sight. Maybe behind some of the other houses, maybe in the garages of the houses still under construction.

She heard the sound of sirens coming closer. The other agent pulled the SUV alongside the sedan so three ambulances could pass.

"Where's my husband?" she asked Agent Rodriguez. "Nick Howard. Where is he?"

The Texan pointed to the radio. "They'll let us know just as soon as there's anything to report, ma'am."

The other agent, a man named Jacobs with a long nose and black hair, talked to Killian, trying to assess his injuries. He made Killian follow his finger with his eyes and asked him what day it was. Through all of this, Killian protested the fuss, said he was perfectly fine and had looked worse than this after a hard night drinking.

Grace tried to be patient. She sat watching the brightly lit house and the flurry of action in the distance. She didn't feel like talking and was grateful the agents hadn't asked for a statement.

She got out and leaned against the car. After a few moments, she noticed Agent Rodriquez staring at her. "What?"

"Sorry, ma'am. I was just looking at the hawk. So that's the Queen's Necklace? That really belonged to King Tut's mother, huh?"

She put her hand to her neck. She'd forgotten she was wearing it. This piece of jewelry that some people were willing to steal, kill or die for. "It's not the Queen's necklace. It's Kavayet's necklace. She was Tut's real mother."

She looked up in time to see a car drive through the gate, one of the big, dark sedans. A reflection told her there was glass in between the front and back seats. As it drew nearer, she saw Laurel in the back seat. He shouted at her as they passed. Of course she couldn't hear what he said, but she assumed it was in Russian and probably involved all the creative ways he would like to see her die. She let out a deep breath as the tail lights disappeared into the night.

The next vehicle to leave was an ambulance, lights flashing and sirens wailing. It was a terribly shrill and lonely sound. As it sped away, she wondered who was inside. Was it Alexsandra, William or maybe even Nick? Or maybe she had hit Hardy with her wild shot and he was the one in the ambulance.

She thought about asking Agent Rodriguez, but stopped herself, as if ignorance of the facts could somehow postpone them. The two-way radios emitted a constant stream of information. She tried to block it out, but couldn't help overhearing when the agents in the house found Clark. They said his name was Pavel Alkaev. Later, when an ambulance left without its sirens and lights on, she knew Pavel was inside.

She thought about climbing back into the car to escape the radios, but the idea of being closed up inside made her claustrophobic.

A hand touched her shoulder. She jumped.

"Sorry, it's only me," Killian said. "I just wanted to thank you. I don't know what you did, but I know I'm out here instead of in there, so…" She relaxed, let him put his arms around her. They stood that way for several minutes, until she realized they were just propping each other up. She pulled back and looked at him. His face was a mess. An EMT had cleaned his eye and gotten most of the dried blood out of his beard, but there was still a trace of the handsome movie star she'd met just a few days before. He let them wrap his injured hand, but flatly refused to go to the hospital in an ambulance. He created such a disturbance that Agent Jacobs finally said he'd be responsible for him.

Killian didn't say anything else, just leaned against the car shoulder to shoulder with Grace and waited, staring toward the house. She couldn't find the words to tell him, but it was the sweetest thing he could possibly have done.

After a few minutes, the third ambulance pulled out of the gate and headed down the hill toward them. Just past the blockade, it stopped. The rear door opened and Nick climbed out.

Grace made a sound like a yelp and dashed toward him. She almost knocked him back into the ambulance. "You're okay. Oh, thank God."

He wrapped his arms around her and buried his face in her hair. He was laughing but his bloodshot eyes told a different story. He hadn't known for sure who, if anyone, he'd shot at first. He stayed with William in the courtyard until the ambulance arrived, and it was only then that they found out both hostages had escaped.

William lay on a stretcher in the ambulance behind him, his leg in an air splint. Whatever they gave him for pain had put a big smile on his face. He looked more relaxed than Grace had ever seen him. "Bye, you guys!" he called. "They're taking me to play golf in this fire truck. Catch you later!"

Nick put his hand up to stop the rear door from closing. He could see Grace better now, bathed in the light from the inside of the ambulance. Her clothes were smeared and spattered with dried blood. She looked like a macabre Jackson Pollock painting.

"You're hurt," he said. It wasn't a question. It was more an accusation, like someone was going to pay for this.

Grace shook her head. "It's not mine."

Nick closed the ambulance door and pulled her back into his arms as it drove away.

A familiar vehicle followed it through the blockade. The brakes on the old Jeep squealed softly as it pulled up beside them and stopped. Anthony had retrieved William's car and all their equipment.

"Want a ride?"

Agent Jacobs spoke up, "Sorry, sir, they haven't been cleared to leave yet. They're going to be needed for questioning."

Anthony flipped out his badge and said, "I'm clearing them."

Jacobs looked at the badge and stood up straight, a flash of recognition in his eyes. "Yes, sir. They're free to go, sir."

They all climbed into the Jeep, Nick and Grace in the back and Killian in the front. Killian said, "Do you three know each other?"

"Oh, yes, sorry about that. I'm Agent Woodruf of the FBI. You can call me Anthony."

"Pleasure. I'm Killian Ross." His tone suggested he was meeting someone for tea, not being rescued from a kidnapper.

Anthony smiled. "I know."

"So, Anthony, would you care to tell me what the bloody hell is going on here?"

With the help of Nick and Grace, Anthony filled him in on everything he had missed. Killian sat quietly, absorbing it all, occasionally running a hand through his now-greasy hair or softly rubbing his red wrists.

"…and as you can see, this was a lot bigger than just me and William," Anthony said. "We were working it full time, but there were plenty of other people involved."

"Like Koenig? Is he FBI?" Nick asked.

"We wish. Koenig is very much his own man. I can't see him working for anyone."

Grace remembered Clifton getting away and felt cheated. "What about Neil Clifton, the owner of The Isis? He's the one they stole the necklace for to begin with. He ran as soon as the shot came through the window. He's probably halfway to Mexico by now."

Anthony shook his head. "Don't worry about Clifton. Agents apprehended him before he got out of the neighborhood."

Grace remembered that shot perfectly, the broken glass, the blood. "I assume Clark is dead," she said, trying to sound nonchalant. "Who shot him? You?"

"No." Anthony caught Nick's eye in the rearview mirror, waiting for him to speak.

"Was it William?"

"No, he fell over a retaining wall before he could make the shot," Nick said. "That's how he hurt his leg."

She looked at him, willing him to meet her eyes. "You?"

He nodded.

She took his hand from where it lay in his lap, pressed it to her cheek, then kissed his fingers. There was nothing to say.

Anthony cleared his throat. "His real name is Pavel Alkaev. He was the second in command in the Krasnyee Coalition and, yes, he's dead."

"What about the woman? Is she alive?" Grace shivered involuntarily, remembering how the fire extinguisher sounded as it bounced off her skull.

"No. Her neck was broken." Anthony caught her looking at him in the rearview mirror and said, "Don't beat yourself up about it. You did a good thing. Believe me, the world is a better place without her."

They rode for a few minutes while Grace composed herself. "Clark was in love with her, you know," she said. "I thought at first she was Volkov's girlfriend, but Clark acted like she was the boss. Does anybody know where Volkov is?"

Anthony chuckled. "I forgot you didn't know."

"Didn't know what?"

"That was no woman," Anthony said. "That was Alexander Volkov."

"What? No, I'm talking about the blonde. He called her…" Grace's eyes widened as the realization struck. "He called her Alexsandra."

"I don't get it," Nick said. "Who are you talking about?"

"The blonde who was in the house," Anthony said. "You saw her through the window. It turns out she was the same woman who was in the adjoining room at the motel, the same one who moved Killian in the rolling suitcase. She was just in disguise, a different wig, you know."

Killian rubbed the back of his head. "I don't remember that at all. They knocked me out with something, put something in my water, I guess, and when I woke up I was on the bed where you found me."

"It's probably better that way," Anthony said. "Alexsander Volkov was the head of the Krasnyee Coalition and one of the most dangerous people in organized crime."

"Volkov was a woman?" The look on Nick's face clearly said he was waiting for the punch line.

"Well, technically transgender. He had the top done," Anthony explained, patting his own chest, "but the word was he couldn't part with the bottom."

Grace turned to Nick. "We saw her in the casino, remember? Playing blackjack with the old man. You clapped for her boobs."

Nick shook his head. "No way. That was definitely a woman."

"And, Killian, you danced with her at die Nacht. She had her hands in your pockets. I thought she was just being fresh, but I'll bet she was looking for your room key. She didn't know who you were, but she knew we were all together."

"Don't feel too bad," Anthony said with a grin. "She fooled us, too. When he was still known as a man, he was very…over the top, flamboyant. You might expect to see him in expensive clothes or lots of gold jewelry, but certainly not a dress and high heels. We had no idea he wanted to be a woman. And it turned out to be a great cover, too. He operated right under our noses for two years as Alexsandra."

"But Clark, or Pavel, whatever his name is, was having an affair with her. He was in love with her," Grace said. "Did he know she was a man? Did he know she was Volkov?"

"Sure. Pavel had been with the Coalition for years. He was her right hand man. How could he not know? And if he was sleeping with her and couldn't tell she had man-parts, he was dumber than he looked."

Grace remembered the way Pavel knelt in front of Alexsandra, the things he'd said to her. He'd been more than in love with her; he'd been obsessed.

"And Clifton?" she asked. "He was in business with her. Did he know?"

"Well, he may not have known she was Volkov, but he definitely knew she was Coalition. I don't know if he knew she was a man."

"What about Sunshine and Shady? What about Skye? Are they FBI too?" asked Nick.

Anthony shook his head. "Nope. They're just good people. There are still some left in the world."

Almost as an afterthought, Grace reached up and unclasped the amulet. Without even looking at it, she passed it over the seat to Anthony. He held it up in the early morning light as he drove.

"So, that's what all this is about?" Killian said. "The last time I saw a piece of jewelry that caused me this much grief, it was an engagement ring."

They rode for a while in silence, Grace staring out the window at the houses and neighborhoods they passed, most of them dark, their inhabitants tucked warm and snug in their beds, safe thanks to the efforts of men like William and Anthony and the other good people she'd met this week.

She looked at her husband who sat lost in thought beside her. For a brief moment, she thought about what would've happened if the shot had been three inches to the left. What if? What if? Then she pushed the thought out of her head. What if's were dangerous. The reality was she was safe and Pavel and Volkov were on their way to the morgue.

She shifted across the cracked, beige vinyl seat closer to Nick and leaned her head on his shoulder. She flinched. Her cheek was sore from the backhand Clark had given her earlier.

"What is it?" Nick asked.

"Nothing," she lied. He didn't need anything else to worry about. He wrapped his arm around her and pulled her closer. She felt something under her shirt and knew it was the talisman Skye had given Nick. She had to remember to thank her. She closed her eyes and felt her body relax for the first time in days.

Chapter 29 – The Real Thing

It was early in the morning when they got back to their room at The Isis, the sun just breaking orange over the surrounding hills. Once in bed, Grace's dreams were filled with lilies and broken glass and blood, lots of blood. She woke several times, but was too exhausted to move. It was like waking after anesthesia. Her head weighed a thousand pounds on pillows that were made of angels and unicorns. She caught bits and pieces of reality; Nick sitting in bed watching the news on TV or a disjointed phrase as he talked on the phone – someone was having surgery – before she fell back under.

When she finally opened her eyes and was able to move, albeit sluggishly, she found that Nick had ordered room service, a Cleopatra's Club Sandwich and Nile River Nachos. She hadn't thought once about food, but now that it was here, she found she was ravenous.

As they finished the last nacho, Anthony and a woman who introduced herself as Agent Lipton arrived to take their statements. When Anthony stepped through the door, Grace embraced him like a long-lost brother. He chuckled, a deep rumbling sound, and returned the hug. He reported that William was out of surgery and resting comfortably. He also said that they'd just come from taking Killian's statement in his suite, and he was anxious to see them.

Agent Lipton was about Grace's age, and looked exactly the way Grace expected an FBI agent to look. She wore her sandy-colored hair pulled back in a severe chignon at the nape of her neck, had a perfect complexion and no makeup. Grace knew as she shook her outstretched hand that she would never be on a first name basis with this woman.

Agent Lipton pulled out a small, leather-bound notebook and Dictaphone. "Do you mind if I record this?" she asked as she pressed the button. For the next forty-five minutes, she asked in-depth questions and took meticulous notes. She asked for a description of the old man Alexsandra had been with at the blackjack tables. Without a word, she pulled a large, black and white photo from her notebook and handed it to Grace. Two men were having coffee at a sidewalk café. One had his back to the camera, but the other one, here with a few less wrinkles and a little more hair, was unmistakable.

"Yeah, that's him," Grace said. "I even recognize the ring." She looked up and, for the first time, Agent Lipton smiled.

"Who is he?"

Agent Lipton took the photo and slipped it back into her notebook. It looked as though she was trying to decide how much to tell them. Anthony answered instead. "That's Boris Kusnetsov, the founder of the Krasnyee Coalition. Until about thirty seconds ago, he was believed to be dead. As for the ring, it's a diamond called the Durban Blue and it's probably worth more than this hotel."

After Anthony and Agent Lipton left, Grace and Nick rode the service elevator, just as they had the night they had met Killian lurking in the shadows of the ballroom downstairs. It seemed like ages ago.

Killian looked decidedly better than when they'd last parted company. A shower and some sleep could work miracles. He moved slower than usual and his left eye still looked like raw meat, but the swelling had gone down some and he could open it a little. A metal splint bound his left pinky finger. The side of his hand was purple all the way to his wrist.

A man stood behind him, stuffing a stethoscope into an old-fashioned doctor's bag. The bag appeared much older than the doctor, who looked almost as young as Brett. Grace guessed he was fresh out of medical school and doing house calls to pay off his student loans. Or his gambling debts.

Killian ushered the man to the door and shook his hand.

"No broken bones other than the finger," said the young doctor. "But you'll have a wicked headache for a couple of days. The human brain doesn't like to be batted around inside the skull like that. And if those teeth still feel loose by next week, you should have a dentist take a look at them."

"I will do. Thank you."

"Put ice on that finger whenever it starts to throb. And follow up with your own doctor when you get back to London. He'll need to take some x-rays. Are you sure you don't want any painkillers?" the doctor asked, sounding disappointed.

"No, no," said Killian. "I'll pop a couple of aspirin and I'll be right as rain by morning."

The doctor shrugged and pulled a copy of *Bright Star* magazine from his bag. It was the same issue Grace had read on the plane. There was a candid photo of Killian on the cover. He was clean shaven, talking on a cell phone and walking a shaggy terrier. Grace now knew the dog was Zeus and the cell phone was in the Bellagio fountain. She wondered if Walter had taken this photo.

Probably not, since there was nothing compromising in it. Just a man and his dog, out for a stroll.

The doctor had the decency to look a little embarrassed as he held up the magazine and asked for an autograph for his girlfriend. Killian obliged with a genuine, albeit now crooked, smile, and signed the cover with the offered Sharpie.

When Doogie Howser finally left, Killian leaned against the door and blew out a deep breath.

There seemed to be an unspoken understanding among the three of them not to talk about what happened. They had to tell the FBI, of course, and that was enough. It only made sense that Killian wouldn't want to relive being kidnapped and knocked unconscious, or that Nick wouldn't want to talk about how it felt to shoot a man, and how it felt to pray that he wasn't about to shoot his own wife by mistake. And Grace didn't want to discuss the blood and the glass and the "ping" of a fire extinguisher hitting a skull. Her dreams were bad enough.

So, they didn't talk about it. Instead, Killian smiled broadly, hugged Grace, slapped Nick on the back, then, on second thought, pulled him in for a hug as well.

Killian's smile faltered and he stepped back almost nervously. "Look, I only have two things to say. First of all, I don't know whether you've seen it yet, but...you will. And I want you both to know that I'm *very sorry*. It was Walter, that repulsive little swine. For him to do this to me is one thing, but he had no right whatever involving you."

Killian walked over to the coffee table in the ultra modern living room of his suite. Plush curtains lined the far wall and Grace couldn't help remembering the breathtaking view of Las Vegas that waited behind them. He retrieved a newspaper from the table and, with a deep sigh, held it out to them.

It was the kind of paper you see in a supermarket checkout line, a celebrity tabloid filled with ridiculous items like "Cher Abducted by Aliens." *IS* magazine, or *International Star*, was not known for tasteful, or necessarily truthful, stories.

The headline read, "Is This Why Killian Has Been Hiding?" Below it, for all the world to see, was the photo Walter took of them leaving the parking garage. Grace remembered the moment vividly. She'd yawned and Killian had put his arm around her shoulders. It was a harmless gesture and she thought nothing of it at the time, but now, in this context, it did look quite incriminating.

There wasn't much of a story underneath the photo, just a paragraph that read,

> "*IS* captured this photo of Killian Ross cavorting with a mystery woman outside Las Vegas hotspot, die Nacht, this weekend. Sources tell us they were inseparable all night. So, here's the real question: Is her "Concealed Carry" Killian's love child? We think we see a baby bump! Could this explain why Killian has been so conspicuously absent from the London scene lately? Oh, my! What will Astrid say?"

Grace laughed. "Hey look! I'm a celebrity and I'm having Killian Ross's love child!"

Nick shook his head in mock disgust. "Great. There'll be no living with her now." Then he laughed as a thought hit him. "Hey, too bad that wasn't a picture of you and *me*, Killian. Maybe *I* could be having your love child then!" It felt good to be laughing again, to be enjoying something silly like this.

But Killian wasn't laughing. He just looked puzzled. "You're not angry? I thought you would be furious."

"Why?"

"Well, for starters, they said you had a baby bump!"

"Oh, I'm not offended by that," Grace said with a wave of her hand. "You know how they are about women in show business: if their ribs aren't all showing, they say they need liposuction."

Killian turned to Nick. "Well, what about you? You're not angry that they made it look like your wife is having an affair?"

Nick shrugged. "Only if I thought it was true. And I was right there. It wasn't like anything was going on. I was ten feet away."

"Yes, but that's not what it looks like," Killian said, stabbing his finger at the photo.

"So, what?" Grace said. "Perception is not reality."

Killian looked at her as if she just said she believed in fairies. "Well, it is in show business."

"Maybe, but *we're* not in show business," Grace said with a smile.

"Look at it this way, Killian: Is this going to be bad publicity for you?" Nick asked.

"No. If anything, it will probably be good." Killian looked apologetic, almost embarrassed as he said it.

"Then don't worry about it." Nick patted him on the back and reached for the newspaper again. "Baby bump, huh?" He tilted his head sideways and put his hand on Grace's stomach.

She batted his hand away and rolled her eyes. "Oh, stop that."

"All right, even though I won't pretend I understand, I am delighted you two aren't angry. Now I have a favor to ask of you."

"After all we've been through together, you shouldn't even have to ask," Grace said. "What is it?"

"Well, you know that Ruth will be here soon – Brett is picking her up at the airport any minute now – and..." Killian hesitated, looking almost sheepish now. "It would really mean a lot to me if you two would be here when she arrives."

"You want us to meet her? Of course, we'd love to."

"It's more than just that," he said. "Remember the lucky numbers I played in roulette – three, twenty-four and eleven? That's the day I met Ruth, March 24, 2011, the best day of my life. It took me a while to realize it, but I'm going to tell her I love her."

His green eyes sparkled. In that moment, despite the hair and the beard and the injuries, Grace could see the dashing movie star again.

"Oh, that's wonderful," she said. "I'm so happy for you."

"That's great," Nick agreed. "But you don't need an audience for that, man. Wouldn't you rather be alone?"

"No!" Killian shook his head. "I need you two here. I'll lose my nerve if you're not. Promise you'll stay."

Grace had to make a real effort to keep herself from laughing. Here was one of the world's greatest sex symbols standing before her like an awkward, anxious teenager, worried about being rejected by the Prom Queen. She reached out and took one of his hands. She couldn't help noticing the raw red strip of skin that encircled his wrist where the zip tie had been, but she held her smile firmly in place.

"Killian, I may not know much," she began, "but one thing I am absolutely, positively sure of is that Ruth Averhart is crazy-mad in love with you."

He looked at her expectantly, holding his breath.

"I spoke to her on the phone yesterday, while you were still in the motel – or at least we thought you were – and she was a wreck. I could barely understand a word she was saying."

"Well, I don't doubt she cares for me," Killian said, "but like a brother. And that's not what I want. Not anymore. Yesterday, when I was…when I woke up in that house and I had no idea where I was or if I was even in Las Vegas anymore, I felt really frightened for the first time. Up until then, I was just *pissed off.* I had no clue who these people were or what they were going to do with me, and for the first time I began to think I wouldn't make it out. I knew I couldn't let myself get discouraged. I couldn't give up. So I started thinking about all the reasons I had to live. And do you know who I kept seeing, over and over again? It wasn't Astrid. It was Ruth." His face softened as he saw her in his mind's eye. "Always smiling. Always happy to see me. Ruth is the one person who would never, ever hurt me, who would never let me down. And while I was picturing her, this feeling began to wash over me, this feeling of calm, of well-being, like…like that feeling when you come in out of the snow and warm your hands by the fire. You know? And I knew then that I had to live, if only to see her again, to tell her how I feel about her, to tell her I love her, even if she doesn't return my feelings."

He looked at them, his green eyes searching their faces for some sign that they understood, that he was doing the right thing.

Grace could feel tears welling up in her eyes. The strain of the last few days had made her even more emotional than usual. She stood on tip-toe and kissed Killian's non-bruised cheek. She wanted to tell him he had nothing to worry about. She wanted to tell him Ruth would be overjoyed to hear of his change of heart. She wanted to tell him she wished him all the happiness in the world, but she didn't get any of this out before the knock on the door.

Killian froze, his bloodshot eyes locked on Grace's. The next knock was louder.

"Aren't you gonna get that?" Nick said.

"You get it," Killian whispered. "I don't think I can move."

Nick indulged him, opening the door with a flourish. Brett stood before him in the hallway, his arm around a tall, attractive woman in a light grey tailored suit. Her straight, fawn-colored hair hung to her shoulders, framing a pale face with grey eyes that matched her suit. She was younger than Grace had imagined her. She might have been pretty under ordinary circumstances, but anxiety seemed to have drained all the color right out of her. It was as if she could blend in to the wall if she stood still long enough. Brett appeared to be supporting her, keeping her steady.

When the woman saw Nick, she looked a little disappointed, like maybe she had the wrong room. But Brett said cheerfully, "Look who's here! We made it," and began to propel her forward.

Grace studied her face carefully, expecting…what? A passionate embrace? A tearful reunion? Professions of undying love? Yes, yes, and yes.

Instead, Ruth put her hands on Killian's shoulders and hesitated, as if hugging him might hurt him. So she patted his arms awkwardly and said, "Ah! There's my favorite client."

Grace thought she must have heard her wrong. She looked from Nick to Brett, but both of them looked just as confused. Brett actually stopped mid-stride, almost tripping over the suitcase he was carrying.

Killian's face looked pained, much more than it had the night before when he thought his jaw might be broken. Mistaking the meaning, Ruth gingerly patted his cheek and said, "Oh, that will heal fine by the premiere. We've got a whole month. You'll be back to your dazzling self in no time."

She brushed past him to deposit her purse and laptop bag on the leather sofa. "On the flight over, I decided how we could spin this." She didn't look at Nick or Grace. Killian didn't introduce them. He didn't speak at all. "Of course, we can't keep the press from running with it, but we *can* play it to our advantage. You know what they say; the only bad publicity is no publicity." She was in full-on manager mode, all work and no play, and Killian was crumbling like an imploding old casino.

Brett caught Grace's attention and motioned for her to follow him to the kitchen.

"What the hell was that?" Brett whispered as they rounded the corner. "I have spent the last forty-five minutes listening to that woman moan like a wounded animal! I thought she was literally going to faint in the elevator on the way up. I almost had to carry her. We get here and she flips a switch and...bam! It's like she's a completely different person. What are these people playing at? Do you think she has a split personality?"

Grace shook her head. She had no answer. Even Killian, whom she was sure ten minutes before was about to bare his soul, was still standing in the entryway, looking haggard and irresolute. Meanwhile, Ruth flitted around the suite like a hummingbird afraid to light, chattering on about talk show appearances and the number of good scripts she'd been offered in his absence.

Nick caught Grace's eye, making a face that definitely said he thought they were both nuts.

It just didn't make any sense.

Then Grace saw her falter. She saw Ruth skip a beat, heard her quick intake of breath when she saw the tabloid photo on the table. Killian with his arm around a mystery woman in Sin City. The shadow that flickered across Ruth's face was only there for a second before she pushed it away. But it was definitely there. And Grace recognized pain when she saw it.

Just like that, it all fell into place. Grace had forgotten who they were dealing with. What had Killian said earlier? Perception was reality in show business. And apparently, the thought of doing something real and honest was terrifying if you were used to having all your realities written for you. Everything she'd seen Killian do — play pool, gamble, speak foreign languages — he'd learned for parts he had played. He'd parachuted out of an airplane, driven a tank and used a flame thrower, all for the movies. And even though Ruth wasn't an actress, she was show business through and through. She knew how to pretend. After all, she had a lot of practice pretending to be happy for Killian when he was with Astrid.

Grace whirled around, running into Brett in the process. As the two of them stumbled back into the living area, all eyes were on them. She caught herself on the firebox, which, without a fire in it, just looked like a table full of broken glass. She straightened up, trying to look dignified.

"The three of us are gonna go. Nick and I have a flight out in a couple of hours and we need to pack, but mainly we're gonna go because you two need to talk. Ruth, Killian has something he needs to tell you, and I think...no, I *know* that you want to hear it."

They both looked at her like they'd been caught stealing.

"Now the two of you can keep pretending if you want to, or you can be honest with each other and start being happy. It's entirely up to you. But remember, this is not a dress rehearsal; this is the real thing."

Nick and Brett had already gravitated to the door and Nick held it open for Grace. It seemed they couldn't wait to get out of this uncomfortable situation. She stopped as she passed Killian. He looked so scared she couldn't resist hugging him one more time. As she did, she whispered in his ear, "Just be you. She already knows and loves you."

They said good-bye to Brett and went to throw their belongings in suitcases before catching a flight out. Grace couldn't wait to sleep on the plane.

Chapter 30 – Home

More than a month had passed since Grace and Nick returned from Las Vegas. Things were almost back to normal. She no longer had to sleep with the light on. She'd almost stopped having nightmares about blood and lilies. Almost.

At first, everyone listened intently, *oohing* and *ahhing* at the appropriate places, while she and Nick told the somewhat edited version of their "vacation" again and again. It had been exciting and terrifying and adventurous and something neither of them ever wanted to go through again.

Her niece loved the book of Native American folklore and immediately began looking through it. Grace could see the illustrations over her niece's shoulder, drawings of Stone Mother and Coyote and the Sun. One in particular caught her eye, making the hair stand on the back of her neck. Molly turned the page. Grace said, "Wait. Go back. Let me see that a second."

"What? That's kind of a depressing picture. Did that woman burn that village?"

"No," Grace said. "She just…didn't stop it. Now it's her burden to try and protect people whenever she can, because she didn't protect her own people."

A young, Native American woman with a tear-streaked face stared up at her from the page. Charred, smoldering teepees surrounded her. She was wearing an indigo blue dress with brown and white stitching around the neck and hem. She wore a small drawstring pouch around her neck on a leather cord, like the one Skye had made for Nick. She was dressed exactly like the old woman Grace had seen in the Smoke Shop, the woman who mysteriously appeared at Red Rock to deliver a warning. The only thing that was different was her face. It was Skye's.

Grace could only stare at the woman, stunned at the resemblance. Then she saw the caption. It was written three ways, first with the Cherokee symbols, then phonetically, and then the English translation. It read *Tsi s qua A ge yv, the Bird Woman*. She sucked in a deep breath. The last time Grace saw Skye, she was asking for protection for Killian, using the ways that her grandmother, a Cherokee medicine woman, taught her. What was it Skye said? That her grandmother told her they were direct descendents of *Tsi s qua A ge yv*. Grace hadn't thought then to ask what that meant; there was a little too much going on at the time. And maybe she wouldn't have believed it anyway. But now? Well, things were different now.

William called one night with the news that Boris Kuznetsov was indeed still alive. It turned out he faked his own death in 2006. Apparently, mob bosses were like gunfighters; the only way they could retire was to die. Kuznetsov was getting older and slower and decided to turn over the reins to his most trusted right-hand man, Volkov, who was still known as Alex at the time. It was the perfect cover. Volkov wanted to move the entire operation to the US and made strides to do so. Now that Volkov was dead, thanks to Grace's home-run swing, Kuznetsov had come out of retirement. William's new mission was to find him.

William said his leg was as good as new now, no more cast and no more crutches. While they'd waited for the ambulance behind Volkov's house that night, William told Nick through gritted teeth that it would be better for everyone involved if no one found out Nick was the shooter. "I'll never live it down," he'd said, but it wasn't just his reputation he was trying to protect.

Grace kept expecting to be called to testify about her part in Volkov's death, but the call never came. The initial statement she gave to the FBI agent the day after must have sufficed. William assured her they'd call her if they had any more questions.

Then one evening, just as things were truly getting back to normal, a courier delivered a box to their front door. Inside was a black zippered bag the size of a camera case, and an envelope addressed to both of them in spiky handwriting. Grace pulled the paper from the envelope and read aloud.

Nick and Grace,

I suppose I could have phoned, but I seem to have misplaced my mobile at the Bellagio and haven't bothered to get a new one. Being without it is quite liberating.

I saw Rooster Hathcock earlier this week. Was able to persuade him to record the title song for our upcoming movie. He had the girl, Misty, with him and they looked quite the pair, holding hands like teenagers.

My main reason for writing is to tell you that Ruth and I were married two weeks ago in a private ceremony. We managed to keep it entirely out of the press and it has been wonderful keeping a secret from the world, not something I get to do often, I assure you. We'll let it leak soon, but at least we will have a few weeks to ourselves.

Speaking of secrets, saw on the news where the necklace was "recovered." Can't believe your federal friend managed to keep all of our names out of it. If you speak to him, tell him I am forever in his debt.

As for the enclosed bag, these are rightfully yours. You two have brought me more luck than you will ever know – or maybe it was just the hat with the dice on it. Let's all four plan a trip soon so you can cash them in. I never got to see the Grand Canyon.

Your friend,

Killian

Nick unzipped the leather bag and pulled out a mustard yellow casino chip with the Caesar's Palace logo on it. He stretched the opening wider to reveal more than one hundred thousand dollars in casino chips.

Grace was shocked and uncharacteristically speechless. The pair stood for a minute on their small front porch, cicadas droning in the trees overhead. Then Nick began to laugh. It was the most beautiful sound Grace had heard in months.

"You know," he said, "I think I like that guy. He's good people."

The End

About the Author

Kelly Adamson lives in Birmingham, Alabama with her husband.

She is a member of the Southern Chapter of Sisters in Crime and the Murder and Sweet Tea writers group.